Louette's wake

a Wiregrass Series novel

Blessings!

by

Sue Riddle Cronkite

Sue Riddle Cronkite

New Hope
Press

More Praise for Louette's Wake...

"I especially enjoyed colloquial phrases that helped give characters depth and create a sense of locale. Recipes and detailed notes on the music round out the book. More than a comedy, it is a struggle to survive. I was pleased to be invited to the wake."

Chester Butler, Naturalist of the Big Bend Oral History Project and author of a series for Coastlines Newspaper on Florida Green Guides.

"Sue Cronkite's novel invites you to pull up a chair, rest your elbows on the kitchen table as Louette, who is deepdish southern, shares her humorous observations, and hints of a quiet grief that has haunted her since the disappearance of her husband years ago."

Persis Granger, Author of Shared Stories from Daughters of Alzheimer's, *and novels* Adirondack Gold, *and* A Summer of Strangers.

"The author puts the heart of the South into Louette's Wake, a tale of a Southern family rambling around in Sue's mind for years while she reported news articles. At last she let her story explode upon the pages with a mastery of southern language and character development. Louette's Wake will touch your soul as her southern family experiences love and loss, and Sue Cronkite reveals her gift as masterful storyteller."

Sharman Burson Ramsey, author of Swimming with Serpents, In Pursuit, On to Angola, *and the* Mint Julep Mysteries.

Other Publications by New Hope Press:

Heart and History of Holmes County
a local history by Anna Paget Wells

Nuts to Us a collection of stories, poems,
and essays celebrating Wiregrass peanuts

The riveting tales of *Mary Dozier Thomas*

Font: Bookman Old Style
Cover and design: Merri Rose Fink.
Cover photo: Lake Victor, North Holmes County, FL, by
Sue Riddle Cronkite.
Cover image balloons designed by vectorpocket / Freepik.
Wiregrass Region Map, Wikipedia

The characters and events in this book are fictitious. Any
similarity to real persons, living or dead, is coincidental
and not intended by the author.

ISBN-13: 978-0-9724101-3-7
ISBN-10: 0-9724101-3-9

First Edition

New Hope Press
Geneva, AL ~ Apalachicola, FL

The Wiregrass

The Wiregrass area includes parts of southeast Alabama, southwest Georgia and the Florida Panhandle.

Wiregrass Pioneers in the 1700s, and into the 1900s, turned cattle loose to ramble, and to graze on this strangely nutritious grass.

Wiregrass sprouted from the ground in tufts, looking like fat, green wires. Fencing laws and progress have largely wiped out the wild-growing wiregrass. Lightning fires under loblolly pines and water oaks cleared places for new wiregrass to grow. Controlled burns in state and national forests may have allowed some to regenerate.

More than just a place, the Wiregrass is a frame of mind, a hopeful preservation of a way of life and language, a holding on to unique idioms and expressions.

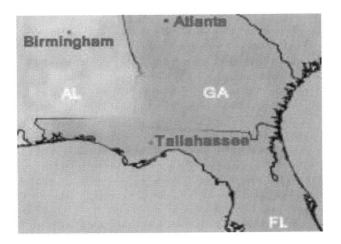

FOR MY GRANDCHILDREN...

who asked me to write about how our small towns
and communities once were.

I remember quiet places where people swapped rakes,
gossip, and recipes, where they knew each other's
personal business and refused to hold it against them.

OUR UNIQUE WAY OF TALKING

Thoroughly depicted in these pages, the expressive
language of the South is an American treasure.

Words and expressions common in frontier times
reflected settlers' origins. Different accents were
musical or guttural, high-pitched or low-pitched, slow
or fast. Here I try to preserve their colloquialisms,
idiosyncrasies of a vernacular still spoken in the
Wiregrass area, as in much of the South.

OUR SOULFUL MUSIC

Chapter headings feature snippets of Gospel songs,
which were an integral part of Wiregrass daily life
during the Great Depression. This was a time of
increased community reliance for maintaining hope
and positivity during debilitating drought, the 1929
Stock Market crash and the onset of World War II.

O they tell me of a home far beyond the skies;
O they tell me of a home far away.
O they tell me of a home where no storm
clouds rise;
O they tell me of an unclouded day.

Chapter One

Louette shifted her bony frame in the car seat and swiped at curly, gray hair. *The whole world is happy,* she thought, *especially me. This time of year, magic floats in the air looking for someplace to light.* She glanced sideways at her grandson Bucky, sitting on the edge of the car seat, his face glowing with expectation.

He doesn't look much like me, except for the auburn hair. He's stocky and filled out, more like Marj and Joseph.

Bucky swung his head back and forth, hunched forward, peering out the window as if trying to see their destination as they passed fresh-plowed fields and early budding peach trees on the way to the farm where his grandmother grew up.

"Did my mom go to the farm when she was my age?"

"She did. She stayed a lot with Mama and Daddy. She loved them, and the farm with all the cows, pigs, and chickens. She liked to filch eggs right out from under the hens."

Louise Etta Kelly, Louette for short, drove slowly down the winding lane to the weather-beaten farmhouse where she had grown up, where her brother Daniel and his wife Mittie now lived.

Six-year-old Bucky gazed at the unfolding scene, his eyes glittering with pleasure. "Look Gramma Lou, an eagle!"

"Likely a chicken hawk," she told him. "We used to watch for them when we played in the barnyard. They'd swoop down and grab up a baby chicken before you could say scat."

"I think I see rocking chairs," yelled Bucky. "Let's go rock on the front porch, Gramma Lou."

She guided the car around the house and into the barnyard with its weather-beaten wood-slatted barn. Shards of once-red paint clung to the rackety old building with bales of hay, rakes, shovels, and a pile of lumber visible through the open double doors.

Memories reached out and grabbed Louette's heart. The ladder still had rungs missing where she had climbed up to pitch hay near feed troughs for horses and cows. The small wheelbarrow her grandfather built for her sat by the door with sticks of firewood in it.

"Roll down your window," she told Bucky. He grabbed the handle. The atmosphere throbbed with animal sounds. Bucky clutched the edge of the car window as he stared at chickens pecking and scratching in a long pen.

An old dog stood, glanced at them, yawned and stretched lazily. "That's Popeye," Louette told Bucky. "We call him that because his eyes stick out. He's not much of a watchdog." Bucky sat as if welded to the window handle, his eyes and mouth open wide.

"When your great-grandmother's health went down so bad," Louette said in his direction though he obviously wasn't listening, "I holed up in the hospital or in the house with her until she died."

The memory was painful but Louette couldn't help rubbing at it. Sometimes it almost scabbed over. Then it broke open again and her other sorrows would also surface, over her husband Joseph leaving and her daughter Marj turning against her.

She wiped her eyes, took in a deep breath. "Let's get out and see the farm." With that Bucky was in motion. His door flew open.

"You don't have to tell me twice, Gramma Lou."

Watching Bucky was balm to Louette's soul. He stopped a few feet from the car, scuffed one foot back and forth in the pungent soil, then barreled ahead as if propelled from a cannon. He dipped his hand into the central horse trough. "Look, Gramma Lou, a big bathtub."

"The water is there for the animals to drink," she said, "horses, cows, and one especially ornery mule. Want to meet old Jobe?"

"Jobe?" His eyes sparkled.

Pursing her lips, Louette whistled, sharp and quick. Right away, from around the corner of the barn, appeared the long face of a gray mule with crafty eyes and pointed ears. "This is Jobe?" asked Bucky.

"Sure is. My brother, your great uncle Dan, got Jobe after Whistler disappeared."

"Whistler?"

"Yeah. When he neighed, the air whistled through his teeth. I think he took off about the same time your grandfather Joseph did, all those years ago. Maybe Joseph rode off on him instead of on the truck he left at the train station."

"Then Uncle Dan got Jobe?" Bucky reached toward the mule. "Can we pet him or feed him?" Before Louette could answer, Bucky climbed the tall square-wire fence and perched on a post. He looked into the mule's eyes.

Louette started to grab for him, then pulled back her hands. *My grandson can climb! Fast too!* She thought. "Better be careful," She told him. "That irritable old mule is apt to bite. He's got big teeth."

From his perch, Bucky considered the mule. Jobe, on the other side of the fence, returned the stare. A low chuckle sounded behind them. "This must be the grandson we've been so hungry to see."

"Here's your Uncle Dan," Louette told Bucky. "He's the owner of this mean old mule."

"Hello, Bucky." Carefully putting down a galvanized tin bucket filled with eggs, Dan extended eager hands toward the boy on the fence post. Bucky sat still for an instant, as if considering every aspect of this elderly person in faded blue overalls and low-brim sunhat. Something clicked. "Hello," he said, leaning into the tall man's arms.

Dan hugged Bucky. "My, how big you are."

Louette looked at the bucket. "I see the hens are laying a lot."

"Yeah. Mittie meant to call you or take you some eggs."

"You've rebuilt the hog pen." Louette hugged her brother. "I'm impressed."

"You ought to be. I got the plans through the Progressive Farmer. Not hard to follow, but I changed some of it."

"A concrete slab with water dribbling on it beside the mud puddle? Never seen that before." Louette picked up a Rhode Island Red hen, petted it then sent it flying toward the central watering trough.

"Yep. Old sow can rub her behind on that all she wants to. That raised platform under the shed yonder is for the pigs to get under to keep the sow from laying on 'em to mash 'em dead."

"Never seen one of those, but it sounds reasonable." Louette rubbed her hand on a fence post. *Treated four by fours. No splinters for the sow to rub on, gnaw, or push over.*

"According to the article, I could've put up a slat fence around the hog pen, but I didn't do that. I wanted to be able to see the pigs. I guess the six-footer is a bit tall. But hog wire seemed a better way to go. I did put planks around the bottom though, dug down some so they couldn't root out from under the fence."

"I've got a soft spot for pigs. Remember how Mama and Dad let us pick out pets, then when the pigs and chickens got big enough, they hauled them off to market?"

"I still feel the separation pain." Dan reached out and hugged Louette. She pulled on the fence, testing its strength. The wires stretched taut. "Seems safe to me." The sow, black with white markings, appearing to be at least four hundred pounds, watched warily, ready to attack if they came too close to her piglets.

"Gramma Lou!" Bucky called out as he ran around the side of the barn. "See the pigs! See the pigs!"

Dan dipped a bucket into a plastic garbage can, filling it with pig starter, then leaned over the fence and emptied the bucket into a food trough.

"Mittie's at the neighbors." Dan's eyes sparkled at Bucky's eagerness. "Wish she was here to see him now."

"She'll see him. We're in no hurry. Got him for the whole weekend. Life don't get no better than that."

Dan turned toward the barn for more pig starter. Louette's eyes wandered to a smelly compost pile beside the lot fence. Her eyes watered from the overpowering odor of cow, pig, mule and chicken manure. She looked toward the slough where she and Joseph had gotten into trouble for throwing wood into the quicksand sinkhole. The fence was still there.

"You planning to put compost on the Retherford field soon?" she called out, as Dan dipped another bucket of pig feed.

A deep, angry screech split the air, then a high keening wail. Louette looked up and froze. Bucky was inside the pen, his hand on a baby pig! The sow ran from the wallowing place near the water pipe, charging straight toward the child. Dan dropped the feed bucket, slapped his hand on a post and flew into the air, propelling himself over the fence.

Pig feed scattered. Louette slipped on it as she ran. One foot tumped over the bucket of eggs. Her head snapped back. Dan called out, "Lou, catch him."

In one motion, Louette's feet held ground as she flung her arms wide. Bucky plopped into them, his weight tipped her balance and she fell backward onto the egg bucket. The jolt jarred her knees and her elbows came down hard on the edge of the bucket. It felt like her arms were being ripped off. Bucky's weight slammed her hard onto the ground. They landed, arms and legs spread out, then sat up, eyes wide, mouths round as O's.

In the scramble Louette saw the blur of Dan's body lunging back over the fence—wallet, keys and penknife flying from his pockets. He landed with a thud.

With a yell almost as loud as the sow's bloodcurdling scream, Bucky ran toward Dan. Then he stopped between them, looking from Dan to his grandmother.

Louette's hand felt wet. She looked down. She was seated in a giant raw omelet, mixed with crushed eggshells and dirt. She pushed slowly to a crouch, not trusting her self to be able to stand.

A skid of brakes, and Mittie came running. "I saw from the road," she gasped and ran to Bucky, feeling his head, arms, legs. "Oh, my goodness. Are you hurt?"

Dan chortled. "You saw who Mittie went to check on first, didn't you, Lou?" Louette nodded.

The scene was unreal. She hurt all over. She wiped her face with the tail of her blouse. "Sorry about the eggs."

Mittie held Bucky, casting a practical eye on the mess, then leaned over and began picking out the unbroken eggs. Dan sat on his haunches near the fence. On the other side of the wide-mesh wire the sow now lay quietly stretched out, her piglets jockeying for nursing positions.

"Don't nobody panic," Dan said slowly, as if he'd rehearsed the words. "But I think old Walrus may have got me."

"Got you?" Mittie's hands were filled with gooey, unbroken eggs. She placed the eggs carefully in the bucket.

"You mean the sow bit you?"

"Seems like." Dan's words were careful, measured. "No pain has set in yet. But it looks like blood trickling over my foot onto the ground." Dan wrapped his arms around his knees and pulled them close. "Maybe it ain't too bad."

Louette rushed to Dan's side and rolled his overall leg to just above the calf. Blood oozed in miniature spurts from punctures made by long, sharp teeth. Dan looked in awe at the wound. "Old Walrus has been wantin' a piece of me awhile now."

"We'd better get you to a doctor," said Mittie as Dan produced a handkerchief from the pouch on the front of his overalls.

"Tie this around it," he said. "It'll pinch the holes shut. Maybe stanch the flow."

"I'll get him into the truck," said Mittie. "Lou, run in and call the hospital emergency room. The number is beside the phone."

Bucky stood next to Dan. "Wait there," Louette told him. "We'll sit in the back."

Tears stopped and Bucky brightened. "We're riding in the truck?"

"You bet," said Louette. "In the back. You and me." She ran to make the call as Bucky scrambled over the tailgate. Then she climbed in beside him. Mittie gunned the motor. Louette used a burlap fertilizer bag to wipe egg from her arms and from Bucky's face.

The truck leaped over the gravel road and soon skidded to a stop at the emergency room entrance where rescue workers in white uniforms ran toward them with a gurney.

"Gored by a hog," one told a nurse at the door.

It didn't take long for the doctor to arrive. "Damn," he said to Dan. "Old Walrus finally get you?"

"Sure did."

"I told you that big sow was dangerous first time I saw her." Dr. Bartow Tippin cuffed Dan on the shoulder. They had been in the same grade in school and had played baseball together.

"Just stitch up the cut, Bart, 'fore I bleed to death."

"Stay off the leg," Dr. Tippin told him when he was done. "There, there" he kept saying to Mittie. "You got him here in time. Dan with a wound is all just part of a day's business. He used to get more cuts and scrapes than any of us boys. Might have been what helped me decide to become a doctor. Knew I'd have plenty of practice keeping up with Dan."

Louette and Bucky huddled together at the far side of the treatment room, Bucky holding to Louette's slacks, his dirt-streaked face peeking around her. "This looks like the place where they give you a shot," Bucky whispered. Louette smiled in spite of herself.

A nurse brought crutches and helped Dan stand and position them under his arms. He looked askance at the supports. "These saplings don't look too strong," he tried to joke, but maneuvered himself down the hall—over the years he'd had plenty of practice.

Dr. Tippin walked with them to the front desk. "These are important people," he told the receptionist.

"You're right about that!" she smiled. "If their mom hadn't sold land and donated money, the county wouldn't have gotten a matching grant to build this hospital."

Louette, Dan, Mittie, and Bucky walked past a painting of Louette and Dan's mother Clara on the wall at the entrance, commemorating the dedication of the hospital in her name. "I'll tell him the story behind the picture when he's older," Louette said at a questioning look from Mittie.

Mittie nodded. "It don't look much like her anyway."

"Don't take him to any square dances!" Dr. Tippin hollered out to Mittie, who tried a polite laugh.

Dan maneuvered the crutches around potholes in the pavement as they made their way back to the truck. They seemed not to hear as the boy chattered on. "I petted the baby pigs. But the mama pig didn't like me."

At the truck, the adults stopped. Louette turned her face toward the sky. "Thank you," she whispered to the windblown clouds.

Bucky chattered on. "The hens let Uncle Dan pick eggs, didn't they Gramma Lou? Hens are more friendly than big pigs."

Louette reached for Bucky and hugged him. *The young know no fear or danger.* Dread formed in the pit of her stomach. She looked at Dan's bandages. His overall pants-leg flapped where the nurse had slashed the denim. There was a chill to the March breeze.

"You sit in the cab with Mittie," Dan told Lou. "I'll get in the back with Bucky."

Mittie's usually serene face clouded. "You sure?"

"I'd better keep the leg moving," Dan put his arm lovingly around her shoulders. A look of trust passed between them. "I'll be all right."

Louette wasn't ready to release the wriggling boy. The horror of the near-tragedy settled around her, and her knees felt weak. "Phew," she told him. "You smell like raw eggs."

"I know." Bucky giggled. He settled beside Dan. "I never rode in a truck before today. I'll have to remember and tell my mom and dad." His voice swelled with pride.

In the cab of the truck, Louette said, "I sure hope he forgets to tell them why we went to the hospital."

Mittie nodded. Her hands trembled on the steering wheel. "Or the fact he rode in the bed of an open truck."

On the way home, the women shared a grateful silence. The fascination of a countryside ready to bloom no longer held Louette's attention. The truck purred along on the blacktop road. Bucky's laughter and Dan's low, calm voice echoed from the back. The realization that the angry sow could have killed them both hung in the air between the two women.

As the truck entered the lane and slowed, Louette could hear Dan and Bucky talking. She motioned for Mittie to listen. "What's that?" Bucky called out. He had noticed the tall wooden privacy fence of pointed stakes along the west side boundary.

Dan chuckled. "That fence separates us from the people in Shady Oaks," he told the boy. "They say fences make good neighbors, like in Robert's Frost's famous poem 'Mending Wall'."

"How can it be true, Uncle Dan?" Bucky seized on the subject. "There's no fence around Gramma Lou's yard. You can walk right over to Aunt Shirley's or Miz Gumby's."

Dan hugged Bucky. "Boy, you can right smartly run a conversation into the ground."

Mittie parked the truck behind the house. The teeming barnyard commanded Bucky's attention, but Louette noted that he walked near to the house, away from the fence. His eyes big with wonder, he kept saying, "Look, look," at the chickens, but didn't mention the sow and pigs. He stayed as close as he could to the adults as they made their way toward the house.

Inside the kitchen, Mittie told Dan, "You sit in your chair. Lou can shower while the coffee perks. Bucky and I will rescue what's left of the eggs."

"No argument from me." Dan leaned back, closing his eyes.

Louette went upstairs to the bedroom, which had been hers in her youth. First her mother, Clara, and then Mittie, had kept Louette's room at the farm as a place to come back to. Occasionally Louette and Joseph had stayed there together, then Marj slept there when she spent time with her grandmother and uncle and aunt.

After Louette took her mother Clara to town to live with her, Dan and Mittie had moved from the tenant house to the big house. After the tenant house burned down, they sold more of the farmland to a developer, leaving just enough so that Dan could continue to keep up the farm place.

"Habit and ritual are important," Dan said. "Activity is what keeps people going. I've worked here most of my life. I want to keep it that way. And, I want to survive for a long time, if I can." He and Mittie lived at the farm alone, content to take care of the fields and animals.

This room should have been for the baby that Dan and Mittie wanted but never had, thought Louette. *When Marj was growing up, she slept in here too. Mittie hadn't changed anything then either.*

A picture of Lou and the other Ponce de Leon High School cheerleaders still sat on the bureau; pennants from the Ponce de Leon Pirates hung beside the door. Over the chest of drawers was a wedding picture of Louette and Joseph as they raced from the church in a shower of rice to a 1951 Plymouth. Beside the picture of Lou in high school cap and gown were photos of Marj's graduation from Geneva High School and from Florida State University. *Happy times, long gone,* she thought.

As she pulled slacks and a blouse from the closet, her hand brushed a shirt of Joseph's. Years after he disappeared, Mittie had grabbed a handful of hangers to help her carry his work shirts and jeans to the secondhand store, but Louette had taken the clothes from her and put them back in the closet. "He'll come home, Mittie," she said. "I just know it." Today, it still seemed natural for Joseph's clothing to hang in the closet in her old room at the farm and in her house in town.

What if Benjamin asked her to marry him? If that was what he wanted, she'd have to clear out Joseph's clothes. Louette shivered. She wasn't sure she could do that. *Maybe, if Benjamin helped...*

Even with the troubling image of Benjamin beside her, clearing out Joseph's things, there was a feeling of peace in the room. It seemed happy times and memories were in the air and they crowded around, comforting her. "I'll have to put a picture of Bucky in here."

After a quick shower and change into clean but musty-smelling clothes, Louette made her way downstairs. Her knees popped when she walked and her left leg looked twice it's size. In the kitchen, the shock of the sow's attack flooded back upon her. Her hands shook as she poured herself a cup of coffee.

Mittie and Bucky clattered in at the back door with rescued eggs. "Let's wash them," Mittie told him.

Louette took the pot into the den and freshened Dan's coffee. She let out a long breath. "You realize, don't you, that the way you leaped over that fence was impossible for a man your age? I thank you for saving my grandson's life."

"Dan's quick," Mittie called out. "When we were young, he used to catch a baseball, fling it home, then run backwards 'til he could stop."

When they finished cleaning up the surviving eggs, Mittie told Bucky, "Now it's your turn for a bath."

He grabbed his grandmother around the waist. "Umm, you smell good."

"Be careful. You'll get Lou dirty again," Mittie warned. She was a tiny woman, short enough to stand under Dan's outstretched arm, more like a ballet dancer than a farmer's wife.

From the bathroom door, Bucky handed Mittie his soiled clothes and she put them in the washing machine with Louette's. "I can wash ours later."

As her grandson bathed, Louette sat on a kitchen stool sipping coffee. There was no excuse for allowing Bucky to climb into the hog pen. If her brother hadn't jumped the fence and grabbed him, the sow would have killed him. The sow's squeal rang again in Louette's ears.

Bucky played in the tub. He was a happy six-year-old, impervious to fear, resistant to calamity. But Louette knew Marj would be angry when she learned what had happened. She'd had harsh words from Marj many times, and not just when Marj was a teenager. Over all those years since Joseph left, the pain had festered beneath the surface. After one bitter exchange between Marj and herself Louette's mother had tried to soothe her about it. "You must be patient," she had cautioned Louette. But patience was not Louette's strong suit. She was more no-nonsense, practical. Even now her thoughts kept returning to what she might have done differently with Marj.

Bucky sang and kicked up a racket. "I have to take a shower at home. This is more fun," he called out.

Mittie walked to the bathroom door, a smile on her face. "You might better get out of there," she told Bucky, "or all that water will turn you into a prune."

Bucky splashed happily. "What's a prune?"

"It's sort of like a raisin, only bigger, all wrinkled and dark." Mittie had changed her clothes and was tying an apron over her old-fashioned house dress.

Though Bucky would have liked turning into a raisin-prune, Louette and Mittie ushered him out of the tub and into his clothes. He skipped to Uncle Dan in the den. "Don't tire your Uncle Dan," Louette warned Bucky. She could see her brother was uncomfortable.

The skin of his spare, craggy face stretched over the bones like a coon hide nailed to the side of a barn. "Leave him alone, he's going to help me take a nap." He pulled Bucky up on his lap and the child watched Dan's face as the man closed his eyes and dropped off to sleep. Bucky held still as long as he could, then tentatively reached out and patted Dan's hand.

At Mittie's nod and her finger pointed toward the front of the house, Bucky eased from Dan's lap and followed the women to the front porch. Popeye the dog was on the porch sound asleep. "Why does Popeye have such long cheeks hanging down?" Bucky asked. Popeye opened one eye, eased himself up, and paced slowly to the rocking chair where Bucky swung his legs back and forth. The dog lay as near to Bucky as he could.

Louette nudged Mittie. "Old Popeye better watch out for his tail."

Now I'm so happy,
No sorrow in sight . . .

Chapter Two

Late in the day Lou and Bucky reluctantly headed toward town, up the river road and back over the levee to Geneva. She hummed "I saw the light," as she guided the car over the winding road. "No more darkness, no more night..." Bucky snuggled against her. A feeling of sheer happiness engulfed her as she drove along with her grandson peacefully napping, his mouth making motorboat sounds. She took the long way around, past Benjamin's place with its carefully clipped hedges in the shape of a long train.

As Louette parked in her side yard, the sun began to slide down its evening chute, dusting the sky gold and mauve. Bucky mumbled.

Louette sat for an instant, admiring the sunset. In the side yard she saw what looked like a reddish-brown cat with a thick tail. A sunbeam flushed the furry animal with a bright glow, turning its coat into a shimmering copper shield.

"Why did you stop, Gramma Lou?" Bucky was suddenly awake. Then he saw the animal. "Ooooh," he said. "What is it?"

"A fox squirrel, I think." A twist of dread formed near her stomach. She realized that when Marj learned about the danger Bucky had faced at the farm, she would never let him stay alone with her overnight again.

"How can it be a fox and a squirrel at the same time?"

"Lord, Bucky, you can ask the most gosh-awful questions. Let's rest our tongues for a change." They got out of the car. The little boy skipped ahead. He kicked leaves under the rain tree and jumped so hard on the picnic table Louette was afraid it would collapse. *Let it*, she thought. It was a joy to see him bounce around her bedraggled back yard.

She reached her hand into her pocket. *Benjamin's note.* She'd found it early in the morning, before Bucky came. She had walked onto the back steps to see a bouquet of roses with the note tucked in them. *That man could make a fence post bloom if he took a mind to.*

She pulled out the note. It smelled like the roses she had put on the breakfast table. *I wish he wouldn't do this. I already told him I couldn't have feelings for him, not with Joseph gone. Me and Joseph said our vows, for better or for worse.*

The pain of Joseph's leaving mixed with her sentiments toward Benjamin. She wanted to be more than friends, but she had to keep her emotions tamped down until she knew for sure if her husband would ever come back. She held the note to her nose, then read it again.

"Dear Louette, I brought these roses for a reason. We need to talk. I understand you're troubled right now, so soon after your mother's death. But Joseph has been gone more than twenty years. I have to know if there is room for me in your life. My cousin Louis insisted I go hunting with him in Tate's Hell. I'll be back in about a week. When I get back, no excuses. I need to know how you really feel about me, once and for all. Love, Benjamin."

Louette crumpled the paper into a wad, held it to her lips, kissed it then shoved it back into her pocket. *I just can't do it, Benjamin*, ran through her mind, even while a flush spread outward over her, enveloping her with its heat.

"Duty and honor come before personal considerations." She could hear the words as if her mother spoke them aloud.

What about love, Mama? My soul is parched. The heartache is like a cancer, growing in me. What can I do?

She listened to the wind rattle the rain tree's leaves. Close by, Bucky's voice echoed over the back yard. Far off she could hear the whistle of a freight train. Pinecones made popping sounds as they fell on the tin roof of the shed in the side yard. But not a sound from her dead mother. *Not a cotton-picking word*, she thought, *when I need it most.* She couldn't stop the hurts from surfacing, like peeling an onion, with fresh tears for each layer.

Bucky bounced around the yard like a bunny, hopping over the mounds where last year's corn stalks had stood. She looked around. The neighbor's orange and black tabby cat sat on the stoop, staring at her. Waiting.

Bucky came running just as she called out, "Let's feed the kitty." Bucky stomped into the kitchen. She opened a can of cat food and spooned it into a broken saucer. *Shirley must be gone again. Some kind of neighbor that Shirley is. Looks like she'd feed her animal before she runs off somewheres, or at least ask me if I'll feed it, or tell me thank you when I do, for that matter.*

"I'll sit with kitty while she eats," said Bucky from the back steps. He stroked its soft fur as it gobbled the food.

From the door, Louette could hear a dog barking. A rooster picked up the rhythm and the mockingbird who lived in the rain tree added its tunes. "It's not even quiet at dark around here," she told Bucky.

Louette rubbed the spot on her back where it ached. The screen door squeaked as she held it for Bucky to come inside. The cat ambled off, full and satisfied. *I should put some oil on those noisy door hinges. Or mop the kitchen floor,* she thought. But her hand didn't reach into the pantry for the oil or the mop.

She and Bucky stretched their arms and yawned at the same time, then burst out laughing.

"We're already clean. Why don't we just put on our sleepers and go to bed?" Bucky agreed. He didn't seem very tired, but he had slowed down with the questions. "You sleep in your mom's bed," Louette told him. "When you get changed I'll come tuck you in."

"Okay, Gramma Lou." He held his pajamas aloft. "It won't take me long." He rushed into the bathroom and then jumped right into the bed. "I'm ready, Gramma Lou," he called out.

Louette came into the bedroom and tucked the covers around him. "You are certainly fast," she said, remembering how quickly he had climbed into the pigpen.

"I know." He smiled and was making motorboat sounds with his mouth before Louette could get a book for a bedtime story. She tiptoed out. As she went down the hall, the sound of the telephone jarred the evening quiet.

Who could that be? Shirley's gone. Probably Deputy Clyde. Clyde was Joseph's fishing buddy from long ago; checking up on her was his usual habit.

"Hello," she said.

"Need anything?" It was Clyde.

"Not that I know of." She almost told him about the pig incident but thought better of it. "Thanks anyway. I'm fine."

She didn't feel fine. Actually, she hurt all over and her knee kept swelling bigger and bigger. She was tired from all that commotion. And so was Bucky. He'd fallen asleep almost as fast as he had climbed over the pigpen fence.

"Bet Bucky ran you a race." She could feel Clyde's smile over the telephone.

"We've had a full day," she told him.

When Clyde was a child, he had been Joseph's shadow. She felt a twinge when she thought about how Joseph had wanted a boy. Not that he didn't love Marj, she was his heart. But Joseph looked forward to teaching Clyde how to fish. He would ask Joseph questions like "When the sun first comes up, the light's pink. Why's that?" Joseph would laugh and give the rambunctious little boy an answer of some kind, which was often followed by another "why?"

After Joseph left, Clyde didn't come around much; he grew up and joined the Navy. Occasionally he'd send a postcard from some mysterious-looking port. "Just want to say Hi." When his father the sheriff died, Clyde came home for good—joining the county sheriff's force as a deputy. After he settled in as an officer of the law, Clyde drove by now and then.

He acts like it's his duty to pester me, thought Louette. Night and day, he'd pop up. "How you doin'?" he'd ask. She smoothed out Benjamin's note. He didn't call or come around as often as Clyde, but he made sure she knew he was serious.

The phone rang. "I told you I don't need anything, Clyde."

"I'm not Clyde, Mom." It was Marj.

"What do you want?" Louette realized her words sounded harsh, but they were already out there, flapping like wet laundry in the wind. She wished she could take them back, soften them somewhat then reel them out slow and friendly.

"Are you okay, Mom?"

"Sure," said Louette. "I'm sorry," she added. "I didn't mean to be so abrupt. Guess my voice is getting rusty." *Had she heard about the sow attack?* Dread, like a dead weight, sank to the bottom of Louette's stomach, and settled there.

"My class reunion committee is in charge of refreshments tonight before Florida State homecoming and I just got a chance to call. You two having fun?"

Louette could imagine Marj on the other end of the phone line, her skinny arm leaning against the desk in the hotel. *She has her grandmother's dark hair, smooth brow and serious expression, but not her big heart*, Louette thought. The sow attack at the farm today would nail another painful plank into the wall between them.

"We had so much fun at the farm that Bucky's already asleep." *So, she hadn't heard.*

"You thought I was Clyde. I heard he was away in the military or something."

"Clyde's a deputy. He comes by the house now and then. Kind of peculiar. Seeing about me, he says. Maybe he's thinking of when he was little and followed Joseph around, or maybe he misses you."

"Misses me? You've got to be kidding."

"I know you insisted you'd never marry a man named Clyde, but you did date him." Louette wished she had married Clyde, instead of that supercilious college professor Snowden.

Snowden taught at the University of West Florida in Pensacola after they graduated from Florida State, then accepted a position as instructor of social studies at Huntingdon College in Montgomery, Alabama. With a degree in business, Marj was now in charge of the registrar's office.

"I'm fine with Snowden, thank you," Marj said with a chuckle. "Even if he is scratchy like sandpaper, sometimes. He's not the only prickly person I know."

It was nice to hear Marj's normal voice. Usually their conversation was more stilted. Louette had long ago given up on getting closer to Marj. She had tried over the years, but that wall around her daughter had been constructed from sorrow when Marj was ten years old. Since Joseph left, her daughter had blamed her for his abandoning the family.

Louette fingered Benjamin's note as she got ready for bed. She wondered what he saw when he looked at her. She knew the years etched her face with hills and valleys turning here and there on her chin and cheeks. The thought of being old affected her like a head cold coming on. Mixed with that was what would happen when Marj found out about the sow attacking Bucky. She'd likely never get a visit from her beloved grandson again.

Love divine, all loves excelling, Joy
of Heav'n, to earth come down!

Chapter Three

Louette woke up early. Marj hadn't called again, so she must not have heard about the sow attack. Louette had Bucky to herself one more day. After that, who knew what Marj would come up with. The uneasiness was lessened by a warm feeling of completeness, like a live thing pulsing within her. She heard him stirring in the other room.

Louette grinned from ear to ear as she rushed to get the coffee ready. *"Some glad morning, when this life is o'er,"* she sang in her clear soprano. *"I'll fly away."* But not today, she thought. *I'm too happy to fly away. After Marj hears about the pigs, that'll be the bad day.*

"Fine morning," she called out, "I am so glad you are here."

Bucky skipped in and gave her a wide-awake hug. "Smells good in this kitchen," he said. "Friendly. Not like Miz Gumby's house." Miz Gumby was Louette's neighbor on the east side. Shirley lived on the west.

"What do you mean, Bucky? Not like Miz Gumby's?"

"It was funny there," Bucky said. "It smelled like a wet cat. You remember the day I stayed with her while you and Mom and Dad got all dressed up?"

"I remember." Louette said.

"She wouldn't let me in the house, except to go to the bathroom. We sat on the porch all day long. I got tired and took a nap on the swing," said Bucky.

"You didn't even go in the kitchen to eat?" Louette asked.

"She brought jelly samwiches to us on the porch. But the cat smell followed her right on out the door. We sat on the swing and ate. The samwiches were good, though," Bucky said.

"Miz Gumby's sort of peculiar," said Louette. Her mind wandered into another memory. One time the old lady lost a pearl brooch somewhere in her house and thought it had been stolen. Louette and neighbor Shirley found it in plain sight on Miz Gumby's dresser. 'I looked in my jewelry box where it was supposed to be,' grumbled Miz Gumby. She thanked them for finding the brooch. But after that, she was stingy about inviting anybody into her house. Said you just couldn't trust most folks. Louette walked to the stove. "How about flapjacks?"

"What are flapjacks?"

"Something like pancakes. You like pancakes and syrup?"

Bucky blinked. "Got any Pop Tarts?"

"I thought those things were just something in television commercials. Didn't think anybody really ate em."

"I like the strawberry ones best of all. Got any?"

"What about eggs?"

"Mom says she doesn't want me eating anything that has a mother."

Louette put her hand over her mouth to stifle a laugh. "I've got cornflakes."

Bucky looked thoughtful. He wasn't through with the chicken and egg. "Does an egg really have a mother?"

"A hen lays an egg, so I guess she's its mother. But she doesn't get to keep it or anything. It's like a factory. They set up the chickens on an assembly line and they drop eggs as a conveyor belt rolls along under them. It takes the eggs right on to where they wash them and put 'em in cartons. I suppose the egg could even think of the egg carton as its mother." Louette stopped. This was getting tricky. "But I get my eggs from the refrigerator section." Disbelief marked Bucky's face.

"Tell you what," she told him. "I'll make biscuits. You can bust one open and put strawberry preserves in it and pretend it's a Pop Tart." Louette greased the biscuit pan and mixed buttermilk in flour, then rolled out the fluffy dough into round biscuits.

Bucky walked about the room, moving his shoulders up and down as if copying a scene from a movie. "My dad said he wouldn't eat at your house, 'cause your kitchen is unsanitary." He peered around, inspecting the entire room.

Typical of Bucky's dad all right. He could mess up anybody's happiness with one little passed-on remark. "Do you agree?"

"It is pretty dark in here." He looked around. "But I kinda like it." He walked over and leaned against the refrigerator, which gave a friendly burp.

Louette took a deep breath and sighed. "To me it's just old, and some of my favorite things are old. The wallpaper does need replacing. The plumbing is ancient. The wiring's about shot."

Louette looked around at faded fruit print wallpaper and the pale trim, once bright green. She had redecorated the kitchen about ten years ago. Since then she had painted the cabinets and woodwork once but washed the woodwork only occasionally. Looking at it with the child standing there, the kitchen seemed shabby indeed.

Bucky's marching route took him to the table where he perched on a dinette chair to look out the window. "You moved the picnic table," he announced.

"My, aren't you smart," Louette said. "Maybe that's why your mom named you for Buckminster Fuller."

"I know, she told me he 'vented a 'desic dome." Bucky grinned. "My dad said that's not so—he copied the design off an Eskimo igloo."

Bucky hadn't seen the back yard since his great-grandmother Clara's funeral, which Marj didn't let him attend. Marj said he might be confused about death. After the funeral, Marj had retrieved Bucky from Miz Gumby's house and they had gone to the attorney's office to hear the will read.

Louette had wondered why Marj thought he wouldn't understand death but took him to hear how his Grandma Clara left most everything to Louette anyway. Sometimes, to her, Marj and her fancy-pants husband didn't act like they had walking-around sense.

Returning to her house after the funeral, the first thing the child had asked was where to find his other grandma. Louette had held her breath at Marj's explanation that Grandma Clara was away. Bucky seemed to accept it.

Louette believed, deep down, that children instinctively knew more than adults realized. Marj had rushed off right after supper. The memory stabbed at her heart.

Louette put the biscuits in the oven. She broke an egg into a bowl. "What did you decide about the eggs? Thought I'd scramble a few. I can eat them if they're against your religion, or something."

"Oh, it's not religion. My mom says it's trying to be a veginarian."

Louette stifled a quick laugh. "What does your dad say?" The skillet made a sizzling sound as she stirred the eggs.

Bucky laughed a high, clear note. He threw back his head. A lock of hair so much like Joseph's bounced about his face. *His nose is like mine. I don't see a thing about the child which favors his parents. Maybe his build, a little. He is sort of stocky, with thick wrists and arms.*

"My dad doesn't like some of Mom's ideas. He says they came from you and that you're ignorant about most things." *Takes one to know one,* thought Louette. *Snowden may be a college professor but he's sure enough ignorant about human kindness.*

She sat on a kitchen chair and pulled the boy onto her lap. "I may not meet your father's expectations, but I do know that I love you very much." *Isn't this what heaven is all about?* Bucky leaned close to her and sighed happily.

Louette rubbed her cheek against the top of his head. "What are you thinking?"

"This is the happiest day of my life." His soft hair felt like spun silk.

"Why?"

"'Cause I am here with you."

Louette couldn't stop the tears. "I am happy too, Bucky. More than you can even guess."

He jumped down then and ran around the dinette, tagging a chair as if playing with other children. *An energetic little boy,* she thought.

"I'd better take up the eggs and check on the biscuits." She stood up. "Want a couple of strips of bacon?"

"Gramma Lou, bacon comes from pigs and pigs have mothers. That old mama pig tried to eat me. She bited Uncle Dan."

"We'll skip the bacon. I'd better find the strawberry jam." Louette split hot biscuits and slathered them with butter while Bucky sat in the chair beside her, watching closely. Louette handed him a spoon and the preserves. "Why don't you dip up some for us?"

"You can put eggs on my plate, too, Gramma Lou." Bucky glanced at her. "I saw you take the egg box out of the refrigerator."

Without thinking, Louette poured a glass of milk for the child. He didn't mention it, so she supposed Marj hadn't talked about cows having babies. Bucky took another swallow, smiled, and hiccupped loudly.

"My mom says you're a little crazy."

Louette laughed. "Maybe it runs in the family."

He changed the subject. "I like to look at the picture of my great-grandma, but it's only got her head." Bucky's voice sounded firm, like Marj's. "Was she like you?"

"Sort of. I'm thinner and taller. She was more petite. Before she took sick she was an extremely positive person, strong-willed. She would raise one eyebrow when making a point. When she raised both eyebrows, you better watch out." Louette bit her lip. "You did see her once when you were little."

"I don't remember," he said.

"Your mom didn't bring you again until the day we went to the church and you stayed with Miz Gumby."

"When I talk to Grandma Clara's picture sometimes at home, she smiles at me." To include Louette, he added, "I like your picture, too. But I don't talk to it much 'cause it's too high on the mantel."

Louette patted Bucky on the head and swallowed around the lump in her throat. *He's so wonderful.*

She looked out the window at a turkey buzzard sailing over the rain tree, hoping that wasn't a bad omen. The angry sow was enough bad luck for anybody's lifetime, especially hers. It had a frightful quality about it all its own, worse than the scare when after a rainstorm she'd seen a magnolia tree fall into the sinkhole out at the farm and the quicksand had pulled it straight down, roots and all.

While she washed the dishes and Bucky ran around the back yard, memories crowded in. She and Joseph had played around that sinkhole when they were kids. Her dad had warned them to stay away from it, that it would eat them alive. But at twelve years old Joseph was skeptical. He had pitched a yellow orange peel into the gray, trembling water to see if it would sink, then threw in Louette's whole orange. Louette had watched, mesmerized as Joseph also hurled a piece of rotten wood from the split-rail fence into the murky water. The wood rolled over, then swirled downward with a sucking sound.

Even now, standing in her own kitchen, listening to Bucky run around the yard, Louette could feel the wind whipping her face. She could smell the wetness of the sand pulsating as it pulled the whole orange, orange peel, and piece of wood out of sight. Louette dried the last fork and shook her head to clear it, her eyes on her grandson.

The farm was a wondrous place if you didn't think of the sinkhole. Even now with only a few fields left and the 200 acres having been sold for the fancy housing development, Dan still enjoyed working those forty acres. He'd soon be out making the cultivated land into plowed rows that would look like a giant's combed hair. The fresh-plowed soil smelling so good, the fields were like the balm of Gilead.

"Come inside, Bucky," she called out. "We'd better get ready for church."

"What's your church like?" he asked.

"Probably not much different from yours," Louette told him. "Let's get dressed and you can see for yourself."

Pride was reflected in Louette's purposeful walk down the aisle. This was her grandson, brought to her church, by her, for the inspection of friends and acquaintances. She saw heads turn and nodded every few feet on the way to the third-row seat.

Miz Gumby moved over and Shirley followed. "Where's Benjamin?" Shirley asked.

"How should I know?" Louette mouthed back. She didn't want her neighbor involved in her personal business. *The nerve of that woman.*

"Pa...a...ardon me," huffed Shirley. "I thought you two were thick as soppin' syrup."

Louette didn't answer. She'd jump that creek when she got to it. But it wasn't today. This was her time with her grandson before Marj learned about the pigs.

"When the ro...o...oll is called up yaw...n...der..." they sang, in full southern drawl. Louette peeked at Bucky. The little scaper was lip-syncing the words. She reached for his songbook and turned it right-side-up, then patted him on the head. "I'll be th...e...e...e...re."

Louette straightened her shoulders and stood as tall as she could. "On the other side of Jordan," she sang lustily. "In the sweet fields of Eden... there is rest for you." She felt rest, deep in her soul, even with the extra helping of dread way down in her stomach.

When the congregation settled with a sigh, Preacher Ed intoned: "There is no joy greater than today." *You got that part right*, thought Louette. "Not yesterday, for it is already gone." Louette wished there was some way she could wipe yesterday from Bucky's memory, for he was sure to tell Marj. And Marj was sure to be mad as a guinea wasp. "Not tomorrow, for we don't have the privilege of knowing what another day brings. Look for today's promise, today's hope, the beauty of the fields, the delight in the harvest."

Preacher Ed has the seasons wrong. He is correct about today though. It is so wonderful to have my grandson here beside me. I'd better cram in as much living with him as I can. This may be the last day I will ever spend with him without his parents.

Patting Bucky on the shoulder, Louette saw Miz Gumby's bony hand reach out and touch him on the knee. *It is one thing to show pictures of your grandson at church and at the grocery store. It is quite another to have the real article sitting beside you.* She thought.

Bucky looked puzzled at the sermon, the same look Marj used to show when she disagreed with someone. Once at a Wednesday night prayer meeting, when the leader, Mrs. Snow, invited questions, Marj stood up abruptly. "I don't have a question," she said. "I have a statement: I have come to believe the Holy Spirit in the Trinity is a woman."

Almost before the loud gasp died, Marj offered her explanation: "It seems strange to me, in a world where it is taught that the family is what holds civilization together, for the Trinity to consist of three male spirits. Surely the founders of religion would have understood that the spirit which cared personally about every human being and helped people to survive must, by definition, be female."

Louette was mortified. Joseph had chuckled. "She's a child, trying to figure out what she believes." That was when love embraced the little family.

She and Marj were so different. Joseph had been the buffer between them. Joseph's absence, instead of bringing them together, had built the terrible wall of grief, which still held them apart.

Bucky closed the songbook and leaned back against the polished pew. When Preacher Ed started talking again, Louette glanced down. Bucky's eyes drooped. In an instant he was asleep. A puff of air escaped his pursed lips. He awoke with a jerk of his head when the congregation stood singing, "We shall come rejoicing, bringing in the sheaves."

"What a sweet boy," Miz Gumby said when the service ended.

"We're going home the long way around," Louette told her neighbor, holding her mouth in plain view. Miz Gumby didn't hear well, but she could read lips. "You can walk with us if you like. I want Bucky to see Benjamin's trains."

Miz Gumby chuckled. "He'll enjoy that," she said. "I won't go with you, Lou; I'd best head straight home." A smile split her wrinkled face. "Enjoy Benjamin's trains. They're special," she told Bucky.

As they walked, Louette thought about Benjamin's note, now smoothed out and settled in her purse. Bucky perked up. "Did I see the trains when I was a little boy, when I was here before?"

"I don't think so."

"Does Benjamin have lots of trains?"

Louette laughed. "Does he!"

Benjamin was one of those people who seem lonely, as if stuck in time. He had told Louette that he had been married, his wife died, and they had no children. He had retired as a railroad engineer after he fell while trying to climb onto a locomotive, and rolled down a ravine. His injuries took a long time to heal. By the time he was well they hired someone to replace him, so he retired. This town was his start on a new, more leisurely life.

To Louette he looked like a young man while wielding shears on the hedges scattered about his yard. Then, again, his shoulders would slump and he looked as if he were hauling around the troubles of the world. Around Louette he laughed and talked, then clammed up when another person came near. "Most people I know aren't very interesting," he told her. "Maybe I'm like what Will Rogers used to say."

"What?"

"'I love humanity, it's people I can't stand.'"

"Maybe they aren't as interested in what you do as you wish they were," added Louette.

"You hit that nail on the head." Benjamin reached out and took her hand.

He said he wanted more from her and she knew she felt deeply toward him. But where did that leave Joseph? She yearned to get closer to Benjamin, but the specter of Joseph stood in the way. Louette felt stuck between a rock and a hard place.

"Benjamin is an enigma," said Louette.

"What's a 'nigma?" asked Bucky.

"A perplexing, baffling, hard-to-understand person."

"Will he let me see his trains?"

"You can't miss them," Louette assured him.

Rounding the corner to Benjamin's place, Louette watched Bucky's expression of surprise. "Wow! Look, look Gramma Lou." He ran to admire the engine, boxcars and caboose carved from privet hedge, jasmine, hibiscus, azalea, camellia, and gardenia plants. "This IS a train!"

After close inspection, Bucky announced to his grandmother: "Benjamin sure draws nice pictures with bushes."

"I never thought of it that way." Louette marveled at Bucky's perception.

"Does Benjamin have a little boy?"

"No," said Louette. "Benjamin is old like me. And he's not lucky enough to have a grandson like you." The last was said proudly as if it were somehow a miracle she did actually have a grandson.

Bucky ran from dining car, passenger car, engine, to caboose. "This is where the flowers you have on the table came from," he announced.

"They sure did." Louette leaned over and nuzzled a rose. It smelled exciting and mysterious.

"I could do this," Benjamin told Louette. "If I had some big-enough scissors." He twirled a jasmine vine around his arm. He sat down on the doorsteps. "Let's wait 'till Benjamin gets here."

"He's out of town and you'll likely be gone home when he gets back."

"Oh." Bucky breathed in the perfume of the just-opening jasmine blossoms.

"I know you're disappointed," Louette told him. "He's looking forward to meeting you."

"You told him about me?"

"I did. You'll meet him when you come to visit another time." Worry gnawed at her. *If there ever is another time.* She rubbed her arms and shivered.

Bucky skipped cheerfully beside Louette as they walked around the block and turned into her yard. He jumped onto the porch swing and started it creaking back and forth. "Didn't you tell me we'd look in the shed for the big gopher shell when we got back from church?" he said. "That place where you keep old stuff."

"The food's ready for lunch," she told him. "Let's eat first. All we have to do is heat it up." She hoped he liked spaghetti. Marj had called it "pasketti" when she was Bucky's age. *At least I know not to put meat in the sauce, since he's a "veginarian".*

As Louette opened the door, she saw neighbor Shirley emerge from around the weathered shed in the side yard. Shirley wound her way through ankle-high grass. *Got to cut that grass.*

"Lou! Bucky!" Shirley called out, now rushing across the yard.

"You should have been with us at Benjamin's," Louette told her. "Bucky saw the trains." Bucky nodded, frowning slightly as Shirley hugged him.

"What did you think of Benjamin's trains?" Shirley asked.

"They were cool." Bucky stared at Shirley's platform shoes.

"I wish I had walked home with you," Shirley told them.

Her husband had died in an automobile accident four years after their marriage, and ever since she had been a grieving widow, living off income from the insurance settlement. At fifty-five, Shirley dressed and acted thirty, as if life was now beginning and an exciting man lurked in her future.

"I'm on my way to the store. Need anything, Lou?"

"Not that I know of." Louette reached for Bucky's hand. "We're going through the shed later. I told Bucky about the gopher-turtle shell Mama used to keep crochet thread in, and he wants to see it. You could help us look." Right then Louette realized she was grasping at anything to keep Bucky's mind on the present. She hoped he wouldn't tell Shirley about the incident at the farm. She held her breath.

"Not now," Shirley answered. "Maybe later." Louette sighed with relief. What had happened was bad enough. She didn't want Shirley blabbing it around before she could even get the story straight for her own self.

As they ate spaghetti, her mind niggled around the memory of the farm disaster. She felt urgency in the need to figure out if she should call Marj and tell her straight out, or just wait and see how the incident came up.

Bucky was bound to tell his mother. And his mother would certainly have another weapon to throw at Louette: that she couldn't take care of Bucky and keep him safe.

Louette thought of the chocolate fudge cake and sweet potato pie she had made before Bucky came. Somehow, she wasn't very hungry for dessert, and Bucky was soon full. *Maybe he doesn't eat sweets, but then growing boys will usually eat most anything, especially chocolate fudge cake.*

Suddenly she felt the resurgence of a strong desire she had been having to take Bucky to see the big oak at the junction of the Choctawhatchee and Pea rivers. *Maybe we'd better do that before we get into the shed stuff. I'll probably never get another chance.*

"I'd like to show something to you before we look for the gopher turtle shell," she told Bucky.

"Do we go in the car?" He jumped up and down. Apparently a car ride outdid the turtle shell.

Louette looked at the houses as she drove through the town snuggled in the V where two rivers join—Pea River from the northwest and the Choctawhatchee from the northeast. In the V stood a giant oak tree. Some called it the treaty oak, some called it the tree of life, some the hanging tree. Louette called it her prayer tree, because she sometimes went there to pray for her mother's health and for Joseph to find his way home.

She felt a sense of satisfaction as she drove through town. Little in the world was more mysterious to her than the huge live oaks, magnolias, and cedar trees that shaded the houses, many of which had been built before the Civil War. Forsythia bloomed on door-yard bushes, and daffodils flaunted yellow blossoms along brick walkways.

Bucky watched carefully. Louette wondered if he was old enough to enjoy trees and flowers, or if he was looking for other children. She waved to the cashier at the door of the Dixie Doodle grocery store.

They passed Gilstrap Drugs, Kresge's Ten-Cent Store, the Osceola Hotel, a square brick post office with a flag in front, Teuten's Café and Halls Oyster Bar. They passed The Grill, a long-ago teenage hangout where she and Joseph went for a cheeseburger and strawberry milkshake after the Saturday movie on their first date.

Bucky's face was serious when he turned toward her. "Gramma Lou, my mother said this town is called Geneva, after a big lake. Is that right?"

"Yes. A man named it when this place was the frontier. He said it was like his home on Lake Geneva in Switzerland. It's a great place to go swimming."

At the word "swimming," Bucky perked up. "I didn't bring a swimsuit!"

"It's a little early for that. It'll be hotter than hades first thing you know, and Lake Geneva is perfect for cooling off. I've got lots of happy memories of swimming and learning to dance at the pavilion. They had good hotdogs there too."

"Did you swim in the rivers too?"

Louette shrugged her shoulders. "When I was little we swam in the Choctawhatchee. It's only two miles from the farm in New Hope, Florida, seven miles south of Geneva, which is in Alabama. I sometimes call Geneva New Home. It's like where I'm from has two personalities."

Crossing the levee, she pointed to the skinny Pea River. "This little stream flows into the big Choctawhatchee River over yonder." She motioned to the left. She had spent many afternoons at the river junction when Marj was little, watching her climb on the big tree's sturdy limbs.

Off the highway, she followed the road at the bottom of the levee to the rivers' junction. She had a heartache in her chest at the resurfacing thought that this would likely be her last chance to show Bucky the big oak. "People here claim it is the biggest oak tree in the world, but then, not many people in Geneva have seen the world."

Bucky leaned forward, peering out the window as if trying to see the river around the fresh-plowed fields and early-budding peach trees along the roadside. Louette rounded a curve in the dirt road. "I didn't want you to miss the Choctawhatchee River and the tree." She pointed. "See there?"

"Wow!" Bucky was suitably impressed. Out of the car, he ran to the big tree and scrambled upon a low limb. "This is a climbing tree, isn't it Gramma Lou?"

"About any kind of a tree you might want." Louette walked from habit to the river's edge. She stared at the water, brown and silver, moving ceaselessly toward the Gulf of Mexico.

Behind her she could hear Bucky laughing. She felt that Joseph and her mother could see him too. *Isn't he something?* Sorrow pulled at her, but the young boy's laughter overrode it.

She heard him call out, "Look Gramma Lou, no hands."

Uh, oh. Last thing we need is another accident. She pulled in her breath and hurried back to the tree. "If we're going to get into that shed, we better step right smart," she told him. Bucky jumped down into her arms. As they walked across the grass, a county sheriff's car drove up and stopped.

Out stepped Clyde Norris, big as you please, in starched blues with gold buttons, big black leather belt and holstered gun. "Wow!" Bucky was impressed.

"I'm Officer Clyde to you," he told Bucky and shook hands with him.

"Look, Gramma Lou, a police car with a bubble gum machine on top."

Clyde turned on the flashing lights. "Want me to turn on the siren?" he asked.

"Can you?" Bucky asked.

Clyde did. The siren echoed up and down the river.

"Are you a real policeman?" Bucky leaped like a jack-in-the-box.

"Clyde is our very own resident police protection," Louette answered. Bucky was completely captivated. His eyes fastened on Clyde.

"I wanted to be sure Bucky saw the world's greatest tree," Louette explained. "Thanks for the show."

"Anytime." Clyde leaned down and shook hands with Bucky. "Come back again and I'll take you for a ride in my police car."

"Could we do that now?"

"Next time." Louette was firm. *Lord let there be a next time.*

Bucky waited while Louette unlocked the shed. "This looks like a house with two windows and a dirt porch."

"It's a storage building. Actually, I suppose you could say it's a place of memories. There's lots in here nobody but me would want." Louette pulled the door open.

"I want to see the turtle shell, if you can find it." Bucky peered inside the darkness.

"Plenty of dust." Louette pulled out a straight chair with a cowhide seat and placed it on the grass. "Sit there and I'll sweep out some." But Bucky wasn't in a sitting mood.

"This is a hairy chair," he observed, rubbing the seat.

"It's made from rawhide, a cowhide that hadn't been tanned properly. It was stretched out on the side of the barn and left to dry, then cut to fit the chair frame."

Bucky wasn't listening. He followed Louette into the shed. "What does a gopher turtle shell look like, Gramma Lou?"

"It's pretty big with designs on it, something like those on a diamondback rattler, and it's shaped sort of like a knight's armor, except it's part of a turtle's body. They live to be real old, you know, turtles. This one may have been a loggerhead, which mainly lives in the Gulf salt water, but we got some down in Dead River. They're about the same as a gopher turtle, only bigger and meaner."

"What's this, Gramma Lou?" Bucky pulled on a box.

"I can't tell. This light bulb's blowed. The wiring's got to be fixed one of these days. Carry the box outside. This shed's been needing a cleaning."

"See?" Bucky held up the chrome-covered figure of a winged Mercury, lightning bolts held aloft.

"A hood ornament from a Mercury automobile." Louette took it and turned it in her hand. "Your Grandpa Joseph got it when we first started going together. Said when he became a rich man, he'd buy the car to fit it. He never did get a Mercury though. Later he favored Buicks."

Bucky pulled out a big round embroidery hoop with a half-finished design. Louette took it from him, sat on the cowhide chair, and pulled him onto her lap. "Mama was stitching this when she had her first stroke."

In the center was a bird with wings outspread. The shape of the bird had been outlined in royal blue, dots of black thread for the eyes. Only a few of the orange-red lines of flames had been embroidered. They emerged from a pile of gray twigs and spread above the bird like a blooming bush of fire. "What is that, Gramma Lou?"

"A phoenix bird. If I remember correctly, the bird was born in the desert and when its life cycle ended, it burned itself to death on a pile of twigs. The heat from the sun sparked the fire, and the bird beat its wings until it died. Then a new phoenix bird rose from the ashes."

Bucky jumped out of her lap. He pulled on a rusty, old bicycle. "Look, look, Gramma Lou."

"That was your mama's when she was about your age."

"There's no training wheels on it. It's bigger than mine at home. Can I ride it?"

"May I?" Louette corrected.

"You'd look funny, Gramma Lou." Bucky giggled. "You're bigger than the bicycle. Can I ride it?"

"With flat tires?" Bucky pulled the bicycle out and leaned it, wheels up, against a pine tree.

"Just a minute." Louette hung the embroidery hoop on a nail. "It looks rusted. Think I saw some machine oil on a shelf." Bucky followed her inside the shed.

"Look, Gramma Lou, we could tie this big rope to the bicycle."

Louette eyed the rope Bucky had pulled from the wall. "My dad used this to pull gopher turtles from their burrows. See the hook on the end? Joseph and I tried it, but all we got was a couple of mad rattlesnakes." Bucky looked skeptical. He dragged the rope outside.

"The hook caught on the edge of the turtle's shell," Louette explained. "We ate turtles a lot when I was little, back during the Great Depression. They had white meat, like chicken, dark meat like beef and middle-in-between which tasted like pork. Mama would make turtle dumplings for Sunday dinner."

"But we're looking for the turtle shell," said Bucky. "Right?" Louette looked up. Bucky was busy dragging the rope over the grass. One end was frayed where she and

Joseph had cut some of the hemp and tried to smoke it when they were teenagers.

She heard a car door slam. "Shirley must be back from the store." She looked up. It was Marj.

"Mama, Mama." Bucky ran to Marj. "You should have been here. We had great 'ventures at the farm. I petted the pigs." Marj picked up Bucky and swung him around.

"The pigs smiled at me." Bucky's words tumbled out. "But the mama pig didn't like me."

"Hello, Marj," said Louette. She held her breath.

"You saw a mama pig?" Marj looked happy.

"We went out to the farm to visit Dan and Mittie," Louette offered.

Bucky didn't stop. "Uncle Dan grabbed me up and I got to ride in the truck to the hospital." He stopped then, for emphasis, though none was needed.

The blood drained from Marj's face. "What? Why did you go to the hospital?"

"The mama of the little pigs bit Uncle Dan when he picked me up in the pen."

Marj turned to Louette. "When were you going to tell me about this?" she asked.

"As soon as I could get a word in edgewise."

"I see." Marj's voice was bitter.

"I doubt it, but I'll tell you anyway, if you'll listen." Louette reached out to touch her daughter, but Marj pulled back.

"As Bucky said, he petted the pigs, the sow didn't like it and tried to attack him. Dan grabbed him and pitched him to me. We fell in a bucket of eggs."

"Next he would have gotten into that damned sinkhole and disappeared in the quicksand." Marj pinched her bottom lip between her fingers.

"There's a fence around the sinkhole."

"There's a fence around the pig pen, but Bucky climbed it, didn't he?" Marj said through clenched lips. "He could have climbed the sinkhole fence."

"But he didn't." Tears filled Louette's eyes.

"Why is it any time that sinkhole is mentioned you start to cry?" asked Marj.

"It seems linked to your daddy in my mind. For some reason, any mention of the sinkhole makes me miss Joseph more than ever."

Marj shook her head. "Maybe you should have thought of how much you were gonna miss him before you made him think you loved this town more than him."

"I did not. Why would you say such a thing?" Louette wiped her eyes.

"Why? Because I heard you two arguing. He wanted to leave this little town. You could have said you would follow him to the ends of the Earth, but instead you told him that you never wanted to leave Geneva Alabama," said Marj bitterly.

"Marj, there is nothing wrong with being from a small town. President Jimmy Carter is from Plains, Georgia."

"Yeah, and he didn't get re-elected, did he? Ronald Regan is president now, if you haven't noticed Mom."

"I just can't accept that he left because he was tired of this town. Your father loved us. Where would he have gone?"

"Somewhere else, that's for sure. His truck was found at the train station."

"I know, Marj." Louette hung her head. What could she say? Joseph hadn't bought a ticket, but he must have left on the train. Louette had filed a missing person's report.

Marj blamed her for Joseph's disappearance. It was hard for Louette to remember what the argument had been about the night before he left. She remembered bits and pieces and sometimes what was said. Marj had stayed in her room. The next morning, she had dropped Marj off at school and gone to work at the print shop. Joseph left and never came back.

"Come on Bucky." Marj started toward the house.

Bucky pulled on Louette's sweater sleeve. "What's a sinkhole, Gramma Lou?"

"It's a place where the ground trembles and sucks everything down into a big hole." She drew in a deep breath. "It can suck the life out of you and the people you love the most."

At Bucky's puzzled look, Louette hugged him. *Love doesn't really go away. Sometimes it comes back in the form of a little boy.* She thought, cheering herself up.

"Come on, Bucky," Marj called out. "Let's get your suitcase. We're going home."

Bucky followed her, protesting. "But we didn't find the gopher turtle shell yet. Gramma Lou said I could have it."

Louette stood beside the door of the shed. She had expected Marj to react in just that way. *Old habits stick fast.*

From the corner of her eye, Louette saw Shirley park and take a bag of groceries from her car. *Lord, keep that busybody from coming over here,* she prayed. She didn't want Shirley to see Marj's anger toward her.

Marj came out the front door with Bucky's suitcase in hand. "Get in the car."

"Wait, Mom, let's get my bicycle. It was yours when you were a little girl. It's the right size for me. Gramma Lou said it is mine now." Bucky trotted behind his mother as she threw the suitcase into the car trunk. "Gramma Lou and I can put it in the car, and we can take it home with us. Right?"

"No. You can leave it here and ride it when you come back sometime."

Bucky's face went white. "But, Mom," he began to cry. "I might not never get to come back to Gramma Lou's house. Remember what you said, for me not to get my hopes up about spending time with my gramma, that she was old and didn't have the energy to look after a little boy? That's what you said."

Louette turned and walked into the quiet confines of the storage shed. Tears coursed down her cheeks. She swiped at them with the back of her hand.

"It's, uh, not exactly my words." Marj stood beside the car.

"It is, too. That's what you told me."

Marj bristled. "Don't talk to me like that, young man. I'll spank your bottom, even if you are a big boy."

Louette walked to the front of the shed. She held the gopher turtle shell in her arms. "I found it!" She called to Bucky. But the child—who until now had been an adorable, bright, energetic and wonderful grandson—had turned into a howling monster.

"It's my bicycle. Gramma Lou gave it to me!" He threw himself onto the pine-straw-covered grass, pounding fists against the ground and howled, "It's mine, mine, mine!"

Louette stood in the door of the shed. The image of a tyke having a temper fit came back to her with amazing clarity. Marj used to try such shenanigans with her. She waited to see how the grownup Marj would handle her own child's tantrum.

Marj looked at the screaming child, then turned toward Louette, puting down the gopher turtle shell. "The car's packed. But I think we've got time for a cup of coffee."

"I'd like that," said Louette. "When Bucky cools down, he might like to have a piece of chocolate fudge cake with us."

As the coffee perked, Marj set out cups and saucers. She placed the chocolate cake on the edge of the dinette so Bucky could see it through the window.

They were eating quietly when Bucky peeked in at the door. His face looked like sunshine after a quick spring rain. He eased into a chair. "Eat your fudge cake and drink your milk." Marj was matter of fact. "We've got to hit the road and get home before bedtime."

"What about the bicycle?" Bucky didn't give in easily. Marj looked from her son to her mother and back.

"Leave the bicycle, Bucky," Louette told him. "I'll get it cleaned up and buy some tires. If your mother don't bring you back, I'll take it to you. I'm not tied down by Mama's sickness now. I can go anywhere I want." It came out in a belligerent tone. Marj gave her a look that said don't push your luck.

But Louette did. She continued in a level, conversational manner. "If you stayed 'til dark, Bucky and I could watch for lightning bugs."

Marj pulled out her car keys. "I thought pesticides killed all the fireflies."

"Not all of them." Louette looked up. "You want to take the rest of the fudge cake?"

"No," said Marj, then saw the stricken look on Bucky's face. "Oh, all right. Maybe half of it."

At the car, Marj stopped. "Get in," she told Bucky. "I need to speak with your grandmother in private." When the door closed, Marj turned to Louette. "You shouldn't have taken him to the farm."

"I took him to see Dan and Mittie. He needs to be acquainted with them. They are his relatives. I don't understand you. They were your favorite people when you were growing up. You shouldn't shun them now because you are angry with me."

"Bucky could have been killed. Do you deny that?"

"No, but he could be killed walking across the street in the city. At least he saw a real farm, with real chickens and pigs." Anger flared on Louette's cheeks. "You turned against me when your father left. You denied my mother the company of her great-grandchild because she was sick. Now you are grasping at straws to keep him from being around me. I don't understand why you think I'm a bad person."

"I don't consider you a bad person." Marj opened the car door. "You always get things mixed up the wrong way." Her words were clear, but her face reflected the still-raw unspoken accusation. She got into the car and backed out of the yard. Bucky waved until they turned the corner. And then they were gone.

Louette stood in the driveway holding the gopher turtle shell. It felt like a switch had been flipped and the light of her life had gone dark. She felt like a turtle trapped in its shell.

Louette's heart reached for a song. "Some glad morning when this life is o'er, I'll fly away," came out softly. The song soothed her. It riffed through her mind, like a kind of mantra. She knew that some glad morning her spirit would fly away, but not today.

Sitting in the cowhide chair, beside the old shed, she took in a deep breath. She imagined Joseph, hands deep in his jeans pockets, his lanky frame leaning against the huge pine tree where Bucky had propped the bicycle. A quick laugh spread wrinkles around Joseph's eyes and a hank of auburn hair swung jauntily across his forehead. She felt as if he looked right through her.

She stood up and put her hand in her pocket, fingered the note from Benjamin. He was a lot like Joseph in his gentle, knowing way. *"Maybe you ought to give Benjamin a chance,"* Joseph seemed to be telling her. *"He is here and I'm long gone."*

Louette cleared her throat. She'd like to be closer than just a good friend to Benjamin. He said he wanted something more of her. But what did she have to give? She could spend the rest of her life waiting for Joseph to come home. She could lose Benjamin in the process.

She walked to the back stoop and sat there, her mind churning with "might have beens" and "what if's." Maybe if she hadn't taken Bucky out to the farm... but that would have hurt Dan and Mittie who had looked forward to being with Bucky. It had turned out all right, except for Marj's anger. She guessed she could deal with that. She'd lived with it for a long time, and likely would have to for the rest of her life.

Shirley came bouncing across the yard. "Thought I saw Marj's car."

"Yeah," Louette moved over so Shirley could sit beside her. "They left."

"I wanted to speak to her, to tell Bucky goodbye."

"I know. Marj said she was in a hurry."

"Well." Shirley got up. "Next time."

"I doubt there will be a next time," Louette said.

"I imagine there will be," Shirley said. "Marj has a boy to raise; she's not likely to give up on gettin' some help out of her Mama. Who else is bound to give her a break once in a while?"

There did seem to be some hope. Marj had said that Bucky could ride the bike when he comes back sometime. So there was some hope; Louette decided to hang on to it.

Lord lift me up and let me stand...
Lord plant my feet on higher ground.

Chapter Four

Louette walked to the front of the house. She could see through the den window of her neighbor to the east. Miz Gumby was inside, watching television. She remembered Miz Gumby telling her: "You don't get wiser when you get old, Lou. All you get is older." Seemed true if old meant spending your time watching reruns of the Beverly Hillbillies.

Louette leaned against the porch railing. Fireflies gamboled around the front yard. "Guess I better put these junktiques back," she said aloud. She rolled up the rope and pulled the cowhide chair across the grass, then leaned it against the open door of the shed.

Pushing the ancient bicycle with flat tires, she heard a low, sexy whistle and turned to see a friend from grammar school, Double Doc Percy.

She laughed. "Whooee, those knobby knees! What you doin' running around in your underwear? You look like an aging basketball player."

"I've taken up jogging to increase my strength."

Louette dragged out a smile for her friend, whose talk about becoming a doctor when he grew up had earned him the nickname "Doc." Then when he actually went to medical school, he was called Double Doc. Instead of a medical doctor though, he became a veterinarian. He said he liked animals better than he did most humans. Louette was an exception. He said she was kind and dependable as a cow and serious and fun-loving at the same time, "like a purebred mare."

"How you doing, Lou? You look sort of peak-ed."

"I feel worse than peaked, Double Doc. I feel like I'm slow-falling into a hole."

"I saw Marj leaving, with a sour-looking son. Appeared like he'd rather have stayed with you."

"I don't get to be with him hardly any at all. I feel guilty sometimes. I been mourning Joseph ever since he took off. Mama's died on me, and I've flubbed it with Marj. I feel so unglued, so alone."

"I thought you and Benjamin had a thing going, Lou."

"We sort of do, but I can't get close to Benjamin with worry about Joseph hanging over my head. I wish he'd come home or let me know where he is."

"Loneliness is normal after what you've been through, Lou. I've been thinking about Joseph. You think maybe the Army took him for one of their clandestine jobs? He was in the intelligence division."

"You might be right. All that spy stuff. I never did understand it. But then he didn't tell me anything about what he actually did during the Korean action."

"If I remember, you checked with the military."

"I did. The veteran's service officer at the courthouse. I keep thinking maybe he just didn't like our life—that he ran off and is working on a boat somewhere."

"But he left his truck." Double Doc patted her on the arm. "If he was running away, why didn't he take his truck?"

"Maybe he hitchhiked or walked to the Gulf. It's not far."

"You may be right, Lou. But that was some time ago. If he was alive, he'd have contacted you by now."

"Unless he's got amnesia?" Louette was being hopeful again. "Maybe he's living close by, just using a different name."

"It's a dead horse we don't need to keep beating, Lou," Double Doc shifted from one foot to the other. "I wish I could help you, but we've all tried, and nothing's come of it. You need to push Joseph to the past and get on with the rest of your life."

"I don't think that's the worst on me now," Louette told him. "I took Bucky to the farm and he climbed a fence and got in the pig pen."

"No way! He wasn't hurt, was he?"

"Dan was, and Marj is madder'n a wet settin' hen." Double Doc laughed at the specter of an angry Marj.

He took the bicycle from Louette and put it in the shed. "Don't laugh. She probably won't ever let me see him again."

"Sorry about the laugh, Lou. You got a real sadness."

"I feel like I'm walking through a swamp, with each step just too much effort to make," Louette told him.

"Sounds like depression to me."

"How do you know about depression? You're a horse doctor."

Double Doc shrugged. "I know depression when I see it. Your shoulders are hanging, and your chin is almost down to your chest. Happens with horses too."

Half a smile moved across Louette's mouth. *I do feel better just talking to the old geezer.* She didn't say it aloud.

"I can suggest something for depression."

"You know how I feel about pills, Double Doc. I'd rather drag through than take pills."

"I wasn't about to suggest pills, Lou. Remember when you were voted the class clown? You and Margaret Powell? You were always full of life and laughter back then."

Louette tried to smile. "That was my cousin."

"You two were just alike."

"I do remember how much fun we had when we were young. You got any laughing pills?"

Double Doc patted her shoulder. "There are ways which work better than pills. Do something, even if it's hard. Especially if it's hard. Think about what would make you happy, then do it. Let the issue with Marj take a back seat for once. Be serious about this. You've got a life. Make it mean something."

"I hadn't thought of it that way. I'll think on what it would take to make me happy, besides being with Bucky and making friends with Marj, of course."

"That's the spirit, Lou. Life's too short to dwell on sadness."

Louette nodded. "I appreciate your concern, Doc. Really I do." She patted her pocket and felt Benjamin's note. A smile skirted across her face. "You're really something, Double Doc. You know that?" With a wave he was off down the street, his skinny legs flitting like scissors over the brick sidewalk.

Louette put the rest of the dusty keepsakes in the shed, then forced one foot after the other, up the steps and into her house. She took a deep breath to drive out the bejeebers. But loneliness, her persistent, unwelcome companion, followed her from room to room. Now that Marj and Bucky had been here, their absence left a blank space. The pain of loneliness was worse than before.

Louette wished she could break through the wall Marj had built around herself. It was like some part of Marj had left with Joseph. Marj had been a bright ten-year-old. She had heard her parents arguing the night before, had taken her father's side, and held to it ever since.

For more than twenty years Louette had replayed what she could remember about the argument the night before Joseph left. When the pain became too great, the memory would retreat. Then it would come back—not all of it, but parts and parcels, unannounced. *Joseph said he didn't want to stay in Geneva, Alabama the rest of our lives,* remembered Louette. *We sold the print shop and he wanted to move, to go someplace else, do something else.*

Louette couldn't understand why he wanted to leave. "This is our home," she had reminded him. He could have gone to the print shop to help out until Willie felt comfortable running it by himself, or he could have gone out and joined Dan at work on the farm. Joseph liked riding that old mule, Whistler. He liked plowing, growing corn and hay. She liked keeping books, she had told him.

Marj was in a good school. "We have family and friends here," was Louette's main emphasis.

She remembered Joseph's serious face as he reminded her that she had never lived anyplace else. He had seen a great big world; that's what the Army did for him. He told her that life was different in big towns; they could live anywhere. There were so many things to see and do to add richness to their daily lives, give them expanded experiences.

But Louette didn't want expanded experiences. She couldn't understand how he could weigh somewhere else that they didn't even know against the place they did know. She felt safe among the people of Geneva, even the ones she might not like much. At least she knew them. Louette didn't want to live far away, among strangers.

She remembered Joseph's level, honest eyes looking squarely into hers. He explained that if they didn't like where they moved, they could always come back.

Louette argued that Willie needed them at the shop until he got used to being in charge, that the schools might not be as safe in a big city. "Let's talk about it some other time," she begged.

But there hadn't been another time to talk. The next day Joseph was gone. Over and over she relived that bright clear morning with spring in the air. As she dressed for work Joseph called out that he'd stay in bed a while longer, he'd check Willie's specs on printing their receipt books for the county clerk the next day.

Louette remembered Marj kissing him on the cheek before they ran to the car. She wished she had kissed him goodbye herself. She wished she had listened to him. Maybe there could have been a compromise. But she'd had no inkling it would be their last conversation.

That was then, this is now, she told herself. Whatever she had done, whatever mistakes she had made, there was no way she could undo any of it. She couldn't bring Joseph back any more than she could have stopped what happened at the farm with Bucky and the sow.

Marj had been ten when Joseph disappeared. *That was the end of my joy,* she thought. All those years since, even when she laughed, there had been a dark undercurrent of sadness.

Louette walked down the hall and into her mother's room. She ran her hand over the carved wood along the foot of the bed and touched the white-painted rocker where Clara had sat when she was able to get up. She stared a long while at a picture of her and Marj and ran her hands over the quilt on her mother's bed.

A book lay open on the nightstand. Louette leaned over and read "Laughter is day, and sobriety is night, and a smile is the twilight that hovers gently between both – more bewitching than either." Henry Ward Beecher.

That was a different poem from the one Clara had been reading just before she died. *So Marj has been in Mama's room.* She felt a glimmer of understanding. *Maybe there is more to Marj than she shows to others, to her mother. Maybe she cares more than she lets on.*

When she passed the phone in the den, it rang at her elbow and made her jump. "What you doin', now they've gone?" It was Shirley.

"Just wandering around." She cleared her throat. "There's some fudge cake left. Why don't you come over?"

"Guess I could. I might ought to be on a diet. But one little old piece of fudge cake isn't going to make too much difference."

A ton of fudge cake probably wouldn't make much difference, thought Louette. "Come on," she repeated.

The chatter of her neighbor was like an old phonograph record. Shirley asked a question, then answered herself. Even as she ate. She would take a bite, talk around it, swallow, then break out in talk again, right on top of the swallow. Louette wondered if she did that at home alone.

She interrupted Shirley. "I didn't tell you where Benjamin was; he's gone hunting down at the coast in Tate's Hell with one of his visiting cousins."

"He needs to get out more. Mostly he stays right there in his house and yard, like a hermit," mused Shirley. "Whatever makes a grown man cut hedges to look like freight trains?"

"They're passenger trains." It felt like a fake conversation. Louette tried to inject a little more meaning. "I enjoy the smell when Benjamin cuts the hedges. It's like a pasture with new-mown hay. Makes the whole neighborhood smell good."

"Whatever," said Shirley. "I asked him one time why he trimmed the hedges like he does and he said so as to remind people that once there were trains, that people traveled on them instead of on airplanes. He wears that striped railroad hat to cover up his bald head."

"You sure Benjamin has a bald head?"

Shirley shrugged. "You never seen Benjamin's head without the cap? Bald as a peeled onion."

"How come you know so much about Benjamin?"

"That's about it. I was taking a walk and he reached up to tip his cap, and it fell, right there where he was trimming all them little sprigs of privet hedge to make it look like the cowcatcher on a train. I sure don't understand why he does that to his yard."

"It's his property. He can fix it any way he likes," said Louette. It did seem that Benjamin spent an awful lot of time in his yard. "Boy, he sure knows how to grow roses."

"He ought to share the roses. I asked him for some once and he just looked at me as if I wasn't there, as if he was thinking about somebody else, you maybe."

"Me?" Louette tried not to sound hopeful. A little flutter began deep in her chest. It warmed her.

"Or somebody else. I don't know." Shirley got up from the table and automatically washed the saucer where her slice of fudge cake had been.

Louette thought about Benjamin. The year before, in the spring, as she passed his house, Benjamin had motioned her to stop. He'd taken her hand and led her around the hedge locomotive. Beside the dining car was a bank of early blooming roses on a trellis, just budding out. Louette sucked in her breath. "How beautiful. Their buds look like little heads hanging in prayer."

Benjamin reached down and clipped a stem with a bouquet of buds on the end. He'd taken a long breath as if trying to pull the fragrance from the tiny buds with his nose, then handed the miniature bouquet to Louette. "Smile, Louise Etta," he'd said. "A smile becomes you." His voice was soft.

At home she had put the rosebuds in a vase on the nightstand beside her mother's bed. She and Clara had shared the delight of watching the buds become blossoms.

Shirley's brash voice brought her immediately back to the here and now. "Men sure are funny."

"Why do you say that?"

"Oh, I don't know. I don't mean ha-ha funny, just peculiar. They're different. But you sure do miss them when they're not around. You miss Joseph, don't you? I mean even if he did run away. I still miss Dexter, and he's been dead all these years. It's like he's still here, saying 'Shirley, do this. Shirley don't do that. Shirley, wipe off some of that makeup. Shirley, you talk too much'." Louette stifled a laugh. *Dexter got the last one right.*

"I miss him, even if he did criticize me." Shirley stopped. "Didn't your mama miss your daddy after he died?"

"Of course, but then pretty soon after that she was so ill and in so much pain she couldn't hardly tell what day it was. She didn't mention him much then."

That wasn't exactly true. A few days before she died, her mother had said, "I'll soon be with your father." Maybe her mother had a premonition of her death. But Louette didn't want to share anything that deeply personal with Shirley. Maybe she was more of a loner than she had always thought. She pushed on the chair arms and stood up. They walked into the den.

"Let's watch TV," Shirley suggested.

"Aw, I'm not in the mood."

"You're sure enough not. You're following a black moon, Louette Kelly. One of them comedies might help."

Louette shook her head. She was suddenly tired. Her neck ached. "No. I don't think so. Guess I'm just out of sorts. I usually wash my hair on Saturday nights. Bucky was here last night, and I plumb forgot."

"It wouldn't hurt if you washed it tonight, on Sunday night. Or why don't you go to the beauty shop like me?" Shirley's frizzy hair looked like a wig.

"I can't abide sitting under the hot dryers. It makes my face red."

"But the red goes away after awhile, and then your hair feels so clean." To illustrate, Shirley fluffed her hair. Louette's lips grimaced then settled into a wan smile. *Must be they wash Shirley's head clean all the way through, brains and all.*

"We could play dominoes," she said.

Shirley shook her hair again, then stood up and stretched. "I guess it's likely long past my bedtime."

"What does it matter when you go to bed? It's not like you have to go to work or anything." *Maybe that is what keeps one going: a set of directions on when to get up, clean the house, wash clothes, cook meals, even if only one person sits at the table*, Louette pondered.

Suddenly she was forced back in time, to when it did matter what day it was, when every day in the week had its own special duties. Louette mulled over the possibilities.

"I wash my clothes on Monday." Shirley sounded defensive.

"I know. But you don't have to. You could wash your clothes on Sunday after church if you took a notion."

"You're right. And now since you don't have to cook dinner for your mother, we could go by the Osceola Hotel dining room and eat sometime, Lou."

"People still go there to eat?"

"I do, lots of times. Dexter and I ate there often, back when I worked at Chapman's Department Store. He said I stood on my feet long enough during the week, that I didn't need to stand over a hot stove unless I happened to want to. I didn't often want to cook dinner back then."

Louette chuckled and crossed her legs. "I forgot how it was to eat out. When we first bought the print shop after Joseph finished his schooling on the GI bill, we'd get a hamburger and milkshake at The Grill for lunch. I always ordered strawberry. That was a long time ago."

"Lots of things that happen 'way back', are still right there in your memory. Whenever I want to, I can recollect me and Dexter having fun, just glad to be together." Shirley's eyes sparkled.

"Memories are fine, but you can't live your life by them." Louette stood up.

"What's the matter with you, Lou? You used to laugh a lot. Now it's like you're in a trance. We got to depend on memories to help us get by. The people in our lives are gone. First it was our husbands, then our mothers. It'll be us next."

A tenderness toward Shirley welled up in Louette.

"We'll last a long time yet, Shirley. At least you probably will."

"What do you mean?"

Tiredness suddenly overcame Louette. "Go home, Shirley. It's time to go to bed so you can get up in the morning and put your clothes in the washing machine."

Shirley checked her watch and sighed. "Guess you're right. This teddybear better get on over to her own cave." She sashayed out the door.

Louette went back to the kitchen, washed the dishes she had used and wiped the table. She pursed her lips and tried to blow a tune. It came out dry and insincere, like whistling on a walk by the cemetery, pretending not to be afraid. She reached for her sweater on the hook beside the back door and stepped outside.

She remembered what Double Doc had said, but she couldn't turn loose of the wonderful two days and one night with her grandson. The new memory took on a life that pulsed in the space around her heart—a lump of hard-core joy, untarnished. She rubbed her foot back and forth on the dry grass. High over the gaunt limbs of the rain tree, a sickle moon winked. She skirted the edge of the yard, watching the moon ride ever higher in the sky.

There had been wonderful, happy times, with her, Joseph, and Marj laughing together. She and Joseph worked at the print shop, took Marj to school plays, baseball and basketball games, to church services and the wonderful dinners held to honor someone in the community. Food was at the center of life in Geneva; that was for sure.

Her mother was there when she needed someone to talk to about Joseph's disappearance. "Mama," she'd say. "I can't help but believe that one day he'll come through that door. He'll be singing an old Hank Williams song, like 'Jambalaya, Crawfish Pie.' Don't you think so?"

Mama would smile. She'd loved Joseph too, even back when Louette and Joseph, the boy from the next farm over, played together as children. She had made oatmeal cinnamon cookies for him. "I can't help it that he left, any more than I can help missing him," Louette said aloud. Her heart felt as if it would explode.

After Joseph left, she'd had Marj to take care of. After Marj grew up, went to college, and married, Louette's mother had a serious stroke and was bed-ridden. Then her precious grandson Bucky had come along, bright-eyed and laughing.

"Marj blamed me for Joseph leaving. She believed I had chased my own husband and her father away. Why on earth would she think that?" The words were the same, except that when she spoke them now, there was no one to hear but herself. The wind rustled the rain tree leaves and the moon skimmed higher in the sky.

She wasn't really alone, she told herself, the universe whirled around, covered with people, many probably as bad off as herself. It didn't make her feel one whit better. *Lord, help me to figure myself out,* she prayed. *I don't know who I am, what I'm here for, or what to do.*

She went into the house to her mother's rocking chair. She pulled her feet up like a child, and rocked, back and forth, unaware as a sob filled the room, then faded away as the rocker slowed.

A scrap of an old gospel song trailed behind her as she left the room. "Do Lord, oh do Lord, oh do, remember me... " At the kitchen table she reached out to touch the vase with the bright pink roses. "Aahh, Benjamin." She sighed.

Louette loved early mornings. Even if she didn't have to get up with the sun, she usually did. She liked to sit on the back steps of her once-yellow wood-frame house, stare at the yard, and listen to the wind whistle in the dried corn stalks and pea vines in the remnants of last year's garden. Grief over her mother's absence hung above her like a winter cloud. But here was a new day.

Dig down, scratch out the pain and throw it to the wind. It's time to start over. Louette stood and rubbed her hands together. According to the wisdom of the old folks, it had thundered in February, so there was bound to be frost in March. She'd thought about sowing a bed of turnip seeds for greens. The onions would come up volunteer, pushing aside rain tree leaves, unless she raked them first.

With her mother dead and gone, and the recent attack by the old sow, it was hard to get her thoughts to firm up, to even think of planting a garden. An earthshattering thing had happened to her and she wished there was some way she could guarantee that her mother's passing mattered, not just to her, but to other people. Her mother, when she was able, would have been out there in the yard digging, even if all she planted were rutabagas and cabbages.

She dragged the rake out of the storage shed. *It's getting rusty, just like me.* But she did clear rain tree leaves from around the volunteer onion rows. Raking under the picnic table she saw wigglers in the dark, rich soil. *Fish bait.* She sniffed. The back yard smelled like spring.

Her neighbor Miz Gumby walked up. "Shifting the dirt around, Lou?"

Louette leaned on the rake. "I need to dig at more than dirt. I need to figure me out a new life, don't you think?" She was careful to hold her face toward Miz Gumby, who was hard of hearing.

"You got a plan?" The old woman took off her sunhat and peered at her old brogan shoes. After her husband died Miz Gumby told Louette she'd paid lots of money for the shoes, and she intended to get the rest of the wear out of them.

"I'm working on it."

"Does it include Benjamin?"

"I don't know, Miz Gumby. I wish it did, but there's complications."

"Don't let anything stand in your way, Lou. Life's too short." Miz Gumby picked up several rain tree leaves. "These are so beautiful. Makes one believe in the pot of gold at the end of the rainbow, the magic, the promise."

Louette watched her shuffle away, kicking at leaves with the too-large brogans. Louette smiled in spite of her gloom. *That Miz Gumby is a card.*

60

It didn't take long for Louette to tire out. She put the rake back in the storage shed. In the kitchen she pulled out slices of bread, mayonnaise and a wintertime store-bought tomato. She knew it wouldn't taste like a tomato out of the garden, but it'd have to do for now. The sandwich became a lump when she tried to swallow.

She got up and walked into her mother's room and reached to touch pictures on the fireplace mantel: herself and husband Joseph, with their daughter Marjoram; Marj on a horse as a teenager; Marj's boy Bucky freshly born, red in the face, waving his arms; Louette's dad in his World War I uniform, handsome, eyes crinkly.

Moments in time were captured in the photographs. Happiness from long ago. Louette wiped dust off a frame with her sleeve. The story of her life. The pictures were still there on the mantel, but the real people had moved on, except for Marj and Bucky. *Pictures persist. People disappear.*

Later, Louette decided she ought to phone Marj. No matter how badly she might feel, she couldn't stay mad at her own daughter forever. It seemed to her that Marj had been angry with her most of her life. If the cycle of anger was to be broken, Louette would have to make the first move.

Bucky answered. "Hello, Gramma Lou." His voice was like a song. "My mom's at a meeting and my dad's taking me to the library. I told him you said he ought to."

"That's nice, Bucky."

"He said it's a great suggestion coming from you." Louette considered whether to take offense at the remark. If there had been a pause after "suggestion," then she could take it as an insult. Otherwise what Bucky said was just a group of words jumbled up to tell her something in a hurry. She decided to let it pass.

"Tell your dad I highly approve of him taking my favorite grandson to the library."

"I will, Gramma Lou."

Louette sat back down, her face split by a quick grin. *I have an idea. I could go to Montgomery to visit Bucky. Marj would have to be pleasant whether she wanted to or not. At least she's still got manners. And it's not as if I haven't been there before.*

Before Bucky was born, Louette had gone to Marj and Snowden's home in Montgomery to deliver a cradle. Marj wanted the cradle Louette's grandfather had made, but her husband was too busy to drive her to get it.

"I can take it to you, in the truck." That was before Louette had sold Joseph's old truck. Clara was still up and about then, but not well enough to ride very far.

"That would be nice," Marj told her. No mention was made of when she should take the cradle. The next afternoon Louette loaded it up, covered it with a quilt, and headed north. The truck struggled when climbing even modest hills, but it made the trip safely.

The memory made her grimace. Taking the cradle without calling first had been a mistake. She should have asked Marj when she wanted the cradle. When Louette arrived, they had company.

"Mom! Why didn't you tell me you were coming tonight?" Marj whispered at the door. She wore a blue cocktail dress covered with sequins. It flounced out as if trying to hide her pregnancy. She was holding a glass of dark-colored wine.

Before Louette could stop herself, she asked, "Should you be drinking wine when you're pregnant?"

"I'm not drinking this." Marj wrinkled her nose. "I'm taking it to a guest."

"I apologize," Louette told her. "I never dreamed you'd be holding a party. With the baby about due, I just figured you'd want the cradle now, so I brought it." She looked down at her faded slacks and shapeless sweater. "I'll drive around, come in the back and go upstairs. Maybe nobody will see me."

But Louette's son-in-law had heard them talking at the front door. He walked up, carrying a highball glass. She knew that rascal was a drinker the minute she laid eyes on him. First time she ever caught him at it, though.

"What's going on?" he asked. "Oh, Lou. It's good to see you." His voice sounded insincere. His eyes moved from her old canvas shoes to her wind-blown hair. "How are you?" His voice dropped an octave.

Wonder who he thought I was—the tooth fairy? She didn't say any of that. She stuck out a hand to shake. "I'll just go around to the back."

"Oh, no, come on in." He pulled her into the living room. With all that glass and sleek designer couches, chairs and chandelier, it looked like something from a magazine's modern home layout.

"This is Marj's mother," Snowden announced loudly. She was dragged from guest to guest, introduced. Louette saw the look of triumph he leveled on Marj. Suddenly she felt sorry for her daughter. Whatever differences she had with her daughter, Marj didn't deserve this despicable man. He was not worthy of her.

"I'm sorry I'm not dressed for a party," Louette announced loudly. "It must have slipped my mind."

"She brought the cradle I was telling you about," said Marj. "The cradle I slept in when I was a baby. It was my mother's, too. My great-grandfather made it." Louette saw Marj shoot a one-up-on-you look at her husband.

"Would you get it from the truck?" Marj asked him sweetly. He couldn't tactfully refuse with the chorus of offers to help.

Louette felt proud when the men lifted the quilt from the cradle and put it among the modern furnishings of the living room. It was like the Hope Diamond among expensive pieces of jewelry. The polished wood fairly glowed. The carefully crafted homemade cradle could hold its own anywhere.

Amid the oohs and aahs, Louette backed to the door and eased it open to make her escape. She got in the truck, cranked up the motor and drove right on back home. It took her until almost midnight, but she wasn't sorry. She had done what she set out to do. Marj had asked for the cradle. She had carried it to her.

Her mother, Clara, thought she had taken leave of her senses to drive all the way back that night. "I just can't imagine driving three hours to get there, staying long enough to unload the cradle, then getting back into that rackety old truck and driving three more," said Clara. "It's a wonder you're not tuckered out slam to death."

"You should have seen how they've fixed up their house, Mama. Everything all modern and glass. And all those guests so dressed up. I was out of place."

"Nonsense," her mother told her. "You are as good as anybody, better than most, and you are never out of place."

"I wasn't dressed for a party," Louette said firmly, closing the subject. Later she was extra glad she had come on back home. The next day her mother had the first in a long line of strokes. Six years downhill, right on to the funeral.

Visitors came after her mother died: Cousins she hadn't seen in many years, old aunts who lived far away, other cousins who lived closer and rarely came around. Many were too old even to attend church homecoming any more. And Louette had not been able to visit them either, with her mother in such bad shape.

Clara's wake had been like a wedding or a christening. Neighbors and church women brought food, like a person could hardly believe. Some came in and cooked breakfast on the day of the funeral, then returned to make coffee and set out hot food for the mourners. *Relatives were a blessing. Especially those close by like Mittie and Dan. Relations who came from far away were an extra helping of blessings. And friends!*

Even people Louette had never met came to pay their respects. "Without her we wouldn't have a hospital here." An elderly man in overalls wiped at rheumy eyes. "She saved my wife's life. Twenty more minutes to Enterprise or forty-five minutes to Dothan and my wife wouldn't have made it." The hospital was a fine facility. Because of Clara and others much more influential in the community, many people had pushed for passage of the government bill that gave rural areas help, with a tug on the old bootstraps.

Louette hoped people would come to visit when she died. *Marj would have the house open, and the phone would ring with people offering condolences. Shirley would probably wander around the house crying. Certainly Benjamin would come. Maybe he wouldn't come to the house, but surely he'd attend the funeral. He hardly leaves his hedgerow.*

Not long ago Benjamin had walked to her house and found her on the front porch swing, considering whether to have lunch. She was thinking about how it didn't seem worth the trouble to cook without her mother there, even with the annoying deputy Clyde popping in for whatever leftovers she had. You couldn't depend on when Clyde would show up, and he usually overstayed his welcome. At first Louette figured it was Clyde when she heard a man clear his throat.

"You okay Lou?" Benjamin asked.

Louette jerked her head around. "I guess," she said, a bit rattled. "I didn't even hear you come up. It's good to see you." He stood on the top step, holding a bouquet. He wore denim pants and a soft blue shirt, and his bald head glistened without the striped cap. "You look nice." Louette couldn't help staring. She had to pinch her lips together to keep from laughing out loud, she was so happy.

Happy crinkles spread around Benjamin's eyes. He had a gentle expression. "Thought I'd wear something besides the train engineer's overalls," he told her. "I like them, but people look at me strangely sometimes. Thought it might be the clothes."

"As my dad used to say, you clean up well." She shifted on the swing. "I like the penny loafers."

"Thank you."

"Come sit," she told him and he plopped down beside her. A strong physical attraction thrummed about them. *What if...* popped into Louette's mind. She reached her hand toward him but stopped it in midair. She couldn't help it, the emotion bubbled to the surface, emotion she had no right to feel, she thought, then sighed.

"I don't know if I'm speaking out of turn, Lou, but I want to tell you something," Benjamin said, shifting about on the swing.

Louette brushed a strand of hair out of her eyes and looked up, expectantly. "Well, quit cat-footin' around, Benjamin. Out with it."

He pushed the swing back and forth. "I might better wait for Clyde to tell you."

"Tell me what?"

"He's come up with something else about the search for Joseph." Benjamin stopped.

"What else? I thought we did everything anybody could do," said Louette with a puzzled look.

"He and I have been gathering pictures of missing dead people to see if your husband is one of those never identified. You'd be surprised how many missing persons cases are never solved."

"I know. We checked missing persons years ago, but never found Joseph." Louette's shoulders drooped. She leaned forward and held her face in her hands.

"Clyde found a file in the sheriff's office with pictures of people found dead and never identified and now he's gathering them from around the country."

"And you help him?" Louette leaned her head back and looked at Benjamin. "That's a nice thing to do."

"He's got a photo of Joseph, and he and I go through the pictures to see if we can find a match. He was a good-looking man, Lou. One look at his laughing face and I can see how you must have loved him very much."

"You're right about that. I wish I knew where he is. It's like my life's been on hold ever since. I feel sad, even when I should be happy. I'm really a lucky person, you know. This is a good place to live. My worst problem is missing my mother and Joseph and trying to come to terms with mine and Marj's grief."

Benjamin reached his arm to the back of the swing. Almost, but not quite, touching Louette's shoulders. "Lou, you got to snap out of it somehow. Your face looks... I haven't seen a smile on it in a long time."

"I know, Benjamin. I feel adrift. I've probably been that way since Joseph left. But this time it's because Mama died. I've lost my best friend, my touchstone."

Benjamin patted her on the arm with a callused hand. "Your mother was your best friend, Lou. Now that she's gone, could I be your best friend?"

A shock moved through Louette. She tingled with excitement. It must have been words she wanted, needed, but loneliness had dug in too deep. A flush, as pink as a radish, covered her face. She took a sharp breath. Time seemed to stop. She could hear a mockingbird start his mating call from the rain tree and a dove murmur from a limb of the azalea bush beside the driveway.

She couldn't help ignoring the question and the hopeful look in Benjamin's eyes. She so needed a real, close friend, but she reluctantly shifted so that his hand fell away. She rubbed her arms, quick and rough, ridding herself of the tingles. "I appreciate that, Benjamin. A great deal." At his crestfallen look, she added, "More than you know." Then she jumped up from the swing. "Coffee's still in the pot. Would you like a cup?"

Benjamin followed her to the kitchen dinette. "This is the first time I've ever been in your house, Lou."

She put out cups and poured coffee. "You'll have to come again."

"I wish I was more like you," Benjamin told her. "You have friends. You care about folks. I came here because I wanted to live in a small town, to get to know people, but I can't seem to get started."

Louette tried a weak chuckle. "Wearing visiting clothes might make some difference, Benjamin. All anybody mostly sees of you, you're working on your hedge train. Don't get me wrong, I love your train, especially the caboose. And..." she paused, "your roses."

"Should I invite people to come see the train? I sort of don't want people handling the hedges, or my roses, though. Is that strange?"

"I don't think so. It's easier if you simply walk up to somebody, shoot out your hand, and tell them who you are and that you'd like to be friends."

"That's all there is to it?"

"It's a beginning. The regular clothes like you're wearing helps. You could go to church. Say hello to people in the grocery store. Go by the court house and chat with the old fellows who sit on the benches outside. Volunteer at the school or the hospital. Volunteers are always needed. You could teach gardening. People want to know how to grow roses."

On the porch, she hugged him around the shoulders. The strong pull, like gravity, wrapped around them; a whirring sound buzzed in Louette's ears. She felt faint. She put her hands on his chest and pushed back, staring in his face. *I can't do this! I'm married to Joseph! I have no right to feel this way!*

She shook her head. "I've got to get to work on this place," she told him, her voice shaky.

He agreed to take a look at the back yard later and offer advice. He also promised he'd try reaching out more, and that he'd let her know if he and Clyde found any pictures that resembled Joseph. Louette immediately regretted not telling him he could be her best friend. She'd really liked that. He touched a sore spot, but his sincerity was quite moving.

Benjamin would come to my funeral. What about Miz Gumby? Would she invite funeral guests to spend the night with her? If she died, who'd take Miz Gumby to the grocery store? Shirley could hardly abide the old lady. She wouldn't even sit next to her at church. Thinking on it now, Louette hoped Aunt Rufus would still be alive and able to attend her funeral. She loved the old aunts and uncles, but Aunt Rufus was her favorite.

Rufus wasn't her name, of course. Her name was Ruth, after the biblical character who stayed with her mother-in-law because the older woman needed her after her husband died. But the child Louise Etta could not say Ruth and had called her Aunt Rufe, then enlarged it to Rufus. After that, all the cousins called her Aunt Rufus. She had rheumatism "real bad," she'd told Louette at the funeral for Clara, but she couldn't miss her own sister's funeral.

A sorrowful song passed her lips as she sat in the dark in her backyard, "This world is not my home, I'm just a-passin' through... "

Clyde would certainly come, wouldn't he? But he hadn't dropped by since Marj had taken Bucky away. Maybe he was busy gathering pictures of missing people, looking for Joseph. She rarely had jobs for Clyde to do, but he usually showed up—sometimes too often, looking like he wanted to say something, but couldn't figure out how.

What about Laverne and Jasper? She and Laverne had been best friends since primary school. Jasper was two grades ahead of them. Laverne and Jasper had married and moved to Apalachicola where famous oysters were gathered from the bay. They had been among the first to show up when her mother died.

She broke into song again: "The angels beckon me from heaven's open door... and I can't feel at home in this world any more." Louette stopped. A pain caught in her chest like a grief attack. *Sorrow can follow you around until it smothers you.*

Louette didn't like the part of the funeral where the preacher said all those words, or when the casket was opened and everybody lined up to get one last look. She especially had problems with looking at her mother in a casket. She had refused to go near her father's coffin when he died. She was younger then, but what was the good of seeing somebody you loved in a puffy satin-lined box, when they couldn't even smile or talk to you?

It would be a lot more fun at a funeral if the dead person could get up and talk with the visitors. Why have a big party like that after you're dead? The thing to do is to have the party now, while I am still alive.

Louette didn't want to wait to get all that company when she was dead in a casket and unable to be a part of it. She had loved her mother's wake but wished Clara had been able to enjoy all that love and celebration while her heart was still warm and beating. Her smile glowing. Hugs and laughter and soul food being shared.

Why not hold my own wake now, before I die? Double Doc said I should do something to make myself happy. Would holding my own wake make me happy? Moping around isn't cutting it. Maybe planning and holding my own wake will help me out of this depression. Maybe it will give my heart a chance to heal. Allow me the feeling of life being lived and celebrated, here and now. Shoot, it's worth a try.

Come home, come home.
Ye who are weary, come home.

Chapter Five

Louette pulled out the Christmas card file box of names and addresses. She felt good to know she had lots of relatives and friends. She'd invite them all. It was one thing to have a gathering when somebody died, but having your own wake was something else. She'd compose an invitation, get them printed at Willie's shop. She could hand out invitations in town, mail others, and get Editor Horace Greeley to put a notice in the Geneva County Reaper newspaper.

Horace claimed to be a direct descendant of the newspaperman Horace Greeley through his mother's side. His real last name was Purifoy. Horace had come to Geneva from Talladega, Alabama. Uncertainty fell over Louette. Horace might not want her wake in his newspaper.

What if everybody laughed at her because she wasn't dead? What if nobody liked her well enough to come?

Louette sometimes felt invisible. An insensitive young person's remark could cut her to the bone. Recently she had gone to B. C. Moore Department Store looking for stockings. All they'd had were pantyhose. When she'd asked the clerk about stockings, the girl had not understood. When a younger customer came in, the girl left Louette standing at the pantyhose rack as if she were invisible.

Maybe that's what happens when you get old. You disappear. What if she can't even see me? "Miss, Miss," she'd called out. The girls had not reacted. Louette walked to a mirror, and there she stood, her own living reflection. But to the young clerk and customer she wasn't there at all. An annoying inconvenience, that's what she was. "Do you have stockings?" she had called loudly.

The girl had turned. "You are standing in front of the display."

"These are pantyhose. I asked for stockings."

"They're the same," the girl had answered.

"No, they're not. Stockings are held up by a garter." The girl had turned back to her young customer.

"That old woman doesn't even know what pantyhose are," she'd whispered, and they'd both giggled.

Louette pulled the chair closer to the dinette and breathed the perfume from Benjamin's roses. *Such beauty.* She fished the note from her purse and spread it on the dinette. He wanted to know how she felt about him. "Joseph has been gone more than twenty years," he had written. "I have to know if there is room for me in your life."

He'd be gone hunting for a week. When he got back, he'd want to know how she felt about him, once and for all. She didn't like deadlines. They'd had enough of those at the print shop. People wanted their printing as soon as they could get it, that day if possible.

What I ought to do is visit Laverne and Jasper. Benjamin was hunting in Tate's Hell, near Apalachicola. Why shouldn't she take a few days off and go to Apalach to see Laverne? See what her friend thought about her having a wake while she was still alive.

On the phone she asked Laverne "You want some company for a few days?"

"If it's you, I sure do. You bringing Bucky?"

"Not this time," she told her friend. "Maybe later. Thought a visit might clear up my mullygrubs."

"Mine too," agreed Laverne.

It took Louette a few minutes to pack clothes in her old cardboard suitcase. She washed the coffee pot, put leftover food in the freezer, including the milk. The rest of the chocolate cake and sweet potato pie she'd made before Bucky's visit went into the refrigerator. She walked over to tell Miz Gumby she was going out of town. She carefully mouthed the words.

"Be safe," Miz Gumby told her.

Louette wrote a note and taped it to the back door behind the screen where Shirley could see it. "Be back in a few days. Going to visit Laverne and Jasper in Apalach." *Let Shirley chew on that one.*

She was putting her suitcase into the car trunk when Deputy Clyde Norris pulled up. "Oh, Clyde, Did I tell you about the old man who bought the Tadlock place on New Hope Road? He might be growing marijuana."

"You did tell me. Hadn't got around to checking him out, but I will. Where you headed?"

"Down to visit Laverne and Jasper for a few days. Give myself a break from myself. Ha."

"Not a bad idea. You going to hook up with Benjamin? I hear he's hunting in Tate's Hell Forest." She shook her head and re-cranked her car, circling around Clyde. *Nothing gets past nobody in this place*, thought Louette, heading south. *Nothing.*

As she drove toward the Florida Gulf Coast on Highway 98, Louette could feel her tension easing. Pine trees and scrub oak edged the highway; gallberry and sassafras bushes filled in the gaps. She rubbed her neck and left shoulder. That tension knot was getting smaller.

As she neared the coast the scenery changed. White sand pushed aside the underbrush and an occasional fresh-water pond lapped at the edge of the road. She zipped through small communities, crossed once-large, now small, spindly rivers. She let down the windows. Smelled the salt water. Happy memories bubbled up: going fishing with her mother and dad, eating a picnic lunch at the old Civil War salt works (ham sandwiches and tart, sweet pickles, canned peaches with a chunk of coconut pound cake).

Once on the coast road, Louette pushed a little harder on the gas pedal. Expectation and eagerness grew. She swore at the tall condos along Mexico Beach, admired the stretch of land where the Port St. Joe paper mill had once been, and meandered down the coast to Cape San Blas. She couldn't resist driving out onto the cape. At the narrow place where she could see St. Joe Bay on her right and the Gulf of Mexico on the left, she stopped, careful not to let all four tires onto the sand at the same time. That had happened years ago when she visited Laverne and Jasper and they had to walk back to the old Raw Bar for help.

She flicked off her shoes and ran toward the Gulf first, then back across the strip to St. Joe Bay. "Nothing feels better than sand between my toes," she said aloud to the pipers picking in the sand behind every wave. Off in the distance she could see gulls flocking around a boat, waiting for fishermen to throw out fish scraps. The afternoon sun burned straight down. *The sky's bigger here*, she told herself, *and the sun's hotter.*

At Indian Pass and St. Vincent Sound, the sweep of Apalachicola Bay came into view. "World's best-tasting oysters." She leaned out the car window. The air smelled like fish. "Best mullet, grouper, red fish, snapper, and flounder anywhere. All you got to do is go after 'em."

Soon her car snaked down Laverne and Jasper's street, Shadow Lane, where live oak limbs held hands over the street, forming a green tunnel. Louette breathed in deeply. It felt like another world. A place to shuck troubles and worries. Deep down in her soul, she felt hope stirring.

As she neared the house she saw Laverne on the porch. Short, with salt and pepper hair, more rounded than Louette, she had a kind face with a wide smile, hardly any wrinkles. *Still got her figger after all these years*, thought Louette.

"Bless my soul. You are a sight for sore eyes." Laverne hugged her then held her at arm's length. "It's been too long."

"Sure has. I don't need to remind you that the road runs both ways. The phone's a blessing but seeing is better."

"I'll put your suitcase in the room at the end of the hall. You drop your tired self on the swing," Laverne told her as she headed into the house. "I'll bring some iced tea."

Louette picked up a throw pillow and leaned back in the swing. Azalea buds looked like they'd burst into blooms any minute. A gull dragging a broken wing hobbled around the house, squawked at Louette, then picked through the yard grass for bugs.

The tea was refreshing, and the plate of sugar cookies didn't last long. "You make the best cookies, Laverne. You were top of the class in Home Ec."

"Think I learned the cookie baking and eating habit from Ma. We did have a good Home Ec teacher though." Laverne paused. A frown wrinkled her brow. "Instead of Home Economics, it's now called Culinary Class. They don't teach things like sewing, or how to manage a household anymore. Just how to open cans and bags of frozen vegetables and meat."

"That settles it: the world's going to the dogs, just like old people say," Louette announced. It would have been normal for them to laugh, but they sat still and stared ahead. *We are the old people now.*

The injured gull squawked and hopped about in the yard, one wing braced against its back. "That's Oscar demanding food." Laverne threw a piece of cookie. "I took him to the bird rescue place where they tried to set the wing. Oscar jerked it out of the sling and hobbled right back here."

"That gull likes you." The swing squeaked. They sat. Comfortable, but uneasy.

"What's going on Lou? You sounded blue on the phone."

Louette swung back and forth a few licks before speaking. "Not much. Marj's mad at me again. She brought Bucky for me to babysit. We went out to the farm and the old sow tried to attack him."

"Tried to attack him?"

"Yeah, Dan rescued him, but was bit by the hog. Injured his leg. Last I checked it was getting better."

"Didn't hurt Bucky?"

"No. Sow could'a killed him if Dan hadn't jumped that fence."

"Wow." Laverne paused. "Can't blame Marj for gettin' mad. A sow attacked my baby, we'd be eating hog meat the next day." The women went quiet, speculating.

"I'm missing Mama too. Something awful." Louette scuffed a shoe on a porch plank.

"That's natural. Somebody we love dies, we miss them."

"Your mother's been dead a long time. Does the hurt get any better?"

Laverne stared down the Shadow Lane canopy of oaks toward the bay. "The pain does lessen, but that lonely hole in your heart hangs on. Or it has for me. Lasts until we die, I guess."

Louette put her empty glass on the tray. "I got another problem."

Laverne stopped rocking and looked at her. "What?"

Louette blushed. "I think I'm in love."

"Who with?" Laverne's mischievous grin popped out. "Anybody I know?"

"No. He moved into town about three years ago. Came from a big city. Chicago."

"Is he nice?"

"Oh, yes." Louette stood up. "He's a retired railroad engineer. Lost his wife to cancer years ago. Wanted to move to a small town."

"He found one. Geneva, I mean. Anything smaller's just a wide place in the road." Laverne hugged Louette, then plopped back into the rocker.

"The trouble is, I get all flustered when he's around, I even get tingles all over when I think about him. Sometimes my heart starts pumping so fast, it feels like it will burst." Louette looked up at Laverne, her eyes sparkling. "I'm a little too old for the tingles, don't you think?"

Laverne's smile matched Louette's. For a moment they were two teenagers, discussing a boy in the next row of desks during history class. Laverne hiccupped, which signaled a big laugh bubbling up like a volcano.

"I don't exactly know what to do." Louette pushed the swing back and forth, matching squeak for squeak to Laverne's rocking chair.

"Go for it." Laverne's laugh echoed like a bomb. She stood up, holding her arms across her chest. "Louette, you beat all." She picked up the tea tray, then put it back when another belly laugh burst out.

"I don't know that it's all that gol-durned funny." Louette sat back in the swing. "What about Joseph?"

Laverne picked up the tea tray. "What about him? He's been gone, what? Twenty years?"

"Twenty years, one month, sixteen days."

"That's been long enough, Lou. Plenty long enough." She held the screen door open and they walked to the kitchen.

Louette took a deep breath. She hadn't intended to tell anyone how deep her feelings were for Benjamin.

"Where's Jasper?"

"Out fishing."

"For me? What kind?"

"He didn't say. Just said he'd bring supper."

"Maybe we could walk down to the pier later and meet him when he comes in?" Lou stretched, flexing her arms over her head.

"We ought to walk around town some too. You won't recognize the place. They've made the Orman House into a museum, like the Raney House, except it's owned by the State of Florida."

"Last I heard a couple had bought it and were fixing it up with antique furniture and such."

"They did, then sold it to the state. I think they took the furniture, but there's plenty there now. It's a sight worth seeing." Laverne took glasses and saucers from the tray and washed them in the sink.

"The library still percolatin' along? I understand that energetic librarian from Boston is raising money for a new building. Wants to name it after Margaret Key, who died and left money from the sale of her mansion."

"Yeah, gettin' a grant and matching money. I'll miss checking out books at that cute little library across from Trinity Episcopal. I love the sight and feel of a real, printed book. The library is the most important place in this town to me. After church of course."

Louette looked out the window. A cat was circling Oscar. *I didn't come here to mourn; I came to heal.*

"The peace and quiet is here, but the pain and heartache about Bucky and the sow stayed right with me all the way down that road to the Gulf of Mexico," she told Laverne.

"It will get better." Laverne told her. "You want to walk downtown now?"

"That might help. I'm sorry, I just wanted to see you, not drag you down into my woe-is-me pit. Looks like I'd have learned better by now."

"You're not too tired?"

"I am a little tired from driving, but it might cheer me up some to walk."

As they left Shadow Lane, Louette slowed her stride to match Laverne's shorter legs. "Red's Service Station still in the same spot?"

"Yes, and the Rancho Inn across the street. Don't know what the owner was thinking when he fixed it up with stucco and cactus like somewhere in Texas." Laverne chuckled. "Did I ever tell you the first thing I saw waking up at the Rancho Inn on my honeymoon?"

"If you did, tell it again. It sounds funny already."

"Jasper was still asleep. I eased open the drapes just enough to peek out. Coming down the highway was a fellow in Eastpoint Reboks, riding a bicycle, a lawn mower tied to the back."

"Eastpoint Reboks?" *Reboks are rich kids' shoes, and there surely aren't many rich kids in Eastpoint.*

"Eastpoint Reboks are them white wadin' boots the fishermen and oyster catchers wear." They both laughed then.

At the library, Laverne introduced Louette. "This is my friend from LA—lower Alabama."

"Panama City Beach?"

"Naw. North of the beach. Not far, though."

They inspected newly published arrivals, fingered oldies in neat rows, and leafed through Florida history shelves. "*The Other Florida*, Gloria Jahoda's book. Tells about where we grew up. She went from Apalachicola to Pensacola, talking with locals. I'll never forget I'm from the Panhandle and the Wiregrass, after reading that book."

Laverne held the door for Louette. "I been here in the Big Bend a long time, though. You want to go by the Gorrie Museum?"

"Not today." Louette kept walking. "I do appreciate Mister John, though. What would we do without air conditioning and iced tea?"

"Best invention I can think of." Laverne fanned her face with her hand.

They walked downtown, pausing at the Maritime Museum and the Tin Shed. They petted some of the resident cats behind the post office. Laverne pulled a small bag from her pocket. "It must have cost a lot for Christo to feed these cats all those years. You could sure tell it after he died. Lots more people feed the cats now. I help out a little."

"It looks like the same cats from when I was here way back, before Mama had the big stroke."

"Probably from the same lineage. The old fellow fed them a long time. Guess they get scraps from the fish houses too. Whole downtown smells like fish. Got to be why we have so many cats here." Cats rubbed their legs, eager to have contact with people.

They sat on a bench beside the fountain in Waterfront Park and watched fishing boats and yachts pass on the river like regular rush-hour traffic. People on the boats called to one another. "Got flounder," a fisherman yelled to a yacht. "How much?" The answer was lost as another distant voice called out. "Where can I rent a canoe?"

The two friends watched and listened. *The Apalachicola River is a happening place.* She trailed her fingers in the fountain water. They walked south past the old baseball field and Battery Park.

"Do you ever hear from Etheline?" asked Laverne.

"What made you think of Etheline?"

"I don't know. She's been on my mind lately for some reason."

Louette turned and walked backward so she could see Laverne's face. "I haven't heard from her for years. Her parents sent her off up north to some rich-people finishing school. I heard later she'd married."

"Guess her folks got tired of her hanging around with us."

Louette shifted on the bench. "You know, I often wondered if that's not where Joseph might have gone. Maybe he was sweet on Etheline, or something."

"Oh, I doubt that, Lou. He was partial to your company, long as I can remember." Laverne had always been that way. Positive and good-natured. She believed the best about everybody.

"I see the *Wayward Son*." Louette shaded her eyes. "I still think it's a hoot the way Jasper's boat got its name."

"Me too, his pa said anybody who wanted a separate fishing boat when he could work on his own family's shrimp boat was a kook. 'I'll let you name the boat if you'll co-sign,' Jasper told him. So, he did."

Laverne waved. Jasper held up a gaff with a huge flounder on it. "Looks big around as a foot-tub," said Louette. "Wonder where he got it."

"Ask him," Laverne's sun-brown face broke into a grin. They rushed through Battery Park while Jasper pulled in at Ten-Foot-Hole, the City Marina. He waved the flounder again and jumped onto the dock.

"Look what I found in the bay," he yelled to Louette. "Thought you might like a little fresh flounder."

"Nothing little about that fish. Biggest I ever seen. Where did you get him?"

"Under the Gorrie Bridge. Where else?" he said as he put the fish in a croaker sack.

"There's a lot of bay bottom under that bridge," she told him.

"He always says that's where he gets flounder." Laverne punched Jasper on the arm. Louette saw the glance they shared and was instantly jealous. *Those two are the halves of a whole*, she thought. She'd felt like half of her self was gone ever since Joseph went missing.

Jasper threw the flounder into the back of his old truck and the three crammed into the cab for the ride back to Shadow Lane.

After the flounder had been stuffed with cornbread dressing and tiny shrimp and baked to a golden doneness, they sat down to eat.

Louette sprinkled salt and pepper, squirted lemon juice and lifted a forkful of flounder. She savored the mouthful, enjoying it to the limit. "It's just as good as I expected," she said. "Thank you two for a wonderful meal."

After dinner they sat on the porch listening to the evening sounds of dogs barking off in the distance, cicadas singing, the low "who-whooo?" of an owl, and an answering "who?" from the top of the live oak. Oscar the gull was quiet after a meal of flounder scraps.

"Did you follow Benjamin down here?" Jasper asked Louette.

"No." *Oh, not the teasing. Jasper is the worst to pick at people.* "He said he was going hunting in Tate's Hell, somewhere around Whiskey George, or Cash's Creek. Hope he don't get lost and wander around with snakes and alligators like old Cebe Tate, then stumble out and announce he's been in hell."

"Not yet. I saw him ogling the manatees across the bay near Cat's Point."

"You've got manatees in the bay? Maybe we can search for them tomorrow."

"Don't you want to hook up with Benjamin? I could go get him for you." Jasper's eyes flashed mischievously.

"Ha! Don't you start." Louette shook a finger at him. "I can find Benjamin right around the corner when I get back home. I didn't chase him down here. Matter of fact, I did know he had come in this direction. But I wanted to visit Laverne, and you, of course."

"Yeah, yeah," Jasper stood up and stretched. "I'll see you women tomorrow. I've got an early start in the morning." He leaned over to kiss Laverne and plunked down on the swing to give Louette a hug. "You come again. With Benjamin. That man's in l-o-v-e with you."

Louette blushed in spite of herself. She was thankful the sun was almost down so they couldn't see her face turn red. "Go on; you don't know that."

"Yes, I do. I saw his eyes light up with sparks when I mentioned you and I saw sparks in your eyes when I mentioned him." Jasper chuckled as he went inside.

"Jasper has a quirky way of looking at things." Laverne chuckled. "He never did quite grow up,"

"Lucky him."

"Tell me what I can do to help you get back to yourself again." Laverne leaned forward, her foot pushing the floor so that the rocking chair moved back and forth.

"You already have helped. Just being in a normal household, watching you and Jasper so close and so happy with each other after all these years, is balm to my soul. I'm just taking Double Doc's advice."

"Double Doc? What kind of advice?"

"He said I can come out of the funks by doing something for myself that I want to do, that I don't have to follow sorrow around. I can change course."

"Sounds good to me. Not bad advice coming from old Double." Laverne stood up. "So, what are your plans?"

"First was to visit you a couple days. I also thought about holding a wake for myself."

"A wake?" Laverne stopped dead still. She shook her head. "You mean like you're dying?"

"Oh, no, no. I'm not dying, not that I know of."

"I'm not believing this."

"Like the gathering after Mama died, when everybody came to the funeral, brought food and visited. That was a lot of fun. Fun is what I need."

"Oh," Laverne eased back down in the rocking chair.

"Like a big party?"

"Sort of, only I want to call it a wake."

"Wouldn't that confuse people?"

"I think it will get people to feel like they should come. Like it's not just any old party. It is a really a revival of sorts. The suggestion was that I do something I want to do. To lift my spirits. I think this is it. Heck, maybe it will revive more than just me."

"If that's what you want. Then do it. Just let me know when and I'll go up there. Had you rather have it here? On Shadow Lane?"

"No, at my own house. I'll let you know when."

"If you change your mind, I'd love to have a big party for you right here in Apalachicola, on Shadow Lane, or somewhere bigger if you invite a lot of people."

"I was thinking of the relatives and friends who came to Mama's wake. It was a sad-happy time. We mourned her, but we also really enjoyed the big dinner, and all the folks we hadn't seen in years."

They talked until the wee hours, then slept late. In the morning, Louette smelled coffee and pulled herself from bed. As she washed her face, she remembered that Laverne had visited her when she and Jasper disagreed over something years ago. That trip had helped Laverne. This trip helped Louette.

It was hard to leave the Apalachicola River and Gulf of Mexico. Driving through pine forests along the coast, she watched the birds. Gulls flapped overhead and pelicans flopped about, diving for fish, looking like prehistoric monsters. Twice she stopped and helped a box turtle from the center of the road to the grass on the other side.

She remembered fondly the quote from Laura Ingalls Wilder about north Florida: "... where the trees always murmur, where the butterflies are enormous, where plants that eat insects grow in moist places, where alligators inhabit the slowly moving waters of the rivers." It seemed like a perfect description of her homeland.

The slap, slap and singsong of the tires kept pulling Louette toward sleep. She stopped at a service station and bought an RC Cola and a Moon Pie. After that she sang, "I've got the joy, joy, joy, joy, down in my heart. . . Bright star of hope, keep on shining for me. . . I come to the garden alone. . . Jambalaya, crawfish pie, and file gumbo." When her mouth got tired of singing, she hummed.

Wide awake and eager to be home, she lowered herself with delight onto a bench in the shade of the giant oak at the junction of the Choctawhatchee and Pea rivers. She had left one river and arrived at another just before the sun went down. She listened to the birdcalls and the whisper of the wind in the pines. *A place of peace and serenity. Here at the praying tree, my soul is rested.* Double Doc had been right. The feeling of dread was tamped down for the time being.

Do Lord, oh do Lord,
oh do Remember me.

Chapter Six

Address cards, pen and paper waited on her kitchen table. She'd used those cards to address high school and college graduation notices as well as wedding invitations for Marj, and birth announcements for Bucky. She hadn't needed invitations for her mother's funeral. With the newspaper notice, church bulletin, and phone calls, family members and friends had passed the information.

She'd have to figure out the proper wording. "*Dear* _____," Louette read aloud. "You are invited to a wake on Saturday afternoon, May 13, at my house on Sycamore Lane in Geneva. I am not dead. I just want to gather my rosebuds while I may, so I can be here myself to share in the fun. Bring a covered dish if you want to. I'll make plenty of coffee and sweet tea. Come around two o'clock if you like, but it's all right to come earlier or later. Those from far away let me know, so I can arrange for beds. I've got plenty of quilts for pallets if the Osceola Hotel fills up."

She'd take the information to the print shop and get invitations ready first thing in the morning. Just looking at the words lifted her spirits. An infrequently used emotion—excitement—surged through her. Plans for a big, happy gathering swirled in her head.

When Louette stepped through the front door to the porch, she felt like a new person. The blue jays flung insults at blackbirds, a pair of cardinals changed places on an azalea limb, and a brown thrasher in the side yard industriously flipped leaves.

"Hello, birds," Louette announced. "I'm taking a walk downtown." She peered at Shirley's house as she hurried past. *Guess she's still getting her beauty sleep.*

Farther down the street she saw Clyde get into his deputy sheriff car. He saw her and waved. *If only Marj had married Clyde instead of that stuck-up Snowden. But it is too late now, and besides, there wouldn't be the same Bucky. And Bucky is just perfect.*

Most of the houses along her street were quiet; the occupants young and already at work or old and sleeping in. A black and white cat scampered across her path. *Uh, oh, I don't need any black cats spooking my mood.*

She saw Double Doc going into Gilstrap Drug Store, still in a semi-trot. He took jogging seriously. But he had always given his best effort at whatever he did.

One of the employees from the shoe department of Chapman's Store was sweeping the front walk.

"Good morning, Lou. You seem perky today."

"Thanks, Royal. I am looking up some."

Double Doc came out of the drug store. He held up a package reading "Prescription for Lem Turner's horse." Then he did a double take. "Why Lou, you look positively happy. Is that a real smile I see on your face?"

"'Fraid so, Double. You helped put it there."

"Me?"

"You told me to do something to make myself happy, and I'm doing it."

"What are you doing?"

"I'm going to the print shop to get Willie to print up something for me."

"Like what?"

"An invitation. Don't worry, I'll send you one."

"What's it for?"

"Me to know and you to find out," Louette sang. She watched as Doc scratched his head and turned to jog down Main Street.

Louette hurried along the sidewalk only to find the print shop door locked. She was early. Waiting, she impatiently shifted from one foot to the other.

"Why, Louette Kelly. What a nice surprise." Willie, the fellow she and Joseph had sold the print shop to, seemed happy to see her. He had turned the small business over to his son and called himself retired, but still showed up every day, greeting customers and friends.

"My son James asked a few days ago if I thought you might like to come back to work, now that your mother's gone," he told Louette.

Willie's face glowed all over when he smiled. That friendly look had helped Louette a lot after Joseph left. Willie looked older now, with white hair, and his back stooped from bending over printing machines. *He hadn't known as much about pricing as Joseph, but he sure knew how to be friendly to customers. And that accounts for nine-tenths of the success of a business.*

"I hadn't considered going back to work," she told Willie. "I have been battling the hard-down blues, though. Tell James I'll study on it."

"I'll do that. Now what can I help you with?"

"How much would you charge to print up about a hundred of these?" Louette handed the draft of her invitation to Willie.

He unfolded the paper, smoothed it flat and reached for an estimate card. As he counted the words he took in their meaning. The color drained from his face. "Lou, is this an invitation to a wake?"

"Sure. How much will it cost?"

"This is a wake for you?" Before Louette could answer he asked, "Lou, are you planning to kill yourself?"

"Why no, whatever gave you such an idea?"

"You're inviting people to a wake. It's kind of obvious, isn't it, Lou? Why don't you have a May Day? People could dance around a Maypole and scatter flowers or take them to old people in the nursing home, or something. I ain't printing no invitations to no wake for you. I don't want you to do no dying around here."

"It's not a real wake." Louette took the slip of paper from his hand. "It's a party. But I thought people might not come to a regular party. They always come to a wake. People are asked to bring a covered dish. I'll make coffee and tea, a chocolate fudge cake, and some other good things to eat. Keep an invitation for you and one for James and his wife, and his oldest girl, Sarah. I like her."

Willie looked dumbfounded.

"Remember the big crowd that came to Mama's wake?"

"Yes." Willie took the paper back. "It was a fine wake. But wouldn't it be better if you just called this a party? When people get it, they'll think you've died."

"See?" Louette's face lit up. "They'll call to find out, and I'll tell them I wrote it to get them to come see me."

"Oh. So, it's sort of like a joke."

"It's not really a joke, Willie. Don't you understand? Old age is like a time bomb; every minute life is ticking away. Who knows? I want my party now, not when I'm stone cold dead in a coffin and people saying how natural I look. When Mama died, her cousin Alton Griswold looked down at her and said, 'Well, you done gone and done what we all gone do.' He was right. We will all die sooner or later. I want my wake now. I ain't waiting until I'm lying in no coffin."

"Okay, Lou. I'll print 'em up. But it's for a party, right?"

"Cross my heart." She held a finger in the air straight out from Willie's nose. Behind her back she crossed two fingers on her other hand. A person ought to be allowed to make up her own mind.

"Does Marj know you're planning this?"

"Not yet. Why?"

"She might think it's sort of, well, unbalanced."

"What do I care what Marj thinks? I don't ask Marj what to do with my life. She hasn't cared a whit about what happens to me since Joseph left. And that's been a long, long time." Louette suddenly burst into tears. *How mortifying*, she thought and willed the tears to stop, but they kept coming.

"I'm sorry, Lou." Willie took her arm, gently guiding her toward a chair. He handed her a handkerchief and patted her on the back until the tears slowed to a snuffle. "I didn't mean to set you off; you're usually such a no-nonsense kind of a person. Death is a terrible thing. You're grieving over your mother. It will be easier after some time passes."

Louette stood up and blew her nose, handing him back his handkerchief. "How much for 100 invitations?"

"Nothing, Lou. I'll print them for you free if you'll promise to talk to James about coming back to work at the shop."

"It's a deal." Louette's step was lighter as she walked out. Leaving the print shop, she looked around, then pulled Benjamin's note from her pocket. She missed him, but she sure hoped he wouldn't come home today. What would she tell him?

Shirley was waiting on Louette's front porch. *Sitting in the swing as big as you please.* "Are you all right?" she asked, moving over for Louette to sit beside her.

"Sure. Why do you ask?"

"I don't know. When I got home, I found your note about visiting Laverne. Just wondering how you are."

"Why?" Louette pushed with her foot and the swing moved slowly back and forth.

"This morning you walked off toward downtown instead of driving."

"I needed the exercise. You spying on me, Shirley?"

Shirley's face flushed red. "No." She got up. "I'll be going home now."

Louette shrugged and went into the house. Sometime she ought to tell Shirley how annoying it was that she just wandered in and out of her yard and house as if she lived there. *She could call or knock.*

The phone rang. *Nosy Shirley*, she thought as she picked up the receiver.

It was Marj. "What the hell is going on?"

"Don't you cuss at me, young lady. I'm still your mother, whether you like it or not."

"Why are you getting invitations printed for your own funeral?"

"Not a funeral, a wake. You know, the big party they hold when somebody dies."

"Are you planning on dying?"

"People don't plan to die. The wake is not about death. It's about life. I am living. I want to see my friends and relatives before one of us dies. What's wrong with that?"

"Nothing. But call it a party."

"I will not. I'm calling it a wake, because I want lots of people to come. They won't come to a party. But they always come to a wake."

Marj was quiet. "A person holding their own wake is about the most stupid thing I've ever heard of."

"Who told you about the invitations?" Louette thought Willie. But maybe he had called Shirley and Shirley had called Marj. "You got Shirley keeping track of what I'm doing?"

"Never mind that," Marj sputtered. "Just tell me what's going on."

"I am holding my own wake because I want it now, instead of after I'm stone cold dead like Mama. It's on a Saturday, so nobody will have to miss work. You can come. Bring Bucky. You can even bring your annoying husband, if you want to. I'll send you an invitation when Willie gets them printed. And I am not stupid." Louette stood still for a long time after hanging up the phone.

The shrill of the phone lashed at her again. Staring at it, Louette started to pick it up and tell Marj what a relief it was to get angry, then to cry. There was some sort of release in that. But she didn't. Marj had cussed at her. Louette had never done that to her own mother.

Finally, the ringing stopped. The feeling of dread came back. A lump in her throat. Sometimes a memory did that, just jumped into her head. Maybe Marj was right. Maybe she was coming down with the crazies. She picked up the phone and dialed the number for the farm. Dan answered.

"Just wanted to tell you and Mittie I'm back from Laverne and Jasper's. What you up to?"

"I put planks on top of that pig fence and went out and built a real sturdy railing around that scary quicksand sinkhole. If we ever get Bucky back, I sure don't want him jumping in no big blob. It looks so innocent with lilies floating on top. But quicksand is bad treacherous."

"I don't think we have to worry about Bucky climbing no fence to pet pigs or wandering into the quicksand. I have a notion Marj won't let my grandson visit for a long time, if ever again."

"Oh, Lou, she can't stay mad. He'll be back and we'll be glad to see him. Don't go anywhere, Mittie went to town and intends to drop by your place. She should be there pretty soon."

Louette looked out the window as Mittie's car turned in at the driveway. She skipped to the front door.

"Come in," Louette called. "I need to apologize to you. I intended to go out and help with chores until Dan's leg heals."

"It's all right. Dan already broke up the fields and spread fertilizer."

"I'll be happy to help put in seeds."

"Much obliged." Mittie held something in her hand. "I brought this for Bucky. It's a whistle Dan made from a bamboo reed."

Louette took the whistle. "Lord, Mittie, I don't know when Bucky'll get to come back. Marj is pretty mad."

Mittie sighed. "He sure is a nice little fellow. Scared the tar out of me when he went in the hog pen." She turned as if ready to leave.

"Don't go." Louette took her by the arm. "I'll plug in the coffee. I kept out a few of the chocolate chip cookies I made for Bucky. The box is ready to mail. I'll put in the whistle."

"That would be nice."

They drank coffee and nibbled at the cookies.

"Bet Bucky don't bother no fresh-born baby pigs anymore."

Mittie stirred cream in her coffee, then stared at the spoon. "I never had any children of my own, but I always liked having them around, especially Marj. Now she's grown up and the nieces and nephews on my side of the family are married and moved away. I never get to be around little ones anymore."

"Me neither. The ones at church are friendly, I guess. Sometimes though they act scared of me. Reckon I'm just old and ugly."

Mittie grinned. "I've thought about throwing out all the mirrors. It sure gets lonely out at the farm sometimes, just me and Dan." She looked out the window. "Be glad you've got neighbors close by."

"Some neighbors. Miz Gumby is deaf as a post and Shirley's loony as a betsy bug." Laughter bubbled up; they couldn't help it. "About the only breath of fresh air in this neighborhood is Benjamin, and the others make fun of him for cutting hedge trains."

"It was a tragedy for him to be so badly injured by the train. They should've given him a conductor's job or something," said Mittie.

"Benjamin said if he couldn't be an engineer, he'd be nothing. Now he grows trains in his own yard and clips them to suit himself." Louette shook her head. "Shirley tried to flirt with him, but it didn't work."

"Where is Shirley? I didn't see her car in the drive."

"Don't mention that woman. You speak her name, and she pops up. She is a real aggravation."

Mittie chuckled. "Now, Lou, don't say that. At least she's a live human being to talk to."

"You're right. But Shirley can sure get on a person's nerves."

Louette thought about explaining her plans for the wake, then decided against it. *Let Mittie get her invitation like everybody else. Dan might not be able to come, if he's not healed from the sow attack, but Mittie could leave him long enough to visit.*

Louette looked forward to the cousins, the old aunts and uncles, what was left of them, the schoolmates from back in the nineteen forties and fifties. A big gathering on a Saturday in May, with her birthday following on Monday... just the right touch.

After Mittie left, Louette raked leaves and pine straw. The blooms underneath the camellia bushes looked like piles of dried blood. She cleared the garden spot and pulled vines and grass from around the bunch onions, singing all the while, "Shall We Gather at the River?" She intended to clean the house, put the rickety chair back in the shed, take the old Life magazines, Smithsonians, and National Geographics to the library.

Louette heard the squeak and groan of Elijah Finney's rackety wagon coming down the street.

"You need some axle grease on your wagon wheels, Lige," she called out.

Lige clicked to his mule and jumped down, holding the lines. "I come by to see if you want me to cut up your garden plot, Lou." He laughed. "I like the squeaky wheels. Gives me some company along the way. They do sound like they fixin' to fall off, though."

"I'm cleaning up, but I want to wait awhile on the garden." She and Lige shook hands. They had been in grade school together, but Lige looked older. His dark, wizened face had a wide smile. He loved growing fruits and vegetables. His tomatoes won first prize at the county fair every year.

"How's your mama and the younguns?" asked Louette.

"They fine," Lige answered.

"I still got some of Mama's fig preserves here in the shed," Louette told him. "Want a jar?"

"Sure do. Your mama made the best preserves. They almost like eating candy. I like 'em, 'specially in a fat buttered biscuit."

"Now you're making me hungry," Louette said with a laugh.

After Lige's noisy exodus, Louette reminded herself she'd better get back to work.

She walked to the front and cast a critical eye on her house. Once sunshine yellow, it had faded to a dirty-yellow hue. The shutters which had been a bright green now needed scrubbing with soap and water. The pine planks had held the paint pretty well, but many were peeling in spots.

She tried to drag the cot and its lumpy mattress from the storage shed. Maybe someone would want to stay overnight after the wake. Lou stood up and rubbed the achy spot on her back. "You miserable old cot." She talked to it as she pulled at the frame. "You're too heavy for me. I'll have to leave you here."

She leaned down to rub the backs of her legs. She wondered why there was a bulge just below a knee and her calves hurt, then remembered the pig pen. It was a marvel she didn't hurt all over. The big scare replayed itself right there in her mind, like panels of a comic strip.

In the first panel, the boy's hand reaches through a wire-mesh fence toward a brood of fat little baby pigs. The second shows him climbing the fence. The third shows him inside the fence and the four-hundred-pound sow snorting, with her head down, ready to charge.

The fourth panel depicts a farmer flying over the barnyard fence, overalls billowing around skinny legs, one hand balanced on the post, his feet catapulting into the pen. The angry sow, head down, barrels toward the boy and the baby pigs.

The fifh shows the man's feet on the ground in the hog pen, the boy in the air, his grandmother outside the fence, arms outstretched to catch him. The sow's head is lowered, her jaws clamped onto the farmer's calf.

The last panel shows the fat, pink baby pigs scrambling for the sow's teats, the man outside the pen, blood spurting from a wound in his leg and the boy, mouth open, safe in his grandmother's arms.

Other details were less clear, like the bucket of broken eggs. Sounds echoed in her head—the high-pitched squeal of the sow, Bucky's scream, Dan yelling "Catch him."

Louette shook her head. She was no longer at the farm. She was at home, moving dusty relics of an earlier time around in the old falling-down shed. She could take a lot of this stuff to Penny's Worth, but they probably wouldn't want it.

Shirley's brakes screeched.

"Hey," she called from the car. "What you doing?"

"Cleaning."

"Oh, I get it." She walked from her driveway over to the shed. "You're cleaning up for the party. My mother said wait until after the company leaves to clean up or you'll be cleaning up twice." She paused, took a deep breath and

and looked around. "If you'd give away some of that old junk, you might have more room."

"Leave my stuff alone, Shirley. That's my memories you're staring at—my personal memories." Her arms were filled with National Geographics.

"You don't have to get huffy. I might remember some of those things. I've been around here a long time." Too long.

Shirley's arms brimmed with bags. "I was going to show you my new blouse and pedal pushers, but you're being grouchy. I'd come help you clean up, but I'm tired from shopping."

"I don't need no help. It's good exercise for me."

"All right." Shirley sounded relieved. "I didn't really want to help anyway. So there." She stomped across the yard to her own house.

It was a relief to be rid of Shirley. Louette put the magazines in the car trunk, then walked over to Miz Gumby's door. *Why am I knocking? She can't hear me.* But Miz Gumby came right away.

"You want to go with me to the library?"

"Huh?" Miz Gumby cupped her hand behind her ear.

"Car ride?" Louette held up the car keys.

"Let me get my sweater and purse." Miz Gumby disappeared inside the house.

Irene, the librarian, helped take the magazines from the trunk. "Thanks, Lou, Life magazines are jewels people look for. And Marcus Willingham keeps asking about when the new National Geographic and Smithsonian are getting here. Remember Marcus? These days he sits in the sunroom and brings the magazines up to show me the pictures."

"I haven't seen Marcus in a long time." Louette mentally added him to her invitation list. "Does he still wear a black suit coat?"

"Winter, spring, summer, and fall," said Irene. One time Louette had dared ask Marcus why he wore the heavy coat in the summer. He gently explained that if it kept out the cold in winter, it ought to keep out the heat in summer. Louette didn't mention the fact that his suit-coat underarms were soaked with sweat.

"Marcus is a bit peculiar," Louette said.

"Aren't we all," agreed the librarian.

The women, arms filled with magazines, passed Miz Gumby sitting on the library steps picking at little nubs of wool on the sleeves of her sweater.

"I thought we were going to the grocery store," the old woman muttered.

"Aren't we all?" Louette said, and they laughed again.

As she and Miz Gumby drove home, she wondered when Benjamin would get back. He said he wanted to talk to her when he returned from the trip to Tate's Hell Forest. She drove by his house, but he wasn't there. Would he be on her porch? Louette shivered with apprehension. Or was it eagerness?

Revive us again.
Fill each heart with Thy love.
May each soul be rekindled,
with fire from above.
Hallelujah, Thine the glory! Hallelujah, amen!
Hallelujah, Thine the glory! Revive us again!

Chapter Seven

"Your, uh, printing's ready," Willie told her on the phone. "You can pick it up anytime."

It was a pretty day; a few loopy clouds cavorted, yet none seemed heavy enough to carry buckets of rain. Louette walked to the print shop. When she asked at the desk for the invitations to her wake, the girl jumped as if ready to run. She called Willie from the back.

"Here they are," Willie carried the invitations wrapped in white paper and tied with a string on top of a box of fine-looking envelopes. "That'll be forty-five dollars."

"You told me they'd be free, but I'll be glad to pay you. You can be sure if they're messed up like Marj's wedding invitations, I won't be sending them out. You'll be printing them over."

"Oh, no, I'm sorry. They are free. I forgot." Willie watched Louette break the string and unwrap the invitations. Lips moving, she read one carefully.

"You made a mistake," Louette told him. "You've got a *g* instead of a *y* on Kelly. My name is Louette Kelly not Kellg." She handed him one of the cards.

"I told you we need you around here," Willie said. "You're a good proofreader. Besides, I put the bad ones on top. It's right on most of them. James caught it after some of them had run on the press. I thought you might use the bad ones as extras, in case you run out. The good ones are on the bottom. See?" Willie held up a printed card. He was right. The *y* was on Kelly, just the way it was supposed to be.

"I've got a hundred of the good ones?"

"Yes."

"Some printer; gives people the culls," Louette muttered, pulling out her checkbook.

"I told you, no charge," Willie reminded her.

She put her checkbook away. "Be sure that you come."

"You gonna make a chocolate fudge cake like you said?"

"I sure am and a butternut pound cake."

"Maybe you ought to put the cake on the invitations." Louette looked up to a twinkle in Willie's eyes.

"I don't know about everybody else in this town, but I'll be there," he promised. "Just be sure you're alive. I don't want to go to no real wake for you."

Louette pulled the door open.

"Lou, remember Buck Renfrow?" Willie called after her. "Moved over near Tuscaloosa?"

"I remember him. He was ahead of us at first, then dropped back in about fourth grade. Why? What'd Buck do?"

"He died last week."

"I didn't hear about it."

"Wat'n no notice in the paper. They buried him up there."

"Wonder why they didn't bring him back home?"

"Don't think he's got any kin left here. The old place sold to them Rowells from over near Marianna. Remember?"

"Yeah. Now I do. I'm real sorry about Buck." Louette closed the door. That's the way it was. You died and they buried you in some other place. *Didn't even have the decency to bring old Buck home.* He wasn't much, but he had been a part of the community. It bothered her that he had been put in the ground way up there in Tuscaloosa.

Louette walked swiftly down the street. She swiped at her eyes. *Looks like my sinuses are acting up again, or I'm tearing up over Buck. Can't imagine why, though. I didn't really care too much about Buck when he lived here. It don't make sense for me to be so upset that he died. But then not much makes sense lately. Could I be coming unglued?*

She didn't see the stately man walking toward her, his head in a book. They collided with a loud uumph. "Why, Judge, I'm so sorry," Louette stepped off the sidewalk.

"The apology is mine." Gray haired, with shrewd eyes under tufted brows, County Probate Judge Simon O'Connor gazed sharply at Louette. He reached out a hand to steady her. "I was preoccupied. I'm re-reading Homer. It is phenomenal how the ancient classics reflect life as it is today. When you come right down to it, we aren't half as civilized as we think we are."

Lord, deliver me from the judge. He talks too much. Louette nodded her head. "It's nice to see you, Simon." She stepped back on the sidewalk and picked up invitations and envelopes scattered in the collision.

But the honorable judge wasn't to be put off that easy. "Did you read Homer, Lou?"

"I did," she told him, "Same time as you in Miss Ruby Beck's high school literature class." She stepped around him. "I'm in sort of a hurry, Simon. I've got some things to do."

"What?" he asked abruptly. Simon could read people like the book he held in his large hands, one finger marking his place.

Louette shook her head. Tears were close to the surface. She grasped at the news of Buck Renfrow. "Had you heard about Buck Renfrow dying, Simon? And that they buried him up in Tuscaloosa?"

The tall man leaned his skinny frame over and laid the thick book on the grass beside the sidewalk. He reached out his huge hands to grasp Louette's shoulders. "I didn't know you were that fond of Buck, Lou," he said gently.

Louette pulled back. "What do you mean? I wasn't fond of Buck at all. Come to think of it, he was actually a sort of no-account person."

"Then why, my dear, are you on the verge of tears over the news of Buck's death over in Tuscaloosa? Death is a part of everyone's life."

Simon looked like a caricature of a person, with his tall body and round pooched-out stomach, tufts of red hair popping over his ears, and his outlandishly large hands. Under normal circumstances, Louette would have laughed at, and with, Simon. He had a way of looking at a person as if through them and right into their secret places.

"I don't know," she said simply. "Maybe it is the idea of death itself that has my attention."

His large hands were busily helping her gather up the invitations and envelopes. He looked at one of the cards. "What are these?" he asked.

"Something I got Willie to print up for me." Louette grabbed the cards and envelopes from him and hastily stuffed them into the bag from the print shop.

"Invitations?" asked Simon.

"I'm really in a hurry," Louette handed him one of the cards, then scurried up the sidewalk. Glancing back she saw Simon standing on the grass as he read, a puzzled look on his face.

Several streets south of the small downtown Louette could hardly see the potholes and lumps of broken cement through her tears as she made her way home. Her flushed face reflected her embarrassment, not because Simon was the county probate judge, but back in elementary school her first crush had been aimed at him. Long before she fell in love with Joseph, Louette had secretly eyed Simon in a childish, romantic way.

Simon had been handsome. He didn't get his big spurt of growth until eleventh grade. By the time he finished high school and entered the university, he towered over most of the other students. Simon had been unhappy in law school. Just before graduation, he married a girl from Tallahassee, came home and settled down to a mediocre law practice. His warmth and personality helped ease him into politics and a county judge seat, which, Louette thought, suited him quite well.

Just before she reached her street, Louette could hear the rain coming. She tucked the invitations into her purse and stuffed it under her jacket. The leather purse would protect the invitations from the rain. Should she run home the few blocks, or meet the rain? *A few sprinkles won't hurt.* The full force of a hard rain caught her at the edge of her yard and she ran and jumped onto the porch. As she sat in the swing, Louette closed her eyes. The rain on the roof sounded like a shower bath.

I shouldn't have walked to town. I should have driven in the car, then I wouldn't have dropped the invitations and gotten all flustered at Simon.

The phone rang. She had practically stopped answering it. She wasn't talking to a daughter who cussed at her and called her ideas stupid. When her feelings were hurt, they were hurt.

I'm doing what I'm doing and it's none of Marj's business. In the house she put the invitations on the dinette and made herself a glass of iced tea. From her address file she picked her favorites first. If Aunt Rufus was too old to drive, would Aunt Juney be able to bring her? She could call and ask, but the embarrassment of her confrontation with Simon was still with her and she decided to stick to the printed word.

As she reviewed the note cards, she counted more than 100 people she wanted to invite. *I guess it's good Willie messed up some.* She arranged the cards in order of who she wanted to see most.

"Dear Aunt Rufus, I hope you can make it to my wake. If Aunt Juney can't drive you, let me know; I'll get somebody to go pick up both of you." Louette soon realized there was not enough time to write notes on every invitation. *They'll call when they get them anyway. It'll be funny when they call to ask about my wake and I answer the phone. Ha!*

She didn't want to forget Marcus Willingham. He wouldn't understand about a wake while a person was still alive and might come over here crying. For others she simply put the invitation in the envelope and addressed it.

She felt a slight sense of release, or closure, as she licked each envelope. The physical act of announcing that she wanted these people as part of her family and community, gave her a sense of inner peace she hadn't felt with certainty since her mother died. She got up and made another glass of sweet tea. The ice tinkled as she sipped.

She had plenty of stamps left over from when she hadn't felt like sending Christmas cards. December had come too soon after Clara's death. Of course, the post office had upped the price since then. She'd have to add on another two cents.

She wondered if she ought to have had Willie print RSVP on the cards. For a wedding RSVP was a good thing. But she was expecting a bunch of folks who'd bring covered dishes. If she ran out of coffee and tea she could just make more.

When she used up the good invitations, she marked a *y* on top of Willie's errant *g* until those for people out of town were enveloped, ready for the post office. She'd take the rest around town to friends and neighbors, tack one up with the church notices, and put one in the newspaper.

With one bag of addressed invitations and one with spares to hand out, Louette opened the front door. The sun had moved past lunch and into afternoon. She felt good. So far she had put in a good day's work getting ready for her wake to celebrate life.

From the porch Louette watched a slim, elegant woman walk across the side yard to the shed. It looked like she was trying to open the rotten shed door. *Is that Etheline, from long ago?* She looked sort of the same, only older. The woman wore bright red designer sweat pants and shirt and had a distinctively classy carriage to her walk.

Louette put the invitations down on the front stoop. She and Etheline had been close when young, but she hadn't seen her often after Etheline was abruptly sent up north. One day she was there, friendly as always, and the next day she was gone. No announcement. No goodbye party.

Louette had called her house, but was told by a frosty-voiced maid, that Etheline had gone away to finishing school. As if she needed "finishing." Louette liked her the way she was. A flurry of speculation followed among the youngsters in school and the adults at home, but Etheline's father was "the boss" at the cotton mill where most of the county's grownups worked, and no one dared question his actions.

Occasionally Etheline had come home for holidays, and Louette had seen her at the funerals of her parents. But Joseph's disappearance, and trouble with Marj, had left an ache in Louette's heart so big it crowded out almost everything and everyone else.

She took a step forward. "Etheline Powers! Is that really you?"

"Hello, Lou." Etheline turned around.

"Where's Joseph? Did you bring him with you?"

"Joseph?"

"Joseph Kelly. My husband."

"Why would I bring Joseph? How could I? I heard he disappeared, or something, years ago." Etheline walked across the yard toward her.

"I always thought maybe Joseph ran away to be with you."

"Me? Joseph wasn't sweet on me." Etheline gave a short laugh. "He'd sing 'Etheline, Ethelina, where you been so long?' I hoped he was flirting, but Joseph only had eyes for you."

Louette looked at her long-ago friend. "In the back of my mind, I thought maybe that's where Joseph went." She'd worried that Joseph might be cold in the winter. He hadn't taken any of his winter clothes. Louette felt relieved.

"If he did, I didn't see him."

"When did you come home? I heard you married. Thought you stayed up in Boston."

Etheline's laugh was short. "I couldn't stay there my whole life. Actually, I came home to die."

Louette stopped. Puzzled. Etheline looked healthy enough. "What on earth do you mean, Etheline? Why would you come home to die? You don't look anywhere near to death. Actually, you are as pretty as ever, maybe even better looking than in high school."

"It's not happening this instant, Lou. Not today."

"I saw them cleaning up your old place after your parents passed, but I just thought it was to be sold. It never did, so I figured you might be asking too much money for it." Louette chattered on nervously, still trying to register what she had just heard. Louette was shocked. Had she heard Etheline right? Had Etheline said what she thought she'd said? It wasn't proper to come out and say you were going to die. There were manners, or decorum, or something mixed in there somewhere, weren't there? But then, she had just finished addressing invitations to her own wake. What right did she have to criticize?

"I came back for sentimental reasons, Lou. I had to come back. The doctors found a mass on my right kidney. They said it might be cancerous."

"Might be?"

"I stopped the foolishness and came home," Etheline said. Louette pulled open the shed door. Etheline peered inside.

"If it was cancerous, couldn't they take it out?" Louette flailed her arms at cobwebs.

"They said not."

"Don't they cure cancers with chemotherapy these days?" Louette looked Etheline full in the face.

"I'm not interested in chemo and radiation. I don't want my insides poisoned or burned up."

Louette mulled that over. What would she do if she had an incurable disease?

"There is no such thing as dying with dignity," Etheline continued. "I saw that volunteering with cancer patients in the hospital."

"I heard you were a great writer," Louette tried to change the subject. "But I couldn't make myself read your books."

"Really? Why not?"

"Well, you know, I thought Joseph took off to find you."

Etheline gave the same mysterious grin she'd had when she was a kid. "I was trying to get a look at your storage building."

"Bucky and I were sifting through things. I keep my memories in this shed."

"What kind of memories do you have stored?"

"All kinds. What you been doing all this time? Besides writing books."

Etheline looked around. "I collect curios, strange objects for museums and such."

"You ain't collecting any of my stuff. But you can come in." Louette pointed to the cowhide chair.

Etheline looked at the chair but didn't sit down. "What is this?" She picked up a sausage grinder from the top of a cast iron wood-burning stove.

"Mama used to grind up hog meat. Everybody came and got her when they wanted their sausage seasoned," Louette laughed. "You asked her once how she knew how much pepper to put in and she said she asked people to bring her their spices. If they wanted it hot, they brought lots of seasonings. Otherwise, she knew they liked their sausage mild. Either way, by the time she was through mixing, they had what they wanted."

"She taught me many things. Your mother did."

Louette peered at this woman who resembled her childhood friend. A twinkle came into her eyes. Joseph hadn't gone to be with Etheline! He wasn't here, but he wasn't in Boston either! Now that she knew where he wasn't, somehow his going away seemed easier on her mind.

"Maybe I ought to read some of your books."

Etheline turned the handle on the sausage grinder. "Do. But you might not like them. I'm not a real writer in the literary sense," she said slowly. "I'm more a teller of tales."

"Tales?"

"Yes. To be honest, my books are sometimes morbid, often sad, filled with sarcasm," Etheline confessed.

"I don't understand. I thought you had a great life," Louette said.

Etheline grimaced. She picked up the half-finished embroidery hoop with the phoenix rising from the ashes. "Did you do this?"

"No, Mama did."

Etheline peered at another article. "Ooh, look at this turtle shell. May I have it?"

"Not hardly. You put that back." Louette grabbed the turtle shell and placed it on a top shelf.

"I could buy that thing from you. How much do you want for it?"

"The shell is not for sale. Come on. Let's go out of here, you're getting those fancy clothes dirty."

"What's in this box?" Etheline pointed to a shelf. "It looks like Japanese writing."

"Marj and her husband brought me and Mama that box of dishes from Japan when he was stationed over there with the Air Force. We didn't use them because they looked too fragile. I wouldn't have wanted to break even one tiny little saucer. They are so pretty."

Etheline laughed. "I have a house full of china and crystal that's thin and fragile looking. You'd be surprised how strong it is."

Louette reached for Etheline's hand, pulled her out of the shed and shut the door. "I'm on my way to the post office. Want to walk with me?" Louette retrieved the two bags from the steps.

"Sure." Louette handed her one of the bags.

"What is this?" Ethelene matched her stride to Louette's.

"Tell me about your husband. What did he think about coming here?"

"He didn't. I left him. He can rot in that cold place. He never was much of a husband. All he cared about was getting his hands on what was left of my daddy's money. Money doesn't buy happiness, Lou."

"Seems I heard that before," Louette nodded. "But it must be nice to know you'll always have enough."

"I suppose. Why are you taking these bags to the post office?"

"Those are invitations to my wake."

Etheline stopped. "You're having a wake? Then you're dying too."

"No, I'm not dying. I'm having my wake now so I can see people and talk to them, not just lay up there in a coffin like Mama did when everybody came to pay respects. Would you like to come to my wake?"

"Sure. What are you dying from?"

"I'm not dying, I told you, unless it's from loneliness since Mama passed away. I'm having a big party. At least I hope it's big. Maybe won't nobody come. I might not come to no wake, if I wasn't the one thowing it."

"I will, Lou. I'd be happy to come to your party."

"Okay, but don't be telling any of them sad tales you say you write in books. This is to be a joyous occasion. I promise." Etheline perked up.

They walked toward town on the uneven sidewalks canopied by ancient water oaks, magnolias and sycamore trees. Louette wondered what people thought seeing them together: Etheline in her fancy bright clothes; Louette in faded slacks and blouse and dirty tennis shoes. Etheline reached to her side as if she had a stitch.

"You all right?" Louette stopped. "We're to the post office."

"I'm fine. It's my body reminding me it's in control. Of all the ways for the elderly to die, I suppose I'm lucky to have only one."

"Etheline, change the subject. I'm tired of hearing about death."

"You're the one inviting people to a wake." Etheline pushed open the door of the Geneva Post Office. She looked around, as if seeing the place for the first time.

"I need these to go out right away," Louette told Angie behind the window. "I'm delivering the local ones. These are for people out of town. I've got stamps on them. But we need to add the extra two cents. You people went up again."

"It costs money to run the United States Postal Service."

"Spoken like a loyal public servant," Etheline laughed.

Angie pushed her glasses over her forehead and peered at Etheline. "What are you doing out and about, Etheline?"

"What do you mean, 'out and about'? I'm home now, for good."

"I heard that. Racie Mae said for me to tell folks not to call you that you needed to be left alone in your grief."

Etheline gasped. "My grief? What do you mean by that? I'm not dead yet."

"About your husband's death, I mean." Angie had found Etheline's loose board and intended to release every nail, no matter how rusty.

"My husband didn't die. I left him. All he could talk about was his secretary. I told her she could have him. So there."

Louette liked the post office. Especially the sign: Welcome to the Town of One Thousand Friendly Folks and One Old Grouch. She'd always considered Angie the old grouch but guessed they ought to add Etheline to it now. *Make it two old grouches.*

"Whoa," Louette said. "You two used to be friends a million years ago, before you had a fight over one of the Griffin boys. He's long dead and gone. What are you mad about now?"

The women were trying to outglare each other. They turned toward Louette. "If Angie knew I was in town, how come you didn't?" Etheline asked.

"Louette's been holed up in her house like a hermit since her mother died," said Angie.

"Lord," said Etheline. "You still throw out the truth, don't you? Like smearing more mustard on a hot dog."

"Well, it's right. The only time I've seen Louette smile lately was when her grandson came for a visit."

Enough is enough, thought Louette. "I want to mail these, if you don't mind." She pointed to the pile of envelopes in the service window.

Angie frowned. "These are invitations," she said more than asked.

"Yes, to my wake on the thirteenth of May," Louette said. "I'm having it on a Saturday, so folks won't have to get off work to come."

"Then the rumor is true."

"Oh, yes. I brought one for you." Louette handed it over. "It's one of Willie's culls, but I marked the *g* into a *y*. He got Kelly spelled wrong." She laughed, a little ha-ha laugh as if making light of the whole thing.

"But, Lou, you're not dead. Why don't you call it a party?" Angie looked to Etheline as if for support. Etheline turned away.

"Because people don't come to parties like they do to wakes. Remember how everybody came when Mama died?"

"I remember." Angie fingered the invitation. "Your mama was a special person, putting up the money she got for the farm land to build a hospital. There are a lot of rich people who wouldn't do what she did." She frowned at Etheline.

"She didn't exactly 'build' a hospital, Angie, she just donated seed money," said Louette.

"Whatever, she turned over what she got from the land to the hospital committee—did this county a grand favor."

"I was referring to how people flocked to her wake," said Louette.

"I know. They knew what a kind person she was. Not like some people... " Angie looked pointedly at Etheline.

"My father closed the mill because it was no longer profitable," Etheline told her in a strained voice. "He sold the land to pay off the cotton mill debts, and to keep his family out of the poorhouse." The fight in Etheline surfaced. She looked as if she'd like to punch Angie.

"Wait! Stop this! Don't pick up on a 50-year disagreement. You two have a chance to be friends," Louette told them. "Let bygones be bygones. There is no place for bitterness between you."

"Fine one to talk," muttered Angie. "A person who don't even speak to her own daughter."

Uh, oh. Tattle-tale Shirley has been to the PO shootin' off her mouth. "I came in here to mail these invitations," said Louette. "Could you please send these out for me, Miz Postmistress?"

Angie swallowed her anger. It was not Uncle Sam's policy for post office employees to argue with customers. She cleared her frown and gave a lopsided smile. "I'll send out your mail and I'll also post your invitation on the bulletin board." She cleared her throat. "And, Lou, I'll be at your wake."

"Fantastic!" Louette clapped her hands in relief.

Now Angie had a real smile. "What you want me to bring? Chicken casserole and my persimmon pie?"

"That would be nice."

Etheline had wandered over to the wall of wanted posters, studying them as if she might find somebody she knew. She snorted.

"Don't you snort at my persimmon pie, Etheline Powers," Angie told her. "You with all your money. I'll bet you can't cook a lick."

"I've got a cook who can beat your pie in a New York second."

"Hah! All that woman can cook fitten' to eat is collard greens."

"I'd put Racie Mae's cooking up against yours any day in the week," said Etheline. "And besides, I might just cook up some dishes myself. I didn't have a cook after I married. Of course, we ate out a lot. Way up there in Boston, home of baked beans. They even ate them for breakfast; believe it or not."

The door opened, and Gordon Lassiter poked his head in. "Is it okay to come in here? I heard what sounded like bickering."

"Do come in, Gordo," Louette told him. "These two women need a referee."

"They fought all the way through elementary school," said Gordon. "You'd think enough years have gone past to mellow them out."

At the sound of his voice, Etheline turned. "Why, the leader of the pack at the Planters Bank," she said. "How are you, Gordo?"

"I'm fine. You look beautiful."

Surprising Louette, Etheline blushed, and stammered, "I intended to go by the bank."

"I heard you were back," interrupted Gordon gently. "Sounded like you were holed up licking marriage wounds. I didn't want to get in the middle of your heartache."

Louette looked on silently. *Gordon is thoughtful and considerate*, she mused.

Etheline turned her eyes downward, as if studying the floor. Gordon reached out and took her arm. He swallowed, and his Adams apple shifted up and down.

Gordon had muscular shoulders, spare frame, and a smidgen of gray tracing his temples. He was a foot taller than Etheline; she'd have to tip her head back to look at his face. Louette began a slow grin. Some sort of magic was happening, right before her eyes. *It's so quiet in here you could hear a pin drop. If I had a pin on me, I'd drop it.*

She and Angie shared a glance. Some spark was being rekindled from long ago, right there in front of them. Angie cleared her throat, interrupting. "Could I get something for you, Gordo?" she asked, a mischievous smile playing around her lips.

"I was expecting a package and didn't want to wait for mail pickup from the box." Reluctantly he turned away from Etheline to take the official-looking parcel Angie poked through the mail window.

Etheline reached out and touched his arm. Laugh wrinkles spread from his eyes to the edges of his neatly trimmed hair. "Gordo, how's your family?"

"My family? Etheline, you know I never married. I told you myself on the phone. My parents have been dead for years."

Etheline's face was bright red by now. She didn't say anything more. *She doesn't have to,* thought Louette.

Gordon's gentle voice continued. "Your dad didn't want me around when we were in school. I was the poorest kid in town. Wonder what he'd think about me taking care of his, or your, money now."

Etheline squared her shoulders. "I'm sure he would approve. You were a whiz at math. It looks like you're a whiz now at just about everything."

"Yeah," interjected Angie. "Look at him. Fawning over the little rich girl come home to lord it over everybody else."

Etheline, Louette, and Gordon turned toward Angie, who swallowed and reached down as if picking up something from the floor. "You've got one of the best-paying jobs in this town," Gordon told her. "I wouldn't be criticizing anybody if I were you."

"Humpf! to you Gordon Lassiter. At least I don't owe you money, which is better than most people around here." She lifted her nose in the air and turned away.

Etheline and Gordon continued to move in some sort of ancient dance, locked in a private realm of rediscovery. Gazing at them, Louette remembered when they held hands in second grade. They had been close, even as children, although their lives had been very different.

Etheline was the daughter of the town's leading citizen, the county's major employer, who had his financial finger in most of the town's businesses. As a child she was petted and coddled in a comfortable home— the delight of both parents. Then abruptly, at fifteen, she was sent away from the close-knit community to a far-away Northern city.

Gordon had lived in a household of fear. At the slightest provocation he and his mother had been knocked about by his father. When townspeople tried to intervene, the beatings became worse, until at sixteen Gordon grew taller than his father. Then the thrashings mysteriously stopped, and the young Gordon blossomed in school and in the neighborhood.

Louette realized with a start that this Gordon Lassiter standing in the post office—her friend, the president of the local bank—resembled Etheline's father a great deal.

The atmosphere in the post office was charged with a kind of electricity, as if Etheline and Gordon were seeing each other for the first time. This fresh intimacy had a foundation dredged not just from their memories, but from Louette's own, long buried.

"I'll call you in a couple of days." Gordon gave Etheline a long, tender look. "And we won't be discussing business this time."

The door shut behind Gordon, leaving a block of empty space. Etheline exhaled. "Whoa," she said, shaking her head. "That was heavy."

Louette still felt the warmth of what had passed between the two. *If what I saw is not rekindled love, I'd still like to have whatever it is.*

"Let's go, Lou." Etheline reached for the door knob. Louette nodded.

The sparks between Etheline and Gordon brought up a memory, quick and sharp, of a similar current passing between herself and Benjamin.

"Get those invitations out," Louette told Angie.

"Okay," she said, "and I'll be at your party with chicken casserole and persimmon pie."

Bright star of hope, keep on shining for me...
My glad heart thrills, so full and free.

Chapter Eight

When they reached the sidewalk, Etheline shook her head. "Oh, my."

"Yeah," said Louette.

Not one to give clues as to what was on her mind, Etheline turned to Louette. "We ought to get Angie fired," said Etheline. "All she does is mind the whole town's business." *Aha! No mention of Gordon. What a new wrinkle.*

"You want her job?"

"No, I wouldn't. I can't think of a more boring thing to do all day long than to keep track of every human being in this town. Maybe all the cats and dogs too."

"You left out horses and pigeons. But she does move the mail along."

"Unless she wants to read magazines, like they said William Faulkner did when he was a postmaster, before he wrote his fantastic books." Etheline laughed. "Let's go by the drugstore for a malted."

"The drug store don't make malteds anymore, Etheline. They just push pills. We could get a milkshake at a fast food place, but they don't put malt in them, just little bits of strawberries or bananas."

"Oh, well, it was just an idea. This town looks so much the same, I thought nothing here had changed."

"Believe you me, everything changes. Just about when you get used to something, it changes. All the time. Not just for you and me, but for everybody."

Etheline sped up her pace. "Want to walk up the hill to my house?"

Louette pointed to a concrete bench in the shade of a tree. "I'm a little winded; let's set awhile."

"Oh, all right." Etheline reached down and retied her shoes, then straightened up. "Did I ever tell you I appreciated your mother getting my parents to let me spend the night with you? They didn't want me getting too chummy with the children of cotton mill workers, but your mother was special."

"She said you might be lonely up in your big house with no other children."

"She was right." Etheline gazed up at the limbs of the magnolia tree. A breeze rustled the leaves and fanned their faces. "Lou, would you do something for me?"

"Sure. What?"

"Give me a hug." Etheline grinned sheepishly. "I haven't had a hug in a long time."

Louette's eyes widened. "Come to think of it, I haven't either, not from an adult." Etheline's long arms wrapped around Louette. When Louette hugged her back, she put her head on Louette's shoulder.

They parted. "That felt good," Louette told her friend.

"I think," Etheline said, "that our age now is the most lonely time of a person's life. Words, and conversations with other people help. But there's nothing more devastating to the human spirit than loneliness."

"I second the motion on that." Louette rubbed her right thumb where it hurt sometimes. "You know, it just occurred to me I rarely even do the cheek-touching thing they do at church. You know, when women kiss the air." A mischievous grin flashed across her face. "Sometimes though, Benjamin looks like he'd like to hold me close and give me a big kiss. One of these days I just might let him."

"Aha!" Etheline latched onto the revelation. "There is someone lurking on the sidelines."

"Not lurking. He lives around the corner and I talk to him when I go for my walks. He wants more, but I'm trying not to encourage him too much."

"Why not?" Etheline grinned. "It would probably do wonders for you to have a personal relationship with Benjamin. It wouldn't hurt you to give him a big ol' hug, like the one we just had."

"Maybe not. But I'm still married, to Joseph. I couldn't take up with another man. It wouldn't be decent."

"Couldn't you get an annulment, or something?"

"I don't know. I wouldn't want one. I'll be married to Joseph until he dies. Course he might already be dead. I don't really know." She tugged on the hem of her blouse.

"After my husband took himself a younger woman on the side," Etheline spit out the words, "the affection stopped, no more embraces, not from anyone. It seems that somewhere in growing older I lost all physical contact with other people. I suppose even a sorry husband who might brush your arm as he walks past you once in awhile is better than nobody."

"Geez, Etheline, didn't you have any friends up there in Boston?" Even as she spoke Louette realized that among the many people she called her friends, people she had real affection for, there was very little physical contact. A wave of longing swept over her.

"Friends?" Etheline mused. "I had lots of friends while I was in boarding school and college, but, after I married, I was too busy trying to keep them from seeing how hard my husband was to live with. He didn't like my friends, so I quit inviting them over, or going out anyplace with them. All except Lucille. She was all I had left," Etheline looked at Louette. "You didn't know her. I met her in college. But then, Lucille died." Etheline caught her breath.

Louette cleared her throat. "I realize now that I cut myself off from many friends when my mother was ill," she said. "But they were out there in the community, in the town. Shirley and Miz Gumby both lived right next door."

Etheline rubbed her face with her hand, pinching her nose in a way Louette remembered. "My parents are dead," she said. "You have all those relatives, your daughter Marj, and your grandson. I don't have anyone. All I've got now is myself. Me and nobody else. Now I wish I had children."

Louette turned to look her friend square in the face. "What about Gordon?"

"What about him?"

"Don't play coy with me. You know what I'm talking about."

A flash of pain crossed Etheline's face. "I just got back home. It's too soon, Lou."

"Looks like to me it's just about the right time. You might have another chance at real love. You going to kick it under the bench?"

"You don't know how I've changed since we were kids. I'm not the same person. To you I look like a wealthy woman who ought to be happy. On the inside I am 'poor in spirit' as the good book says. Even as unhappy as you are right now, inside you're a whole lot richer than me."

"I wouldn't say that." Louette gave her a long, serious look. "If I were you, I wouldn't throw away what I saw in Gordon's eyes."

Etheline sighed. "I just can't get involved right now, Lou. Besides, I'm dying. Remember?"

"Then you'd better quit wasting time. You are involved, whether you admit it or not. As to dying, all you know is what you were told about a mass on your kidney. We have fine doctors these days. You just might get cured. You could live a long time."

"You don't know the future, Louette Kelly."

"And neither do you, Etheline Powers. Give yourself a chance."

They sat, each lost in thought. "Listen." Louette cocked her head.

"The field lark?" Etheline stood up. "I'd forgotten how beautiful it sounds." They were quiet for several minutes, listening to the bird's clear, melodious note, breaking in midair.

"When I was little I thought the bird knew its own name. I called it a fee-lark."

Etheline looked at Louette and smiled. "Thank you. You've made me feel a whole lot better."

"Maybe you ought to check out the doctors around here. Think positive, Etheline. Think negative, you get bad results. You don't want to die no slow agonizing death if you don't have to. You are a beautiful human being."

"You sounded like your mother then, Lou; she was always telling people they were 'wonderful creatures of God.' I'm not afraid to die. I just wanted to come home for it. You know, like it's a special event, sort of."

"Don't be in such a hurry, Etheline. The 'practicing' doctors have come a long way. They might be able to cure you. And, be friends with Gordo again; it could help you to smile."

Etheline blushed. "It was nice seeing him in person." She ducked her head. "It's not the same talking to someone on the phone about business."

Louette stood up. "We all have to give up this life eventually. You don't want to suffer in order to die."

"I'll think on it," said Etheline. "I think I'll walk on home now, Lou."

"Me too," Louette walked east and Etheline climbed the hill. Louette thought how different their lives had been. Etheline, whose family owned the cotton mill, had no children. Louette had gotten to be a mother.

Louette walked slowly over the broken concrete sidewalk. She might as well go over to the newspaper and put in her notice about the wake. She looked around and saw green grass, trees, and a swirl of daisies. *No getting around it, this is a beautiful place to live. Spring is busting out already.*

The newspaper door was locked. A notice stated: Closed for a couple of weeks. Gone to Talladega to see my mother who's ailing. Signed, Horace Greely Purefoy.

"Well! Whoever heard of closing a newspaper?" Louette looked at the date on the note. Horace had left town this morning. Looks like any one of his employees could have kept the newspaper going while he checked on his mother's health. *What on earth will the town do without the news coming out once a week?*

With purposeful steps, Louette retraced her way toward Commerce Street. It was almost lunchtime. She stopped in front of the big window of Chapman's Store. "That's the prettiest dress," she said aloud. Without hesitating, she walked in. Maxine Carpenter greeted her.

"Why, Louette Kelly. I haven't seen you in a coon's age. Can I help you with something?"

"You sure can, Maxine. I want the outfit in the window, the lavender one. Looks like it was made for me."

"It's a nice dress, all right. You want me to check on the price?"

"I don't care how much it costs, Maxine. You can see if you have it in my size, though." Maxine walked to a rack and pulled out a replica of the dress worn by the mannequin.

"I ought to look right smart in that dress at my wake, hadn't I, Maxine?"

The sales clerk's face paled. "Oh, you mean your big party? Yes, you'll look lovely in this dress, Louette. Want to try it on?"

"I don't have to. If it's a size 10, it'll fit."

"Sometimes they size 'em wrong, what with orders being sent to other countries these days."

"Oh, all right. Hand it here." She was pleased with the way the lavender dress fit close around her shoulders, and the little swing of the skirt when she twirled—not that she expected to be dancing in it. She wondered what Benjamin would think. If he would like her in the dress. Did it matter to her what he thought? It did matter very much, she realized.

"Why that dress looks perfect for you," Maxine gushed. Louette couldn't tell how much of Maxine's appreciation for the dress came from her own opinion or how much was sales pitch.

"What about shoes?"

That's how it is. Give a sales person an inch and they'll push for the mile. "I'd planned to wear my regular Sunday shoes, but it might not hurt to look."

"We have a nice selection," Maxine told her. "You haven't been in lately or you'd know we got in a fresh batch of spring shoes. Or maybe you saw our advertisement in the paper. The regular shoe salesman is off today, but I can help you."

"I try to skip over the ads. They just tempt a person to want something they don't usually need. Let's see what you got." Louette followed Maxine across the department store.

Her choice of a pair of black, patent-leather pumps took less than a minute. The shiny shoes made Louette feel like a kid again. "They remind me of the Mary Janes Mama bought me for Easter," she said, as Maxine rang up the purchase.

"Me too," Maxine said, and it didn't sound like a sales pitch anymore.

Now that she's got the money, she can be herself. Louette turned at the door. "Don't forget you're coming to my wake, Maxine. I'm expecting you."

Oh happy day, oh happy day.
When Jesus washed, my sins away.
He taught me how to watch and pray,
To live rejoicing every day. . . .

Chapter Nine

Louette awoke with anticipation she hadn't felt for some time. She opened the back door. Her visit with Etheline on the park bench had been a fine moment. This would be a marvelous wake. She knew she didn't have time to get the outside of the house painted but wondered what she might do about the inside. Maybe she had time to replace some wallpaper.

"This house won't clean itself," she said aloud. "May as well get back to the kitchen." She began pulling cleaning supplies from under the sink.

"Knock, knock." It was Shirley. "Thought I'd help you clean house for the party. I can go through your kitchen cabinets and the pantry."

Before Louette could protest, Shirley pulled down a quart jar, stared at it and pursed her lips. "We could throw away this syrup. The expiration date was five years ago."

"Leave that alone, Shirley. For heaven's sake. Anybody with one eye and half sense knows syrup don't go bad. They found cane syrup in the pyramids."

"That was honey," protested Shirley. "Nobody ate this syrup, and it has crystallized into rocks." Shirley peered at the Mason jar as if it was a laboratory specimen.

"I'll be," Louette took the jar and searched a drawer for the rubber jar opener. "We ate crystallized sugar for candy when I was little. It would cling to the underside of the tin bucket lids. We called it Depression candy."

Louette opened the jar and broke up the rock sugar with an ice pick.

"Can I have a piece?"

"Sure." She sucked on a piece of the candy as she removed it from the jar. "Here I had a treasure in my pantry and didn't even know it." There was very little syrup in the jar. Most of it had crystalized. She put some of the rock candy in a bag and handed it to Shirley. "Take this home with you and enjoy it."

"But I want to help."

"I know, and I appreciate it. If you don't mind, I'd rather clean up in here by myself. Thank you. I'll call you when I need you."

"Promise."

"Sure, I promise. Now go." Shirley left, reluctantly.

Suddenly it was quiet in the kitchen. Sucking on a piece of rock sugar from the jar, Louette continued to sort and wipe, scrubbing shelves where she could reach. "Guess I need the step-ladder," she muttered. "Wonder where I put that thing?"

The phone rang. *It can't be a response to the wake invitations; they haven't had time to get through the mail.* She hoped it was Etheline. "Hello."

"Mama."

Louette aimed the receiver back toward its cradle. "Don't hang up, Mama. I'm calling to tell you thanks for sending the cookies and reed whistle to Bucky. He wolfed down the cookies and is having fun blowing on the whistle. Tell Uncle Dan he appreciates it, will you?"

"Why not tell him yourself? The number's the same as it was when your grandmother lived there."

"I'll do that. Bucky would enjoy talking to him, too."

"I am sure he would." Louette's tone had a formal cast.

"Mama, can you forgive me? I'm really sorry for whatever I did to hurt your feelings."

"You don't even remember what you said to me?"

"It must have been terrible, whatever it was."

"You said I'm stupid." Louette's voice cracked. Etheline had said she was wise. It was as if her own daughter didn't even know her.

"Mama, you are not stupid."

"I sincerely hope not, but you said the word, not me."

"I'm not sure that's exactly what I said."

"Are you calling me a liar, Marjoram?"

"No, of course not, Mama. I don't know what on earth would have made me say such a thing."

"I invited you to my wake. It's May thirteenth, the Saturday before my birthday on the fifteenth."

"So, you're still going through with that... idea?"

Aha, she almost said stupid. "You are invited, you and Bucky. You could bring your husband, too, if he might accidentally want to come."

"I'll ask him. Do you accept my apologies?"

"I guess so." She'd forgiven Etheline for flirting with Joseph all those years ago. She supposed she'd have to forgive Marj for her sharp tongue. "Mothers and daughters shouldn't stay mad at one another. How's my favorite grandson?"

"I'd give the phone to him, but he's not here. He wanted to go to the farm to see the animals, so his dad took him to the zoo."

"Be sure he don't let Bucky climb no fences."

Marj chuckled. "I told him. Several times. I don't think after his scare Bucky will be tempted to pet baby pigs again."

I'd better change the subject. "Remember your old doll, the one named Mary Ann?"

"Sure do. Got her for Christmas when I was six."

"I put her out in the storage shed, in the box holding your diary and report cards."

"Did you ever clean out the closets and give away Daddy's clothes?"

"No. I just can't. Not yet. He may come back, and he'll need those clothes."

"Mom, the clothes are outdated. It's been a lifetime. I don't understand you hanging on to them. It's not natural. Have you had a physical examination lately?"

"Why should I? I'm not sick."

"You are sick with grief from Grandma Clara's death, and you're still grieving over Daddy's leaving."

"I realize that. I will clean out his clothes. I do want to move forward. You and Bucky and Dan and Mittie are the closest relatives I have now. I want to be friends with you, Marj. I love you." *A gentle moment.*

"If you'll go get a physical exam it would make me feel better."

There it went. "I don't need anything from no doctor. Not after what happened when I was fifty-eight—all those tests."

"But you learned you were healthy."

"After the rascals took me for thousands of dollars and the insurance company for thousands more. Just for an examination. Then they tell me there's nothing wrong with me, that I am a 'healthy specimen of womanhood.' It didn't make no sense."

"You could ask for fewer tests this time. You know, just get your heart checked and see if you need any medicine."

"I don't need anything."

"It wouldn't hurt. I'll pay the insurance deductible, if that's what's bothering you."

"What are you talking about? Insurance deductible? After the big health examination fiasco, I cancelled that insurance."

There was deep silence, then Marj exploded. "You cancelled your health insurance? You can't do that! A person HAS to have health insurance!"

"Not me. After they paid that high bill for all those tests that weren't needed, they sent me a notice they were going up on my premium again. It would have cost me twice as much a month as before. If I get sick, I'll just die."

"I can't imagine living in today's world without health insurance. If you had a heart attack, any kind of disaster, Snowden and I would be left holding the bag. You do have life insurance?"

"You don't have to worry about it. There's enough to bury me with, and you are listed as the beneficiary. Also, I've got a bit Mama gave me from sale of the farmland for the housing development."

"What about the house? You do have homeowner's insurance?" Marj's tone was anxious.

"When I borrowed the money from the bank to replace the roof a couple of years ago, they made me take out regular insurance on the house. As long as I owe them money, I have homeowner's insurance," Louette said.

"When you come down to it," Louette continued, "insurance is like the emperor's clothes in that children's story. It has evolved until it covers nothing. Homeowner's insurance used to be called fire and theft, now it's for everything under the sun. I even got a bill for windstorm insurance and when I asked about it I was told since I live near the Gulf coast, my house is in danger of damage from wind if a hurricane hits. I'll have them know, I'm a right smart distance from the Gulf Coast."

Marj breathed out loudly. "Mama, just go ahead and get a physical checkup."

"If I get sick, I'll go to a doctor and I'll pay the bill, if I can. It's only recently people decided they had to insure everything in the world. When I was your age, people didn't run up bills they couldn't pay and they didn't turn their troubles over to no insurance company at a high price every single month. Insurance companies can't take care of people. People have to do it themselves. When I was a little girl, all the banks failed. Mama kept her money in quart fruit jars. Later on, before she died, she had a bunch of fruit jars stuffed full. All the money's still in the jars. She didn't spend any of it."

"Money, like change?"

"Some change, some bills rolled up tight, so as to get more in the jars."

"How much money did she put in the jars?"

"I don't know. I never counted it. It wasn't mine. You know me well enough to know I don't bother nothing that belongs to somebody else. I believe a person ought to respect other people's property."

"You ought to count it. Now that Gramma Clara's dead, you might be a wealthy woman."

"I doubt that. Mama was never rich. The money from the housing development company wasn't in the bank long enough for even the county to earn much interest. In later years she gave away about as much as she took in. She couldn't have stored up more than she had."

Another audible sigh from Marj: "There could be a great deal of cash in those jars, and you don't have any health insurance. Where are the jars?"

"Mama made me promise not to tell anyone."

"What if you die?"

"Don't worry, I have a note for you in my safety deposit box," Louette told her.

"Grandma Clara didn't believe in banks, but you have a safety deposit box?"

"I had to have someplace to keep deeds, birth certificates, mine and your daddy's marriage certificate. Other important things I have in a strongbox in the shed."

"In the rickety old shed? For heaven's sake, Mama."

The third sigh from Marj cut deep into Louette. She stiffened. "My belongings are safe in there. I have it way in the back. Things somebody might want to steal are in the front. Nobody'd go back there with all that dust and cobwebs."

"Grandma Clara would have wanted you to use the money."

"I am not my mother. Just because I love her, don't mean I'm all the way like her. But I don't owe anybody anything."

"You borrowed money for the roof."

"That was different, I wanted to run up some credit. Just in case I got into a money problem."

"If you became ill, you might need money."

"If the bill was too high, I'd just go ahead and die. I'm not quite old enough for Medicare nor Social Security, but if it happens it happens."

"Mama, it's hard to believe the way you keep living in the past."

"That's how it is when that's all you've got," said Louette. She cleared her throat. "Let's change the subject.

You can go through the storage shed and take whatever you want next time you come down."

"You're not getting off that easy. I'm calling my agent and putting you down for health insurance. Maybe I can add you to mine, now that you're... older."

"I'm not that old." Louette hung up. *She didn't say she'd attend the wake, but she didn't say she wouldn't.*

Louette sat in Joseph's lounger in the den, gazing out at the back yard. When she closed her eyes, she could hear her heart beat. If she did like Benjamin wanted and joined up with him, what would she do with Joseph's old lounge chair? Life was easier if she held on to Joseph's memory, kept him as a presence in her life, even though he had been gone a long time.

"That's the lazy way," she seemed to hear her mother say. She stood up and walked to the kitchen and pulled petals from the bouquet of roses on the dinette. In the lounger she smelled the lovely aroma of crushed rose petals. It would be nice to be close to Benjamin. No matter what Marj might think about her she wasn't too old for romance. She dozed, dreaming of walking down the aisle with Benjamin, roses banked on both sides of the church.

A sound at the back steps roused her. The den window framed the sun getting on over about supper time. Shirley called out. "Yoo, hoo, Louette."

"You don't have to yell." Louette rose from the lounger and headed for the door. "I'm not deaf. I told you I'd call you if I needed you. Weren't you supposed to be going out of town or something?"

"I went to see my niece in Hartford, but I'm back. Remember?"

"What do you want, Shirley? Can't you see I'm busy?"

"Why, Louette Kelly, you were asleep in the lounger. I saw you through the picture window."

"Come on in, then."

"I didn't come to visit, Lou, but to invite you for oysters. My cousin Cecil and his wife Lucy brought them."

"I saw a notice in the paper not to eat oysters out of Mobile Bay. They're polluted. That's where Cecil lives."

"The oysters didn't come from Mobile Bay. They're from Apalachicola, Florida. Cecil and Lucy went down there for a few days, and he raked them up himself. He brought a bushel, iced down already. Lucy's with him. And my cousin George is eating with us."

"I didn't know you had a cousin named George."

Shirley stamped her foot. "Lou, I am inviting you to come over and eat oysters!"

"All right then. I'll go, but I may not eat any oysters. I don't want to take a chance on getting sick before my wake if they happened to come from Mobile Bay."

"They're from Apalach, I told you. And it's March. Don't you remember—you can eat raw oysters during months with r's?"

"Should I bring my oyster knife?"

"No. Just yourself."

"Who's going to shuck?"

"Cecil. He's like you. He likes to hull oysters."

"Tell 'em I'll be right over." Louette slipped her oyster knife into her purse, just in case Cecil couldn't shuck as fast as the rest could eat.

She took her time crossing the yard. It looked better since she had raked some of the leaves. In spite of herself she perked up. The sun slanted across the rain tree. It looked like a person could walk right up the sun's rays, into the sky.

She hugged Lucy and shook hands with Cecil. "Nice of you to bring oysters."

"I noticed you don't have your garden rows in yet, Lou. Want me to come help you put in the plants while I'm here?'

"I may not bother with a garden this year, Cecil."

"But you've had a garden every year, Lou, long as I been knowing you. You used to always be out there digging and hoeing, planting something in the dirt."

"You're right." Louette nodded. "Guess I've had food from the garden year 'round since I can remember—onions, cabbage, rutabagas, collards, turnips and tomatoes and corn... and squash in season."

Cecil laughed. "Everybody had a garden back during the War, but you kept right on going."

Shirley spoke up, visibly annoyed. She pushed a man forward. "This is my nephew, George."

Louette looked the newcomer up and down. He was thinner than Shirley and Cecil. He didn't actually look like them. They were both squarish, hefty people. Not tall, but substantial. George was tall with coal black hair and a pencil-line moustache. He looked much younger, maybe about forty. His handshake was firm and clung to hers.

Cecil had put the oysters in a large tin tub, already iced down and ready. He pulled out an oyster, pushed the oyster knife into the lip, twisted it and the oyster opened. "Look at these," he told Louette as he placed the opened oyster on a cookie sheet.

Louette opened a sleeve of crackers and shook out a toothpick from an empty hot-sauce bottle. She speared and lifted the oyster off its shell, dragged it through a dish filled with horseradish mixed with catsup, and put it on a soda cracker.

She smelled the oyster before plunking it, cracker, sauce and all, into her mouth. She chewed, with a dreamy expression. "That is by far the best thing I have ever tasted."

"Set down. I'll shuck you all you can eat," Cecil told her. He dumped the empty oyster shell into a garbage can and reached for another one. Louette sat in a folding chair beside the makeshift oyster bar. George and Shirley sat across from her.

"It's pleasant here in your back yard," Louette told Shirley. She turned toward George. "Where you from?" she asked. "You don't look like anybody from around here."

"What does that mean?" George shifted uncomfortably in his chair.

"It means she knows all the people in Geneva," Shirley said with a laugh, patting George's shoulder. "He's from Pensacola, Louette. Isn't he handsome?"

Louette blushed. *Shirley's quick at blurting out the obvious.* "You got enough horseradish and catsup?" Louette called out to Cecil. "I could have brought some."

"Got plenty of everything. Even the Nehi grape drinks you like," Cecil said.

"Have you lived in Geneva long?" George spaced each word, sort of tasting it before letting it out through his teeth.

"Since I married back in the '50s," answered Louette.

"I see you like to eat raw oysters…"

"I sure do. We're not too far from the Gulf. I like freshwater bream, bass, and catfish, too."

"Panhandle restaurants are known for excellent seafood." George's voice sounded artificial, as if he was speaking from a script. "I imagine they serve oysters and shrimp," he added. "Do you ever go to Pensacola?"

"Not often. I have a daughter who used to live there." Shirley was right. He was handsome; she'd give him that much. He didn't appear to be eating oysters though. Instead he munched on a dry cracker.

Louette felt uneasy around George. He seemed to pay her extra attention, looking straight at her when he spoke. His eyes twinkled and he gave the impression he was interested in everything she said.

"These oysters are powerful good," Louette told Cecil. "I brought my shucking knife in case you get tired."

"You know how to open oysters?" George seemed surprised.

"Don't you?"

He smiled condescendingly. "I never learned."

Cecil laughed. "Louette can flat-out beat most people any day in the week when it comes to shuckin' oysters."

"Tell me how you came to learn. I'm interested."

George peered intently at Louette. *A red-tailed hawk. That's what he looks like. Sitting on the fence. Just waiting to pounce. There's something strange about this George person.*

"Let me put more catsup in the sauce," Cecil suggested.

"Put more ketchup in yours. I like it just like this, hot with the horseradish." Louette snagged an oyster with a toothpick and plopped it on a cracker. "It's perfect. That last one was so good. He looked at me and said 'eat me quick, before somebody else does'."

"Oysters talk to you?" George stroked his thin moustache.

"Not often. That one did. But he's gone now."

"He?"

"A figure of speech. It could have been a she. I didn't ask, just chewed it up and swallowed."

"How did you become familiar with opening and eating oysters?" George nudged Louette.

"One of my daddy's favorite things was to load us all up in the Model A Ford and head for the bay where the Choctawhatchee river runs into the Gulf of Mexico. It was great fun. We'd take lunch and stay all day, raking oysters off the reefs."

"Raking oysters?"

"Like raking leaves, except they're a lot heavier than leaves. You reach down into the mud with the rake. It was during the Depression. Real oyster tongs cost too much money. Sometimes my dad used a potato digger with bent tines, to bring up oysters. Four or five croaker sacks full."

"Potato digger? Croaker sacks?" George fiddled with his suit coat pocket, like there was something in it. He appeared to be as nervous as a suck-egg dog caught in a hen house.

"A potato digger, or tater digger, is a pitchfork with the tines bent. A croaker sack is a big sack, made of loose woven burlap. I don't know why they're called croaker sacks. Somebody said they used to catch frogs and put them in the sacks. We put our oysters in a croaker sack. It'd hold a bushel to the sack. My dad got several sacks and we took them back up home."

"Still in the shell?" George asked.

Shirley, Lucy, and Cecil laughed.

Louette looked at George as she would a creature from the Black Lagoon. "Like these," she said. "We put them in wash tubs with chunks of ice from the ice house, then added cold water from the well to the ones we brought back home. Sometimes though we'd be getting tired of raw oysters by the time we got home. Mama made oyster stew or put them in Mulligan stew and sometimes in gumbo. After we'd had our fill, my dad would sell or give away the leftovers."

"Mulligan stew?"

This guy is getting crazier by the minute. "Mulligan stew is just tomato soup with whatever meat and vegetables you have on hand pitched in. I liked it with fish, scallops, or oysters added, especially oysters."

"I put ice in these oysters," Cecil noted. "As the ice melts, they take in the water and spit it out. It cleans out the mud."

"Spit it out?"

"Yes."

George looked askance at the oyster on Louette's cracker. "You're putting me on. They die when the shell is opened. Right?"

"Cecil just opened it. See the oyster squinch up? He don't want to be dabbed in hot sauce and chewed." To illustrate, she plopped it on a soda cracker, topped it with ketchup and horseradish sauce and put it in her mouth. Chewing made her face go all dreamy. "Tastes almost as good as when I was little."

"Ought to," said Cecil. "Harvested them myself from Apalachicola Bay."

George's face had turned a bilious green. He hadn't even as much as tasted an oyster, Louette noted. "Y'all are making George sick," said Shirley.

Louette wasn't through. "Daddy made me an oyster shucker out of an old butcher knife. He filed it down himself. Said it was strong as Fort Knox." Louette pulled it from her purse.

"You have your own oyster knife?" George's face looked pale in the dusky glow of Shirley's back yard security light.

"This one," she said, reverently. "We always had raw oysters for supper on Christmas Eve. Santa Claus was stingy at our house. We usually got oranges, apples, raisins on the stem, and some of that chocolate-cream bell-shaped candy. Sometimes I got a box of chocolate covered cherries, my favorite. One year I got this oyster-shucking knife. Had it ever since. Didn't care after that whether there was anything for me under the tree."

Louette held out the knife. George gave the blade a tentative touch. "Daddy said anybody who could shuck oysters as fast as I could would never starve. I could always find a job shucking oysters. There weren't many jobs then. My daddy wanted me to go to college."

"Did you?"

"No."

"Why not?"

Lord, this man is dumb. She didn't state the obvious, that there wasn't any money. "I married. While my husband went to printing school on the GI Bill, I worked in the shirt factory. When he opened his own print shop, I kept the books." She looked George square in the face. "My daughter went to college, though."

George didn't look surprised. "You miss your mother a great deal, and Joseph, too, don't you?" His voice was low. Louette turned in surprise. She would have expected Shirley to have mentioned her mother died recently. But Joseph?

"How do you know my husband's name?"

"Maybe Shirley told me." George was obviously embarrassed.

This slick stranger now looks like a kid with his hand in the cookie jar. Louette was angry. She dealt out her words slowly, one at a time.

"If you want to know, I do still miss my husband. I don't know where you learned his name. Because somebody's not around don't mean you forget them."

"Do you miss him because you're supposed to?"

What a strange question. For Pete's sake. This guy don't give up. He's shaking my tree for all it's worth. Louette put her hand to her head. *What is going on here? George, who obviously isn't related to Shirley or Cecil, sounds like some sort of nut doctor.*

"Hey, we're getting too deep." Cecil told George.

Out of the corner of her eye, Louette saw Shirley shush Cecil. "After I got that fancy homemade shucker, I was the center of the party when somebody in the neighborhood had oysters." Louette's voice was low. She turned toward George. "You got any stories?" she asked him.

"Me? Well, uh, no."

"Why not, George? You never have anybody you loved leave you, or die?"

"Not yet. What about your mother? Didn't your mother expire recently?"

"She did. Expired. Just like an old library card."

Shirley broke in. "Oysters are really useful. And not just for food. The shells are nice in the driveway. Ain't they, Louette?"

"I suppose." Louette stared hard at George.

"Want these shells, Lou?"

"No, thank you, Shirley. My driveway is fine the way it is."

"It's better than paying all that money to pave a driveway in ugly concrete," Shirley chattered. "Dan might want these oyster shells at the farm to put around that muddy hog pen."

"Got any pie?" Cecil interrupted. "I'm about full of oysters."

"Sure." Shirley looked relieved. "I'll get it."

"I'll help," George offered.

"What about coffee? Anybody for coffee?" Shirley was visibly shaken.

Cecil wiped his hands. "I'll come with you."

"Oh, no, we'll manage. Won't we, George?" Shirley ushered him across the yard and into the house.

Louette watched the stranger walk beside Shirley, who almost ran. Louette was past anger. *Marj sent that man to spy on me, to see if he thought I was crazy. The nerve of Marj, and the nerve of Shirley for going along with her.* She placed the oyster knife back in her purse.

"Think I'll go home," Louette told Cecil and Lucy. "Thanks for the oysters. It was nice seeing y'all." She crossed the yard and walked swiftly to her house.

Louette felt relief when she slammed the door. She crept across the family room without turning on the light, walked past the ringing telephone, down the hall, into her bedroom and fell onto her bed. Tears sprang from her in a flood. Her body trembled so hard the bed rattled.

Precious memories, unseen angels,
Sent from somewhere to my soul.

Chapter Ten

The morning sun pushed around the window shades. "Don't mock me," Louette muttered. "I saw the dogwoods ready to bust out any minute. And them azalea bushes; I bet they've bloomed some already. I can tell it's pretty without looking out the window, but you can forget sticking your sunny fingers in here. I ain't going outside today." She pulled the chenille bedspread over her head.

There's no law says I have to get up now that Mama's gone. I don't have to empty the bedpan, fix her breakfast, or bathe her. I don't have to cook anything. I can eat store-bought cereal. She put her feet to the floor, needing to use the bathroom. "Got to get myself out of these mullygrubies."

She heard a commotion at the front door. Holding her breath, she waited in the bathroom. She didn't want to talk to Clyde right now. The knocking stopped. Then the back doorknob rattled. *May not be Clyde. Probably that crazy Shirley with another fake cousin to give me the third degree.* She eased out of the bathroom and climbed back into bed.

The knocking started again on the front door. Louette pushed the window shade aside. Lord'a mercy! It was Mittie. She rushed to open the door. "Gracious, Lou! I was getting worried. Thought you might be dead or something."

"I'm fine, Mittie. I was trying to stay clear of that nosy Shirley taking directions from Marj. She comes bouncing in here at all hours. She might be sociable sometimes, but she ain't neighborly. She don't never leave a person alone. Her and that fake cousin of hers."

"Louette, whatever are you talking about? And answer that phone, why don't you?" Louette lifted the ringing phone, then hung it up.

"It might be somebody about your party."

"The mail ain't that fast."

"I know, but Post Mistress Angie and her mouth sure are." The women laughed and walked to the kitchen. Louette plugged in the percolator.

"I'll have one cup," Mittie told her. She put a bundle wrapped in brown paper on the counter. "Redhorse suckers!" she called out triumphantly.

"You didn't go fishing with a seine net? Not with Dan's sore leg!"

"No, but Jack Larson did. Didn't you notice the dogwood trees blooming? Redhorse suckers run last of March, first of April. Jack said to give you a mess."

"Much obliged, Mittie. But they need to be cooked now."

"Put them in the freezer and save them for the... uh, gathering."

"It's a wake Mittie. You can say it. You coming?"

"Wouldn't miss it for the world."

As they sipped coffee, Louette told Mittie about the night before. "That shyster was no cousin of Shirley's. He was a nut doctor, sent by Marj, sure as I was born. Shirley, by playing into Marj's hand, has squashed my hope of having fun. They don't understand how hard it is to let go of Mama. I have to. I know that. I've got to let go of Joseph too."

Mittie patted her hand. "The young have to get old before they begin to fathom how close life and death are."

"What say I go back to the farm with you and we cook the fish there?"

"That's a grand idea!"

Louette walked toward the bedroom, untying the belt of her housecoat. "You got enough corn meal? I've got a peck, and I won't eat that much in a year with Mama gone."

"You can bring it just in case."

She thought to ride in the truck with Mittie, but decided to follow in her car. That way, if she stayed until dark, she wouldn't inconvenience Mittie by needing a ride home. Driving away, she saw Shirley in the rearview mirror running across the yard, waving. She waved back.

Dan met them on crutches at the farmhouse door. "I told Mittie you might rather come out here, but we weren't sure, with you fixing for a party and all."

"I'm getting ready for my own wake and y'all don't have to be nervous about calling it what it is. A wake is bigger and more important than just any old party."

"I got a hand-printed letter and a picture of Bucky," announced Dan. He pointed to the framed picture atop the television set. "We had a phone call, too. Don't remember when Marj has called us—not for a long time." Mittie hefted a large iron skillet and a jug of peanut oil from the pantry.

"I imagine she's trying to mend her fences," Louette said.

"You two having trouble?" Dan eased onto his recliner.

"She thinks I'm crazy, because I'm holding a wake for myself."

"You have to admit, it does sound a little strange." Dan chuckled.

"It may not make logical sense to anybody else, but it sure does to me."

When the grease started spitting, Mittie and Louette busied themselves rolling pieces of fish in corn meal and plopping them into the skillet. "These fish sure cook up fast," said Mittie.

"Jack is the best at rashering down the bones on a redhorse sucker," said Louette. "He cuts right to the skin. No way a person could get bits of bone in their teeth while eating these fish."

"Y'all want cheese grits?" asked Mittie. She rummaged in the refrigerator. "I found the right amount of hoop cheese to go in them."

"No," they said in unison.

"Fish gravy." Mittie chuckled. "Figured as much. I took a couple of bags of tomatoes out of the freezer too."

"Let's not forget to ring the dinner bell for Jack," said Dan. "It'd be a shame if he didn't get to eat any of his own fish."

"My goodness. Is he here? I didn't see a vehicle."

"His truck's behind the barn," said Mittie. "He's shaping up the hills for a ribbon cane patch."

"I told Bucky we used to make cane syrup. I meant to cook him some flapjacks. But the little fellow was gone so fast, I didn't hardly even have time to get properly acquainted with him."

"He'll be back." Millie dropped spoonfuls of hushpuppy batter into the grease. She dipped out the fried balls of cornbread, now a golden brown. "I've chopped some onion. Lou, see if the tomatoes are thawed. I'll pour up the grease."

Mittie dumped chopped onions into the fish and hushpuppy drippings, stirring them until the onions turned golden yellow. Louette opened the tomatoes and put them into the mixture. "One of the best memories of my childhood was when we all went fishing on the river. Mama'd fry fish and hushpuppies, then make tomato gravy, all thick and oniony. Just about the best thing I ever tasted." Louette sighed.

Dan hobbled toward the door, swinging his crutches. "I think I can reach the bell rope to call Jack in," he said, clomping out the back door.

Louette watched her brother and his friend. "Is it all right for Dan to walk that much?"

"I think so," Mittie told her. "The doctor said for him to use the crutches for awhile longer, and Dan's going to play out the doctor's orders to the minute."

Louette stared out the window toward the barn. "Marj siccin' that shrink on me is about the worst thing I can think of," she said slowly. "I feel betrayed, violated."

Mittie reached out a tentative hand and patted her shoulder. "I know. It must be awful."

Louette turned toward her, buried her head on Mittie's bony shoulder. After the tears subsided, the women moved away from each other, embarrassed. Mittie turned aside, her lined face flushed with concern.

"This was the best fish I ever tasted." Louette leaned back in her chair. "I appreciate you bringing it, Jack. Do you go fishing often?"

"Not often enough. When the dogwood started budding out, I knew redhorse suckers were running. I caught these where Pittman Creek joins with the Choctawhatchee River."

"I hope you didn't go by yourself," said Dan. "At our age, we ought to be careful."

"Yeah, way I heard it you were all there when Bucky tried to pet the baby pigs," said Jack with a wry grin. They laughed.

"I came in on it just as the action was over." Mitti rose to get more of the fried fish. "This is a welcome feast," she said.

"I did try to get Sully to go with me when I caught these, but he wasn't in the mood." Jack looked thoughtful.

"Imagine," said Dan. "Sully's about as useless as tits on a boar hog. I took him deer hunting with me one time and he went missing. I found him in the truck. Said he wasn't shooting at no Bambi's mother."

"I took him to town with me for a haircut and he kept railing on about how we shouldn't have gotten into the Korean action; big as Ike, right in front of God and everybody. I was mortified. 'Sully,' I told him, 'these fellows are younger than us. They fought in Vietnam. Lighten up.'"

"Y'all ought not to talk about Sully," Mittie chided. "He's your cousin, Jack."

"You're right Mittie. He ain't much for a relative, but he's the only cousin I got left. They been dying like flies. Old age gets around to grabbing ahold of all of us."

Louette changed the subject. "We considered saving these fish for the wake, but thought better of it. Their taste is best soon after they leave the water. Be sure you come to my wake, Jack."

"I'll do that and I'll go over to Dead River and get you a mess of bream."

On the way home, Louette stopped by Mayor Warren Roberts' hardware store and bought an answering machine. "I'm getting so many calls about the wake, I need a secretary," she joked. "You and Mandy better be there."

"Oh, we will, Lou. Ought to be some party. I'd be surprised if the whole town don't show up."

"Maybe I ought to move it to the school stadium," said Louette. "But then it wouldn't be as personal as having my relatives and friends come to the house. You think there's room in the yard?"

"Clyde could block off the street." Warren was serious. "You want me to see about getting some benches?"

"I think we'll be all right. Preacher Ed said the men's brotherhood would bring over tables and chairs from the church fellowship hall."

"Are they bringing the big coffee pot? I have one that'll make fifty cups."

"That would be nice. I can keep my percolator going too."

"You don't need to be watching no percolator, Lou. With all that company, you're going to have yourself a good ol' time."

"I'm looking forward to it, Warren. So looking forward to it."

She stopped by the Dixie Doodle for milk and eggs. She added extras like celery and onions. Before she realized it, the shopping cart was full. She'd have to mark items off the refrigerator list. Charlie, one of her favorite bag boys, carried her groceries to the car.

"What's wrong, Miz Lou?

"Why do you ask?"

"You look kind of spacey. Getting ready for your big party is lots of work, huh?"

"No, I was excited about that. Now I'm upset with my daughter."

"Worry can make you pretty sick, huh?"

"Sick? I don't think so. I guess I'm suffering from poverty of the spirit. I was all-fired ready for my wake yesterday, but now my daughter thinks I'm crazy."

"I don't think you're crazy Miz Lou. I think you are a nice person. I could go on my bike and put up fliers around town."

"That's an idea. I'm mailing most of the invitations. I put one on the bulletin board in the store. I went over to put a notice in the newspaper but Mr. Purifoy was out of town."

Louette rounded the corner to her street and saw Benjamin up ahead. He stepped to the curb and waved for her to stop. She felt his note crinkle in her pocket.

"Lou. You've got to see the American Beauties."

"They're blooming? Wait just a minute for me to take in my groceries."

"I'll help you," he said and got in the passenger's seat. It seemed right for him to be in the car and to help carry groceries into the kitchen.

Louette plumped a grocery sack onto the dinette. "I went down to Laverne and Jasper's. He said he saw you at Cat Point watching a herd of manatees."

"There was a group, a pod I think it's called," he said. "They were mating." He turned beat red.

"How was your hunting trip?"

"It was fine. Bud took the deer he killed to be butchered and wrapped."

"You didn't shoot anything?"

A flush spread over Benjamin's face. "I, uh, didn't go along for that. I went to the state forest to think." Her hand at the refrigerator door, Louette didn't say anything.

"I owe you an apology Lou. I'll give you as much time as you need to decide about us. I understand your grief for your mother, and about your husband being gone."

"I appreciate that," Louette told him. "I've done everything I could over the years to find him. Wouldn't it be something if he showed up at my wake?"

Benjamin cleared his throat. "I hope you don't mind, Lou, but I talked to Clyde and he said he's still going through police files of unidentified dead people."

"Has he... found anything?" She held her breath.

"He said you'd be the first to know if he did. I was surprised at the number of people found dead and never identified. Clyde had a picture of Joseph and he said as soon as your big party is over, he'll get you to look at the pictures he's gathered to see if Joseph might be in them." Benjamin stopped.

"We tried everything but pictures of dead people," she whispered. "Joseph didn't take any clothes. Not even his toothbrush. I checked at the bank and they said there were no withdrawals that day. All the print shop money was still there." A fresh dose of pain drained the color from her face.

Benjamin put his arms around her. "I'm here if you need me, Lou. I care about you very much, and I want to help."

Louette shook her head to clear it. "Thanks for helping look for Joseph, Benjamin. I really do care about you too." *More than you know.*

The whole specter of Joseph's absence loomed in the kitchen. Instinctively she leaned inward to Benjamin but turned abruptly aside when he tightened his arms around her. It wasn't time. There was too much heartache. She turned and opened the refrigerator door.

As they walked down the street to Benjamin's house, a cardinal flashed red and landed on the sidewalk. "An omen," said Benjamin.

When they rounded the corner, Benjamin made a tentative grab for her hand. Louette almost let him hold it, then slipped it into her pocket, touching the note. Her fingers tingled. She ached to hold his hand. She desperately wanted his embrace. *He's moving too fast*, she thought.

She followed him around the caboose and to meet a flowerbed filled with newly blossoming roses. "I declare," she said. "You've got more beauty hidden behind this hedgerow train than most people see in a lifetime."

"This one, I'm naming Louise Etta of Geneva, Alabama." Benjamin pointed to a small rosebush covered with buds and a few purplish blooms flashing color.

"Benjamin! You're naming a rose for me?"

"Yes. Well, you and the town. It is a nice town, you know."

"You're right about that. And you are a fine person. Thank you, Benjamin. You've brought beauty into my day."

"Stand there, I'll get some of them for you to take home."

"No. They are too pretty to cut. I'd rather think of them the way they are right here, so all the people in the dining car can look out and see them."

"Yes." His face turned crimson. "They are a sight. They have your essence, Lou, a brisk outspoken color, but gentle on the inside, reflecting a hopeful glint of sunlight."

Sounds poetic, she thought, *which I'm not. There's sure more to Benjamin than most people see.* She held out her hand and took his. "Benjamin, you said once you'd like to be my best friend. You can be, if you still want to." She leaned toward him then, and he held her shoulders as he placed a gentle kiss, right smack on her mouth. A warm tingle started at her lips and spread. She hadn't felt this particular kind of weakness in the knees since long years past with Joseph.

Louette wouldn't let him walk back home with her. "I need to do some thinking too, Benjamin," she told him. "By myself." He smiled so wide his face glowed. At the corner, Louette turned. Benjamin stood beside the engine hedge, waving at her. Looking at him made her feel shaky inside— happy and fearful at the same time. She waved back.

The phone, off its hook, clicked as Louette entered the house. She noticed Shirley's car was gone. *Thank goodness. I won't have to face that Judas yet. When I do, I am going to give her a piece of my mind—a big piece.*

"If you'd like to make a call, please hang up and dial again." Louette slapped the receiver back on its cradle. She unpacked the answering machine, muttering as she read the instructions. She dialed the telephone company.

"I just bought an answering machine, and it says plug it in."

"So? Plug it in."

"How am I going to do that? My phone don't plug."

There was laughter at the other end of the line. "Lou, you need updating. I'll send Carl to put in a phone jack for you. Then you can unplug your phone when you want to."

"Ain't that a marvel? What will they think of next?"

Carl arrived by the time she had swept the kitchen. "I didn't know there were phones still straightwired, Miz Lou."

"I don't know what you call it, but I'm ready for the new-fangled way, if it will let me use an answering machine."

"Did you buy a new phone, or do you want to keep the rotary dial?"

"I'd rather keep my old phone if that's alright."

"They are kind of obsolete, you know," Carl shrugged and put in a wall jack and attached the plug-in to the phone wire.

"I'm not surprised. Everything about me is obsolete too, I reckon."

Carl stood up. "Want me to help you connect the answering machine too?" He took the machine out of the box.

"Sure," Louette told him. "I knew they existed, but never tried one before."

Carl punched buttons. "Say whatever you want to tell people. Don't clear your throat, or anything. Put your finger in the air when you're ready."

"This is Louette Kelly. Leave your number and I'll call you back." They both grinned. "Maybe I ought to do it over and tell them about my wake."

"Your wake?" Carl's face turned beet red.

Uh, oh, he hasn't heard. "I'm expecting you and your family at my wake on May thirteenth," Louette told him, a twinkle in her eye.

"Miz Lou, you not planning on dying, are you?"

"Of course not, Carl. I'm having a big gathering so I can see my relatives and friends before I die."

"Then you are planning on dying?"

"No," Louette assured him. "I'm planning on living." Carl shifted uncertainly. Louette touched his arm. "Just come to the party, Carl. Okay?"

"I will, Miz Lou," he told her and left, shaking his head in bewilderment.

Louette eyed the machine. The phone rang immediately. Louette smiled as she listened to her voice intone the message. "Mother!" Marj's voice burst out. "I want to know what's going on. If you're there, pick up."

"Fat chance," Louette said to herself. "You're the reason I bought the contraption. You can talk to yourself until you're blue in the face, Missy Marjoram." She poured cold coffee into her mug, chuckling as she headed for the picnic table beside the rain tree.

Louette noticed Clyde circling the block in his deputy car. She stood up. *Maybe he'll let me look for Joseph in the pictures of unidentified dead people.* He didn't stop.

She knew she'd have to talk to him and to Marj sooner or later. Or Marj might show up, and they'd have a yelling match. It was indecent what her only child had done. Sic'ing that mental doctor on her.

When Louette came back inside, Marj had figured out a clincher. Bucky's voice reached across the family room and straight into Louette's heart. "Gramma Lou, I can blow a tune on the flute Uncle Dan made for me. Want to hear it?"

Up went the telephone receiver. "I certainly do!"

The tune sounded vaguely familiar, something like the song from church, beginning "Joyful, joyful, we adore thee." It couldn't have been more beautiful to Louette had it been played by a famous orchestra at the Lincoln Center in New York City.

"You know what that is?" Bucky asked. "It's Ode to Joy. My mom showed me how to play it. Want to hear it again?"

"Sure do," Louette said. The resemblance to the tune was there, though Dan probably hadn't put enough holes in the flute.

"I'll play and you can dance when we come to your house," he said.

Louette caught on. "When are you coming?"

"Soon. My mom said she wants to talk to you."

"Sneaky trick," she told her daughter. "Using your own child to deliver messages you're too chicken to deliver yourself. You should be ashamed."

"That's the only way I could get to you, Mama. You have to listen to me."

"I've been trying to avoid you. Unpleasantness is best kept away from. Especially when it's your own daughter. In case you're interested, you have been un-invited to my wake. I only want friends around me on my special weekend."

"I am your friend, Mother."

"You call somebody a friend who'll sic a nuthouse shrink on you? And uses your own looney neighbor to help her?"

"Dr. Waverly is not a nuthouse shrink."

"He sure convinced me he was. Besides that, he didn't eat oysters. Just munched on a dry cracker, like a sneaky little mouse, twitching his moustache."

"Shirley said he was pleasant toward you. Didn't you like him?"

"To tell you the truth, he seemed sort of like Cowboy Bob, Dennis the Menace's hero."

"What are you getting at, Mother?"

"Don't you remember? Dennis said Cowboy Bob didn't smoke, drink, cuss, or kiss girls."

"Oh." Marj was quiet for an instant. "I'll have you know, Dr. Waverly is a well-known and respected psychiatrist."

"So, you admit you sent him?"

"I thought Dr. Waverly could maybe give you something to ease your grief."

"No pill can help the hurt I feel. A person has to barrel right on through grief, or it never goes away."

"But, you've never 'barreled through' on Daddy. After all these years you're still grieving that he left."

"Your father was a different case. It has never been resolved. It's still in there where no pill can reach. It won't go away until I know why he took off. Or if he's happy where he is." Louette breathed deep. "If you thought I was crazy, why didn't you just tell me?"

"I did."

"What I remember is that you said I was stupid." Louette hung up, her hands trembling. She placed one on her heart and held to the backs of chairs until she reached the couch.

She must have dozed because it was dark when heavy footsteps approached. The back door opened.

"You in there, Lou?" It was Shirley.

Talk about a bad dream.

Shirley walked to the middle of the room. "Lou, you all right?"

It was me, I'd go look in the bedroom.

Shirley stood for an instant, then shrieked. "God, Lou. You scared me nearly to death. What are you doing sitting there in the dark?"

Louette didn't answer as Shirley leaped to the light switch. "Are you all right, Lou?"

"Sure, I'm all right. Can't a person take a nap in their own home without some neighbor running in uninvited?"

"But I'm not just a neighbor, Lou. I'm your best friend."

"First, let's get something straight. You are not my best friend. Of the two best friends I ever had in my adult life, one is gone and the other is stone cold dead. Neither would have done what you and Marj did."

"But I didn't do anything. It was Marj."

"You said that man was your cousin, but he's really a nut doctor."

"How do you know he's not my cousin?"

"He don't look a bit like you or Cecil, who is actually kin to you. You and my daughter are un-invited to my wake. I don't want no enemies visiting me, only people who like me."

"But I do care about you, Lou." Shirley's round face puckered.

"Don't you start your crying on me. It won't work. I've had my fill of you and Marj. If she weren't my grandson's mother, I might drive up to that fancy house of hers and shoot her right between the eyes." She advanced toward Shirley, who backed up against the door. "And if you don't get out of here, right now, I'm liable to pop you one."

Eyes wide with fear, Shirley reached back for the knob and ran from the house.

"Good riddance," said Louette, flipping the lock. She unplugged the answering machine and placed the phone receiver on the couch under a pillow. Then she turned off the lights.

All creatures of our God and King,
Lift up your voice and with us sing.

Chapter Eleven

An old dream came back. The one where the quicksand sinkhole bubbled and throbbed, sucking everything in the pasture into its maw while she and Joseph watched. Tree limbs falling into the sinkhole made popping sounds as they sank. In her half-sleep, half-hallucination, Louette thought the sinkhole was a nightmare come for her. She struggled to wake up.

As her eyes opened, she realized the popping sound hadn't stopped. Someone was rapping on the front door. *Maybe it's Millie come to tell me Dan needs me to run the tractor.* "I'm here," she called, bedroom slippers slapping the floor.

On Louette's front porch stood Clyde, all dressed up—a fully-outfitted law officer. "My aren't you handsome in your uniform, Clyde, but you scared me nearly half to death. What on earth are you doing here this early in the morning? Did you find a picture that looks like Joseph?"

"It's not early Lou, it's nine o'clock. And no, I haven't found a picture. This call is not about Joseph. It's about something else."

"Come on in then." Louette held the door open. "I'll plug in the coffee. Make yourself at home while I change out of my sleeping clothes." Louette left Clyde in the living room, nervously fingering the edges of his big hat.

Louette threw off her bathrobe, wondering what on earth could be wrong. There seemed to be something formal, or menacing, about Clyde's manner. She returned to the living room in slacks and blouse. "Is something the matter with Dan and Mittie?"

Clyde followed her into the kitchen. "Why do you ask about them?" He held a piece of paper in his hand.

"You are a county officer, and they live in the county."

"I've got jurisdiction here, too. The Geneva police don't answer, the call automatically comes to me."

"Set a minute. I'll scramble you some eggs."

"I already had breakfast. Coffee's fine. Maybe you got a cinnamon roll?"

"I can cut you a piece of cake left over from Bucky's visit." Louette uncovered the cake, cut a big piece and placed it on a saucer. "Why did you come to see me? Not that I'm not proud of the company."

Clyde picked up his fork and took a bite of cake. A look of pure bliss came over his face as he chewed slowly, then swallowed. "I came out here to bring you this." He reached a piece of paper across the table.

"What is it?" Louette poured cereal into a bowl.

"You have to promise not to get mad at me, Lou. I didn't have nothing to do with it." He was clearly embarrassed.

"I promise."

"The paper is a restraining order. . . . a peace warrant."

"From who? About what?" Louette's eyes lit with astonishment.

"Shirley says you threatened her. Said you were going to shoot her, and Marj too."

"I did tell Shirley I ought to pop her one after she busted in here in the dark yelling at me."

"What about Marj?" He looked around as if searching for Marj.

"She's not here," Louette told him. "And I did say I ought to shoot her. But you know I wouldn't do no such a thing as that!"

"Even so, I have to ask you to hand over any guns you have."

"Guns?"

"The law says I am to confiscate any guns on the premises."

"But, after Joseph left I sold all his guns to your daddy, who was the sheriff back then. Don't you remember?"

"Oh, yeah... so what were you going to shoot Marj with?"

"My mouth, I reckon. You know how Marj is." Louette poured a glob of milk into her coffee cup.

"She was pretty hard to get along with in school," he agreed. "She was always bossing everybody, including me."

When they had finished their coffee, Louette pointed to the warrant on the table. "Why don't you go on? I'll look the paper over and apologize to Shirley, though Lord knows, it ain't going to be easy."

"Lou, you sure you don't have a gun?"

"What on earth would I want with a gun?"

"Lots of old ladies get them for protection. Maybe you ought to think about it now that you live here alone. But you got to have a permit. And I don't know if I could give you a permit after you threatened somebody. I'll have to ask the sheriff's opinion on it."

"I don't want a gun; I'm all right by myself. I don't much like living alone, though." She guided him toward the door. "I do want to look through the pictures Benjamin mentioned. It would really be something if you found him, dead or alive. When can we do that?"

"I don't know, Lou. They're still coming in." Clyde left. She looked at the hall clock and realized he had been there eating cake and drinking coffee over an hour. He sure seemed like he had something heavy on his mind.

The day rolled on as Louette continued cleaning, and she was walking toward the shed with her arms full when Clyde returned and parked in front of the house. "Hi," she greeted him. "I haven't gotten over to apologize to Shirley yet. I'm working up to it though. You want a pressure cooker for canning?"

"I tried to call you, Lou."

"I got one of them answering machines now. I must have been out in the yard."

"I hate to tell you this, Lou." Clyde shifted from foot to foot, unrolling and opening a sheet of official-looking paper.

I've seen that look before. Most every time he comes around here. Maybe he's going to enlighten me on whatever he's been chewing over for ever-so long. "What is it you hate to tell me, Clyde?"

"I had already typed up about half of a search warrant to look for guns, and the sheriff says I can't throw it away because of the numbers printed on the form. So I got to come in and look through your house for any kind of firearms." He let out a long breath.

"Sure, if you say so. Seems like a lot of trouble to me, though. Would you like a sandwich? It's nearly lunch time."

"I'll take a cup of coffee if you've still got some and another piece of cake if there's any left."

"We didn't eat it all up. There's still plenty. I was going by the courthouse today anyway. I mailed out invitations to my wake to those who don't live here, but I kept some to deliver around town."

"I heard about it. Sounds like a great idea for a wacky party. I'll be here, Lou. You might need security or help with parking all the people."

"Hope I have lots of the same visitors who came when Mama died." They sat in silence as Clyde ate cake and they drank coffee.

"Clyde, you think the wake is the cause of all my troubles lately? The row with Marj—she thinks I'm crazy. She said I should call it a party."

"There ain't nothing wrong with inviting folks to come see you, Lou. Don't worry about it. You sure got Shirley riled up though."

"Yeah, I know. Let her stew for awhile. I forgot to ask you, is that paper going to cost me any money?"

"No. It just tells you to leave Shirley alone."

"It ought to tell her to leave me alone. I can't imagine Shirley being afraid of anybody. She's big as an eighteen-wheeler and twice as ugly." They laughed.

"How can a piece of paper protect a person if somebody gets mad at them?"

"Beats me. Got to look through your house now, Lou. Don't get mad at me. Okay?"

"I promise. Go right ahead. I'll wash up these dishes. How do you hunt for guns?"

"I look through the closets and pantry... you know, places like that." Clyde's footsteps echoed down the hall.

Louette looked out the window toward Shirley's house. The storage shed stood between her and a clear view of Shirley's front yard.

Clyde stopped. "You'll have to come down to the sheriff's office with me, Lou." His expression was serious. "I found a gun behind the coat rack at the front door."

"What! That's a BB gun, Clyde. I use it to shoot crows in my garden."

"It's a gun." If Clyde was anything, he was persistent. "And this paper says to arrest you if I find any guns in your house."

"Well, okay. Give me time to get my purse and change my shoes." She seethed as she closed up the house. *That dumb Clyde! I'd like to get my hands on Shirley. She started all this. Her and Marj.*

"Could I see that paper?" He handed her the search warrant. She glanced at it. There it was in black and white.

He had a right to search her house because she had "uttered a threat."

Louette followed Clyde to the official sheriff's department car. He was extremely formal. He held open the back door of the patrol car for her. A thick wire screen separated the back seat from the front.

On the way downtown, Louette read through the official document. It ordered him to confiscate any guns. She'd never thought an old BB gun that couldn't even hit a crow would classify as a firearm. The offending weapon rode in front with Clyde.

"Did you find any BBs?" Louette called out from the back seat. "I couldn't find any in the house last year when the crows came. I had to chunk pine cones at the rascals."

Clyde didn't answer. His face was fixed in an official expression. It was against regulations to carry on a conversation with a prisoner in the back seat. You weren't to get the prisoner riled up in any way, even with a strong wall of wire mesh for protection in-between.

"Is there any way I could look at your pictures of the unidentified dead while we're at the courthouse?" Louette asked from her perch in the back seat of the patrol car.

"I haven't found any that bears the least resemblance to Mr. Joseph," Clyde told her, with straight back and stiff neck.

"Since it's been so long, maybe he'd look different."

"Most of the pictures are real old. Some are terrible to look at. I'll let you know when I find one that resembles him the least bit." Clyde's voice was firm.

Later, in the lobby of the sheriff's office, waiting for Sheriff Messer to come back and explain to Clyde what he was supposed to do next, Louette wished she had brought more invitations to her wake. Lots of people she hadn't even thought about inviting walked by.

"Come to my wake," she told them. She almost told one of her Sunday school class members Shirley had promised to bring her famous coconut cake. Then she remembered Shirley was the cause of this mess with the sheriff's department—her and Marj together.

As Louette looked around the office for something to read, a loud "Harrumph" sounded at the door. "What have we here? Is that you, Louette?" Judge Simon O'Connor stood there, with sprouts of red hair framing his face, his thick eyebrows like a benediction.

"It is me," said Louette.

"Judge O'Connor." Clyde rushed to pull out a chair. "Here, set a spell."

"I don't need to sit, Clyde. What are you doing in the sheriff's office, Lou, bringing him an invitation to your, uh, wake?"

"That too," Louette told him. "But Clyde arrested me for threatening Shirley and having a BB gun in my house." Judge O'Connor reared back and gave out an enormous belly laugh, which echoed down the cavernous halls of the ancient courthouse.

"Somebody needed to threaten Shirley," he said, as he wiped tears from his eyes. Did you actually shoot her with a BB gun?"

"No. But Clyde found one in my house. He said a person with a peace warrant on her oughtn't to be harboring a gun."

"Where's the peace warrant?" Judge O'Connor held out his hand.

"Here it is, but that ain't the big problem," said Louette. "Look at this." She handed him the gun arrest warrant.

"Wait 'till the sheriff sees that," O'Connor placed the paper on the sheriff's desk, still laughing.

"Be sure and come to my wake, Simon." Louette couldn't stifle a grin.

"I will be there, with bells on," he told her as he walked, chuckling, out the door and down the hall.

Clyde's face was red with embarrassment. He shifted in his chair and shuffled his feet.

Louette glanced at the clock. She didn't have time for this foolishness. The only magazines in the office were police periodicals. She picked up one with pictures of the country's most wanted. She reached it out toward Clyde. "At least I'm not in there, yet," she told him.

He made the wait seem longer and more miserable by his constant apologizing. "I'm sorry, Lou. I wouldn't have done it, but the search warrant tells me to, right there in black and white."

"It's okay, Clyde." The morning was wasting away. She needed to get back to cleaning her house.

When the sheriff came it didn't take him long. He looked the deputy straight in the eyes. "A BB gun is a child's toy, not a real gun. Take Lou home, and try not to tell anybody you arrested her."

"Does the peace warrant still stand?"

"Until Shirley cancels it." He turned to Louette. "Please accept my regrets about this incident."

"Just you be sure and come to my wake, sheriff. Bring your wife and some of that wonderful barbeque you make," Louette told him.

In the parking lot, Clyde held the door open, his face red. "Uh, you can sit in the front this time, if you want to, Lou."

"I'd prefer to sit in the back." She wasn't angry, just tired. It was noontime. The courthouse square was empty of people. Benches in front of the gray stone building were usually lined with old men chewing, spitting, and telling tall tales. The dog curled at the feet of a granite statue had the place to himself. Pigeons walked on the soldier's hat and shoulders. Louette held a square of printed cardboard, the last invitation.

As the deputy climbed into the squad car, Louette tapped on the wire barrier. "Wait, Clyde! Do you have some of the yellow tape y'all put around crime scenes?"

"Sure. Why?"

"I just had a thought. Why don't we make a loop on the tape and hang my last invitation around the soldier's neck?"

Clyde turned the key in the ignition. "He's too tall."

"If you pulled the car up there on the grass a little bit, I could jump on the hood, throw the loop over his head and the invitation would hang down right in front of him."

"Lou! I couldn't drive the car on the grass. See the sign 'Stay off the Grass'? Want to get me fired? Besides, you're too short for it to reach."

"But you're tall enough."

"Not me. I'm taking you home."

"Remember when you and those other boys got caught for hanging something around the soldier's neck. How did you do it back then?"

"You don't want to know." A grin curled at the corners of Clyde's mouth. "It was not easy."

"How?"

"We tied rocks to the ends of a rope and threw it." Louette jumped out and got stones from a flowerpot.

"These big enough?"

"Told you I ain't doing it, Lou."

"Think how nice an invitation to my wake would look hanging on the soldier. People would say, 'How on earth did that thing get there?'"

Indecision disturbed Clyde's face before he gave in and picked out two stones. He wrapped and tied them to the ends of a strip of crime scene tape, rolling each end until they met in the middle. He walked to the back of the monument, looking furtively up and down the street, then up at the gray face of the courthouse.

"Hurry! I see folks on the next block coming back from lunch." Louette held onto the open door of the squad car.

Clyde cocked his arm, took careful aim and swung. The only sound on the courthouse lawn was the crack of the tape ball as the stones peppered the back of the soldier's neck. Pigeons fluttered into the air. The stones rolled down the front of the soldier's tunic, stopping level with his gun butt. Clyde ran to the deputy car and jumped into the driver's seat.

Louette used a safety pin to attach the invitation before joining Clyde in the getaway car. She looked back at the soldier's yellow-tape necklace, the invitation to her wake hanging like a pendant. Pigeons resettled on the monument's head and walked placidly across its shoulders.

"There ain't no way everybody who comes to this courthouse won't see my invitation. Thank you so very much, Officer Clyde." Clyde drove back to Louette's house as fast as the law allowed.

"I'm plumb glad to be back home," Louette told him as he finished off two tomato sandwiches and a large chunk of chocolate cake. They drank the last of the heated-up coffee.

"I sure hope that row with the mama sow don't scar Bucky for life," Clyde said.

Clyde clearly has time on his hands. "We could run back down to the courthouse," Louette told him. "You might have gotten in some more pictures. Maybe Joseph is in one of 'em."

"I'll go by and look later today," he said.

"You find anything out about the man who bought the Tadlock place down near New Hope?"

"I still haven't got out there. Been busy," said Clyde. "I will get to it though. Saw him when he first moved in and he was mighty grouchy."

"He yelled for me to get off his property when I checked my tires by his pasture fence."

"Maybe he's got health problems," mused Clyde. "Sometimes that makes people cantankerous."

"May-be," said Louette. She took the dishes to the sink and ran water over them. "He coulda been afraid I'd see a marijuana patch. Told me not to set foot on his land."

"I'll get on it, Lou."

"Back in moonshine days people without crop land had stills. For most of them that was the only income they had during the Depression. Maybe you ought to leave the old man alone."

"I can't do that, Lou. Now that I've been informed, I'm bound by law to check it out."

"Heck. I wish I hadn't told you."

"Me too." Clyde picked up his hat. "I got to get back to work, such as it is."

"You're right. My jaws are tired. I don't see how you do it, talking back and forth with people all day long. Sure hope you find Joseph among the pictures. Even if he's dead, it'd help to know what happened to him."

Wish he wouldn't do that, get that look, then shift back and forth from one foot to the other. "You got something else you want to talk about, Clyde?"

Clyde ignored her question. "Lots of folks come by the office," he said. "Out on patrol though, it gets kind of lonely."

"When you get lonesome, just come on by and I'll heat up the coffee." *Hope he don't show up in the middle of night when he's on the graveyard shift.*

By the time Louette had cleaned up the kitchen, it was late afternoon. She made a list of food to cook for the wake: two chocolate fudge cakes, two butternut pound cakes, a ham, a turkey and dressing, green beans, butterbeans, field peas with snaps, Ferris peas, tomatoes, okra, and creamed corn.

Garden vegetables occupied the freezer in the shed. She'd better clean off some shelves out there; she'd surely run out of room in the kitchen pantry.

She stuck the list on the refrigerator and walked outside. *Guess I better go apologize to Shirley.* But she went to Miz Gumby's instead. She told Miz Gumby to be ready at ten the next morning to go grocery shopping.

Louette noticed a curtain move at Shirley's. *You have to apologize, you know.* She stood at the edge of the yard.

Shirley emerged from the back door holding a plastic container. "I want to donate a coconut cake for the party. Here it is." She took a few nervous steps then stopped. "I'll make some of my popular coconut pineapple pies and a gallon of potato salad, too, if you want them."

A lump formed in Louette's throat. "I'm sorry, Shirley, for how I talked to you."

"It's all right, Lou. It's all right." Neither moved for a long moment.

"Let's take this cake to the shed. I'm putting the pies and cakes on a shelf. The pantry's gettin' fuller by the minute with napkins, paper plates, plastic forks and spoons and cups."

Shirley wrinkled her nose at the thought of putting fresh-baked pies and cakes in that dusty shed. "Why don't we bring the stuff to my house, Lou? The tent with coffee and tea will almost be closer to my back door than yours."

After the women transferred pies and cakes, paper napkins, plastic spoons and forks to Shirley's pantry, they returned to Louette's house.

"Come visit with me while I check the fridge and freezer." The coffee perked.

"What's Ferris peas?" Shirley asked.

"I guess they're what some call White Acre peas. Mr. Manuel Ferris, who lived near us, shared the seeds with his neighbors; after that folks called them Ferris peas."

"If it's them little baby-green peas they call 'white peas' they sure are good." Shirley leaned over and took in a big sniff at the roses in the middle of the dinette.

"I plan to cook a big bowl of them. Field peas, too. Sure hope they'll be a crowd."

"There will be," Shirley told her. "Everybody I've talked to said they're coming. What about Marj?"

"What about her?"

"Is she and Bucky coming or not?"

"You tell me. You talk to Marj more than I do."

"Not since I swore out the warrant. That made her mad as blazes."

"It did?"

"She said I went too far, that I should have known you weren't dangerous, just a little, uh..."

"Crazy?"

"She said Dr. Waverly told her you're probably more sane than most people, for us to leave you alone." Louette harrumphed.

Shirley changed the subject. "Saw you with Etheline the other day."

"Yeah. She's back in town."

"She was in a higher grade than me in school, but I always thought she was stuck up."

"I think Etheline was more like lonely."

Shirley rounded the counter and tried to put her arm around Louette's shoulder, but Louette moved away. "Lou, I sure am glad we're friends again. I've missed you."

Louette couldn't suppress a smile. "Let's don't fight anymore, okay?" Shirley stuck out her hand and Louette took it.

"Okay by me. Lou, you think Marj will forgive me?"

"Don't worry about Marj, Shirley. She's all right, just fractious sometimes."

"You think she'll come to the party, Lou?"

"Sure. Marj and Bucky will be here."

"How do you know?"

"I know Marj. She'll come. She's got a little boy to beg and wheedle at her. I told him the date and to mark it on the calendar. I can bet he's been counting on it, every day."

Shirley smiled and took a loud slurp of coffee. "Think you're something, don't you?"

"Yeah. I'm not sure what, but I am something."

I'll meet you in the morning,
by the bright riverside,
When all sorrow has drifted away.

Chapter Twelve

Louette watched the sky, hoping it wouldn't rain. She changed the message on the answering machine: "This is Louette. I'm not dead or dying, and I'm expecting you at my house for a big gathering on May thirteenth."

Friday, the day before her wake, dawned bright and cheerful. She sang snatches of "Joyful, joyful, we adore thee... fill us with the light of day," as she worked in the kitchen.

She checked her list on the refrigerator. The ham was baked. She'd wait until bedtime to put the thawing turkey into the oven. She'd made two bowls of her special cranberry sauce on Thursday. All the sweet potato soufflé needed was marshmallows for the top and a few minutes in the oven to brown.

She couldn't find her recipe for corn pudding, so she baked a pan of creamed corn. Plus several bowls of peas. One zap in the microwave and the vegetables would be ready. She'd put the okra on top of the peas to steam.

The backyard was filled with voices as Benjamin directed men from the funeral home on where to erect a tent with tables and chairs and Clyde marked off parking places around the houses and across the street in the vacant lot. Folded furniture from the church fellowship hall leaned against the storage shed.

The peas smelled so good. She wondered if she had put in enough salt. It wouldn't matter about the okra; it would pick up flavor from the pea soup. She tasted the corn; it had browned on the top just right. She could almost eat a bowl of peas right now.

As she dipped the spoon into the bowl, the back door flew open. "Aha," called out Etheline. "I caught you tasting the peas."

"Somebody has to. They might not have enough salt."

"I'd be happy to carry out the tasting function for you." Louette laughed and held out the spoon. Etheline rolled her eyes and her face took on a blissful look. "Lord, you don't know how bad I wanted Southern peas while I was exiled up in Boston," she said, licking the spoon.

"Got enough salt?" Louette asked.

"Just right. What about the okra and the corn? You want an expert taster for those?"

"No, I already did that myself."

"I thought I'd come and see if I could help," Etheline told her.

"Just having you back home helps." Louette embraced her friend. No embarrassment this time.

Willie from the print shop knocked on the back door: "Where do you want this?" Louette and Etheline stepped outside. He held a roll of plastic as tall as himself. Clyde stepped up and pulled out one end, unrolling the longest banner Louette had ever seen.

"Wow!" she said. "Happy Birthday to me! I almost forgot my birthday's Monday. You didn't print such a big sign at the shop, did you?"

Willie laughed and patted her on the shoulder. "Sent all the way to Tallahassee for it. Marj ordered it."

Louette swallowed back the tears. "It's about the most beautiful thing I have ever seen."

"I'll help them hang it while you go back to the kitchen." Etheline pushed her toward the door.

"A little higher on the north end." Louette heard Etheline call out as she directed the hanging of the banner; the big plastic sign with huge letters in bright red, whorling this way and that, reached all the way from the rain tree to the clothesline.

Louette, back in the yard with a tin tub and dish cloths, pulled over the garden hose. She and Etheline washed and set up the church's coffee pot, then tackled the one Mayor Warren Roberts had brought from the hardware store. While Louette ran extension cords from the shed, they placed the coffee pots on a table underneath the funeral home canopy. She looked at the sky again. *Not a smidgen of rain in them white clouds.*

They piled containers of plastic cups beside the coffee pots and set out sugar bowls, artificial sweetener, and two family-size jars of coffee creamer. They covered the table and its contents with a red-checkered cloth, anchoring it at the corners with bricks.

"We might as well set out the soft drinks and go ahead and ice 'em down. Young people can't hardly get along without cold drinks." They lined up Styrofoam coolers at the edge of the tent and filled them with an assortment of Coke, 7-Up, Dr. Pepper, orange and punch-flavored drinks.

"We should have asked those men, or at least the teenagers, if they'd stay and put these heavy coolers on the table," Etheline remarked. "I didn't think about it until they left."

"They don't have to be on top of the tables," Louette told her. "We can drag them up under the table near the coffee pots."

They were pulling at the coolers when Shirley called out from her back door. "Miz Gumby says she's got camp cots she can set up for two of your relatives if they want to sleep over there."

"Tell her the Osceola Hotel donated enough rooms for an army. Some of them ought to be coming in pretty soon." As Louette and Etheline entered the kitchen, a frizzy head popped through the back door. Marie Ann Thames.

"Lou, I'm settin' up the baby pen under the tent if you don't mind. I don't want the twins getting wet if it happens to rain on your party."

"Good idea, Marie Ann." *That woman is bringing them brats!* Louette hadn't forgotten how the twins had howled all the way through her mother's wake.

"I want them right in the middle of the party, Lou, so they'll grow up sociable." Marie Ann's head disappeared and the door slammed.

Shirley walked in with a note pad in her hand. "Sociable ain't the word. Aggravating's more like it."

Louette and Etheline exchanged knowing looks, their eyebrows raised. "Takes one to know one," Etheline muttered.

Shirley hadn't noticed. "I was trying to keep a list of who said they'd be here, but I've about run out of notepad paper."

"Is Marj and Bucky on the list, Shirley?" asked Etheline.

"Not yet. Lou says the answering machine hasn't heard a peep." She turned to Louette. "You got more paper?"

"Don't worry about it, Shirley. The wake's tomorrow. They come or they don't."

"What if we run out of food?"

"Guests are supposed to bring a covered dish, remember?"

"I'm bringing my famous Southern spinach with boiled eggs sliced on top," piped up Etheline, striking a pose.

"Southern spinach?"

"Poke sallet, Shirley." The women laughed.

"Where did you find poke?"

"Plenty of it growing in my backyard up on the hill, and it grows everywhere in the woods." Etheline laughed. "Green as grass and twice as tall."

"Humpf." Shirley put the notepad down. "I thought Nervie Johnson's sister was your cook. She can't cook poke. Best I remember, she can't cook diddly squat."

"Racie Mae is a great cook, thank you so much. But I am preparing the poke recipe myself."

A lopsided grin flitted across Shirley's face. "Where'd you learn to fix poke?"

"Louette's mother taught me years ago. I've already got a big bowl of it, boiled two times over and in the refrigerator. Hardboiled eggs are in there, too. Waiting to be put together on one of my mother's fancy platters."

"Hope you don't make a bunch of people sick." Shirley said. "I'm gone home. I've got plenty to do over there."

Etheline gazed at the roses Benjamin had placed on the table soon after sunrise. Drops of water clung to the leaves and petals and they glowed with reflected sunlight. "I wish someone would bring me a big bouquet of roses," she said wistfully. "Remember the song, somebody, Ernest Tubb maybe, sang? 'I'm sending you a big bouquet of roses... one for every time you broke my heart'. Or was it Eddy Arnold who sang that?"

Louette looked up. "You can have these roses if you want them. I'd rather look at roses growing in Benjamin's yard. That man has a way with plants."

"I'll bet he was a good train engineer," said Etheline. "He's still handsome, sort of, but he's not too good at growing hair."

"Maybe that's why he wears an engineer's cap so much. How do you know if he grows hair or not?"

"Shirley told me." Etheline laughed.

"She told me too. Said he tipped his head and his cap fell off." Louette rolled her eyes. "I've actually seen him without his striped engineer's cap. He's very handsome, even with his bald head."

"It is a mystery how Shirley knows so much about everything." Etheline laughed again. "She is one bottomless pit of gossip and misinformation."

It made Louette feel good to watch Etheline carrying on, enjoying herself. "You got that appointment all set up with the doctors?"

"Signed, sealed, delivered, next week I'm theirs..." sang Etheline. "Those doctors will either cure me or kill me." She quick-stepped around the dinette beside the kitchen window. "See you early tomorrow," she sang, high-stepping out the back door and across the yard to her car.

Near dusk Benjamin came to Louette in the kitchen and hugged her tight. Being close to Benjamin made her whole world feel alive and purposeful. She turned for his kiss, which lasted longer than custom allowed, she thought. She leaned into his chest and kissed him back. "I'll see you early tomorrow," he said.

As soon as he had gone Louette listened for Marj's car. She had fresh sheets on all the beds. Her house was as clean as she could get it. She had decided against painting: there hadn't been time. She'd have to get into a painting mood soon. She wished she had the old cot from the storage shed set up for Bucky. But it was way too heavy. The mattress didn't look that good either, even with the plastic cover zippered over it. She'd likely buy a new mattress, so Bucky could have his own special place in her house. Just in case Marj ever let him come back for a visit.

She took a last tour around the outside. Spaces for parking were marked off with yellow tape, courtesy of Deputy Clyde. In the back yard, the grass and remnants of last year's garden had been mowed down to the nub, the rain tree's forlorn leaves raked and taken away. Under Benjamin's direction, tables had been set up in a long row, ready for the food Louette had prepared and that guests would bring. Chairs lined up, with more stacked against the shed. The old picnic table stood over against Shirley's chrysanthemum bed, the flowers neglected but ready to come up again anyway, dry leaves holding back tiny green sprouts.

The sun trembled on the western horizon, colors streaming out like spilled bright poster paints, outlines of houses and trees intruding on the perfect globe. The sun dipped lower as if tilting its hat for good luck on tomorrow's grand gathering, then plunged into the abyss, leaving a faint glow at the edge of the darkness.

Louette smiled. Her mama would have been proud. She basked in the thought. The location of Louise Etta Kelly's wake was as ready as she and a large number of the town's population could make it.

Shirley's backyard security light came on. Louette saw her peek out a window and look up the street. She's watching for Marj and Bucky, too. I'm not the only one who will be disappointed if they don't show up.

Louette thought about calling Marj, just to check on their arrival. But calling might suggest she was overly eager. It would show Marj she had the upper hand over her own mother. Maybe not. *If Mama was still alive, she would have already called and demanded to know when they'd be arriving.* Louette cleared her throat. "I miss you so," she said aloud as she checked out the yard.

At that moment the phone rang. *Is Marj calling to say she's not coming?* But it was Mittie.

"Just want you to know I'm bringing a pile of paper napkins. They had a sale at the dime, uh, dollar store. Anything else you need you can think of?"

"No. It sure looks like we're going to have plenty of food. I'll put the turkey in at bedtime," Louette said.

"I'm cooking a tenderloin and bringing a quart jar of pepper jelly to go with it," said Mittie.

"My mouth's watering already. Thanks Mittie."

Mittie's voice dropped. "The doctor told Dan he can go, but to take his crutches."

Louette hung up the phone and stared. She really wanted to tell Marj about the pictures Clyde was collecting of the unidentified dead. Maybe they could look at them together. But she couldn't force herself to call her daughter.

Louette put the turkey in the oven, then chopped celery and onion for the dressing. Vegetables and desserts were at Shirley's and in the shed. After she finished in the kitchen, she took a long, soaky bath. She carefully hung her new lavender dress on the closet door and put her new, black patent-leather Sunday shoes underneath.

It was too quiet. Her feet kept moving stiffly. The house creaked, settling for the night. She could smell the turkey cooking. Her ears strained for sounds of a car motor. She hadn't thought through to the possibilities of Marj not bringing Bucky. It would hurt. It would be a long day tomorrow.

Sleep came hard. Her room had a strange closed-in smell. This house needed more than painting—it needed an airing out. She shifted about on the bed. Heartache slipped over her, like a great smothering hand that snuffed out all other feeling. She put her finger to her wrist and sure enough there was her pulse. It seemed strange that her heart kept beating.

Maybe a glass of warm milk would help. She put her feet to the floor. There was still that strange odor. She had turned off the turkey. It was done. But something just didn't smell right.

She lay back down. She couldn't bear it if her grandson and daughter didn't come to her wake. She switched on her bedside lamp to see the clock. *Ten at night and Marj's not here. Maybe she decided against it, or maybe they'll get here tomorrow.*

She heard a car door slam. "Gramma Lou, Gramma Lou!" As Louette opened the door and hugged Bucky, she recognized the singed odor of smoke and turned.

"Mama, look!" Marj dropped her suitcase. "The kitchen's on fire!"

"You're right. Grab Bucky and get out of here! I wondered about that smell." Louette ran through the hall to the bedroom. She pulled her pillow from its case and stuffed in her slacks and shirt, underwear, and new dress and shoes. She ran into her mother's room and, in one sweep of her arm, dumped pictures off the mantel into the pillowcase, then threw in her mother's Bible.

The hall filled with smoke. Flames licked at the bathroom wall. Louette raised her bedroom window. She punched the screen with an elbow and climbed out. She heard tearing sounds as the screen ripped her chenille bathrobe, then felt the scrape of breaking camellia limbs as she fell into her mother's prize bush.

"Are you all right?" Marj and Bucky embraced her.

Shirley ran across the yard yelling, "I called the fire house."

"Thank you," whispered Louette.

She, Marj, and Bucky ran to the storage shed. Benjamin was instantly there, hugging Louette. No cap, bald as a peeled onion. He grabbed a water hose and turned it toward the house. Louette and Bucky held each other as the tiny stream of water fizzled into steam.

"I got up to get a drink of water and looked out the window." Shirley's voice was shrill. "A red ball whooshed up on the roof over the kitchen." She jumped up and down.

164

"Come here, Shirley." Marj pulled her into the circle of arms.

They stood that way as the Town of Geneva fire truck roared into the front yard, crushing the stakes Clyde had carefully placed around the parking area. Fire hoses dragged across last year's petunia bed and big feet in rubber hip boots stomped Louette's dwarf azaleas.

"Move back, move back," yelled a fireman. "Go over there." He pointed to the vacant lot across the street. "You're in danger from sparks."

They ran across the street, Shirley right with them. At the corner of her eye Louette saw Clyde stringing yellow tape to stop traffic at the end of the street. Sparks dropped into the yard where they had been.

In shock, Louette kept her eyes riveted on the house where flames gobbled up the roof. Firemen held bulky hoses spewing vast sprays of fire-eating chemicals.

"Maybe they can save the pantry and the refrigerator. Lucky we put the desserts and cooked vegetables at my house. What about the turkey?"

"Just be quiet, Shirley."

Bucky sobbed. "Your house, Gramma Lou. The fire is eating your house." The women patted and hugged him.

"It didn't get us," Marj told her son. "That's the most important thing."

Clyde ran up. "Gimme your keys, Lou and I'll move your car out of the way, across the street." Louette held tight to her purse, her eyes fixed on the fire.

Marj retrieved the keys. "Please do, Clyde, Mama would die without her old car."

Louette roused. "I worked a long time for that Dodge Dart. It better last me the rest of my days."

"Count the dents and you could probably get it in Ripley's Believe It or Not," said Clyde. He drove the car two blocks down the street.

Marj parked her own car right behind Louette's. "Thanks, Clyde," Marj told him. "Looks like we got the cars just in time."

Louette noticed Benjamin at the edge of light, shock on his face, still holding the garden hose. She reached toward him. "Come stand with us, Benjamin."

He ran to her and patted Bucky on the head. "I'm Benjamin," he whispered.

"I saw a note you wrote my gramma," Bucky told him. "She read it over and over, then put it on the table by a big bunch of roses." Louette blushed and hugged Benjamin tighter. Bucky held to Louette's bathrobe. He reached out and circled Benjamin's leg with his other arm.

After a moment, Benjamin removed Bucky's arm. "I'd better go see if I can help. Look after your gramma for me, and your mom too."

"I will," Bucky promised him.

Louette watched the flames boil among the chemicals like a giant whirlwind. "Oh, Lord, don't let that thing eat up my whole house."

Cracking and popping sounds came as the inferno reached the south end of the wood-frame house, then consumed walls, joists and roofing. It inched to the north where firemen aimed chemical and water avalanches in an effort to douse the flames. More firemen turned giant spraying hoses toward Shirley's house and Miz Gumby's, drenching roofs and yards.

A fireman stumbled past. "Move farther back, the heat could get to you. We're going to soak down the shed and the funeral tents."

Louette gazed at the fire in a trance, seeing the flames swirl in on themselves. They seemed to shoot straight up, then with a boom the rest of the house imploded. "Miz Gumby!" cried Louette.

"I'm right here." The old woman stood behind Marj, wrapped in a quilt.

Bucky grabbed the old lady around her waist and pulled her into the family huddle. "Look!" Bucky pointed at her feet. "Miz Gumby's got on Mickey Mouse slippers."

"The young ones wear them; so can I." Miz Gumby tried to hide her feet with the quilt.

Bucky hung on to his mother's pants leg. Louette and Marj were quiet, staring at the flames which seemed to sigh and cluster as if taking a short rest before roaring up again. Heat drove them back, blowing across the paved street, onto the shoulder of the road and farther into the vacant lot that Clyde had marked for parking.

A moan escaped Miz Gumby' mouth and she turned her head. "I just can't bear to watch." She pulled the quilt tight around her, still holding to Bucky's shirt sleeve.

Louette wiped her eyes. "Can't believe this is happening." She had been so happy, then sad because she thought Marj and Bucky weren't coming, and now this. Her daylight had turned into dark again.

People ran among the firemen. Some carried sandbags, encircling the burning site, then sprayed water over the sandbags. She saw Benjamin among those soaking the sandbags. Mayor Warren Roberts plunked down more sandbags, one after the other. Cries could be heard, and footsteps. Then when it appeared the worst of the fire had slowed down, they stopped and stared.

Benjamin returned and put his arms around Louette. "There's not much else can be done," he told her.

The diminishing light revealed disbelief and dismay on the faces of Louette's friends and neighbors. Huddled in a group, they watched while the house burned. Showers of sparks exploded in the air, white and yellow, then fell into the dying embers. Small bonfires spewed the last of the flames. The house, no longer a home, had burned down to an oblong pile of cinders and ash, with the unburned frames of stove, refrigerator, and iron bedstead forming squared-off silhouettes.

The acrid smell of water on burnt wood hung in the air. Ash swirled around the feet of firemen moving about on the charred rubble. Heat still radiated from the fire; smoke stung Louette's eyes and throat. Louette's birthday banner was in tatters along with the clothesline. Shirley's backyard security light glowed, and Miz Gumby's house lights helped illuminate the dreadful scene.

"I'm sorry, Lou." The fire chief walked up, removing thick gloves and smudging his forehead with a grimy hand. Ashes clung to his fireproof overalls. "It was too far gone by the time we got here. That tongue and groove pine was fat as lightered knots."

"Oscar, you did what you could."

"Looks like you might could have kept the pantry from burning, and maybe the kitchen!" Shirley spat out. "Some fireman you are, Oscar Mills!"

Louette put her hand on the fireman's arm. "Oscar, please don't pay no attention to Shirley."

"Looks like she's got a point there, Lou. I'm sorry we weren't able to save your house. A few chairs and a swing; that's all we could retrieve."

"I'm not blaming you Oscar. You helped. And your boys were here to protect us."

She looked up. Shirley stood before her, clasping and unclasping her hands. "The wake! Lou, what are you going to do about the wake?" Shirley had read her mind.

"Yeah," said Oscar. "What about the wake?"

"The wake?" Louette shook her head out of its daze. "I want to have the wake, of course. But this burnt-out house stinks so bad, Oscar. Is there anything we can do about the smell?"

Oscar nodded his head. "Not a whole lot right now, but we've got some chemicals at the fire house, and we can round up some big fans once the place begins to cool down. By daylight we can start to work on it."

"Could we have the wake?" Louette asked. "Not on the ashes, of course, but in the rest of the yard. We can spread out over to Shirley's and Miz Gumby's if we need to, and maybe on the vacant lot where we stood to keep out of reach of the fire."

"I think so," said Oscar. "My wife's made chicken pie and three gallons of sweet tea." The fireman wiped his face with a red bandana.

"Tea! I knew there was something else I forgot to bring outside." Louette pointed toward the tent at the edge of Shirley's yard. "Ain't that something?" She shook her head.

Oscar laughed. "We can put our tea on that table beside the coffee machines. With water on the tent top, the coffee setup stayed put."

"We could fix up you boys some coffee right now. I plugged the extension cord in at the shed. That ain't burned, thank God."

"But, Lou, I had to turn off the power." The fireman waved his arm toward the house ruins.

Shirley had crossed the yard. "I can plug up the extension cord to my outside light," she called. "Benjamin hooked the water pump to my power. We can get water from the spigot beside the shed. I'll bring the big coffee can. Go ahead and get a coffee pot ready." Then she laughed. "You better not turn one of them big hoses on the pot. It'd wash it to China."

"I wouldn't do that, Shirley," Oscar told her as he turned Lou's garden hose on at the spout.

Louette pointed to the Styrofoam coolers. "We've got cold drinks too. There might be somebody who'd rather have cold drinks."

"Not me. I prefer coffee or tea." Oscar slapped ashes off his boots. "Finish rolling up the hoses," he called to the other firemen. "Lou's got refreshments."

"Marj, why don't you follow Shirley and get one of the cakes and cut slices. Give the men a reward for their trouble." Bucky, wide-eyed, clung to Louette and Benjamin as Marj followed Shirley across the yard.

"I'm going home to change," Miz Gumby announced to no one in particular and left the yard, still holding the quilt tightly around her.

Shirley's outside light made patterns on the charred pile of rubble that had been Louette's home, and it was impossible for Louette to look away. Others stood transfixed by the scene.

Etheline rushed up. "Holy rat killer!"

"Lost your Boston accent there for a second," laughed Oscar, chewing on a mouthful of cake. "Welcome home, Etheline."

"Some fireman you are. Nothing left. Hope my house don't never catch fire."

"It's sure a good thing we took desserts and vegetables to Shirley's house," said Louette. "At least that much's saved. The turkey's gone though. And the ham."

"We saved the shed, and Shirley's house and Miz Gumby's. We kept the fire from spreading."

"Thank God. . .and thank you and the boys, too, Oscar," Louette told him.

Etheline stared at the rubble as little fires flashed, then fizzled out. "Oh, Lord," she said. "I can't bear it."

"It's done and gone, Etheline," Louette told her. "Ain't nothing to do about it now."

"But, Lou, where will you live?"

"Haven't got that far yet, Etheline."

"You could come live with me up on the hill," Etheline told her. "It sure is lonesome. But Racie Mae does come in the daytime."

"You don't need me up there," Louette told her. "You already got somebody wants to live with you."

Etheline's face glowed bright pink. "Oh," she said.

"Etheline, you deserve some happiness." Etheline gave Louette a long look, then turned to help Marj and Shirley cut cake.

Louette sat in a chair and pulled Bucky onto her lap. Benjamin sat at what was left of the old picnic table pulled up against the shed. Marj, Shirley, and Etheline cut large slices of pound cake, red velvet, and coconut cake, and served coffee to the volunteer firemen. She glanced aside at the still smoldering fire. An occasional cinder burst into flame, popped into the air, then fell like a burned-out meteor.

Etheline glared at Oscar "You couldn't put the fire out before it completely burned down?"

"We tried our best," Oscar told her, taking in a long pull of his coffee.

"Your best wasn't good enough, Oscar Mills."

"That's what Shirley told me." Oscar looked surprised. "You two kin?"

"Not on your life," Etheline stormed. "Even if we were, I wouldn't claim her."

"Good point." Oscar smiled. He reached for another piece of cake. "She sure knows her way around a kitchen, though."

Marj spoke up. "You and Shirley leave Oscar alone," she told Etheline.

Benjamin got a cup of coffee for Louette and one for himself. A fireman held out his cup for a refill. "You have any money hid in your house, Lou?"

"No." *Phew. Good thing I moved the fruit jars of Mama's and hid them in the shed.*

Marj's eyes took on that wild, scared look again. She turned them full on her mother. Louette shook her head, put a finger to her lips and pointed to the shed, hoping Marge would catch on.

Oscar plunged a fork into a big slice of Shirley's prize-winning coconut cake. "My wife's got clothes about your size, Lou."

Louette gave a wry chuckle. "I'll be all right. I got a few things in a pillow case." She pointed to a spot beside the shed where firemen had piled chairs and the swing.

Marj ran toward the pillow case. "What did you get?" she asked.

"I grabbed a blouse, a pair of slacks, my new church dress. And my new black shoes."

"What else is in there?" Marj's face was ashen.

"All the pictures off Mama's mantel, and her Bible."

"Nothing else?"

Louette motioned toward the shed. "I took some other things you talked about to the shed when I stored your doll. I had already moved the strong box with some important papers. The rest are in the safety deposit box at the bank." The color returned to Marj's face.

Oscar laughed. "The house burns down and Louette Kelly saves family pictures and a Sunday dress!"

"Wanted to look pretty for my wake." Louette grinned.

"I'm glad you grabbed Gramma Clara's Bible," said Marj.

"Me too. She loved that Bible," said Louette.

"I meant to look through it when I had time," Marj told her mother. "She used clippings, pictures and notes as page markers. I've been meaning to ask you about some of them."

"Like what?"

"Wedding announcements of people I'm not sure we are kin to. Baby pictures people sent her. A church bulletin from a church over toward Black, called New Zion."

"Mama was baptized at New Zion, when she was a little girl. She used to take me to that church for homecomings."

The fire chief cleared his throat. "You did some quick thinking, Lou. Don't know what I'd rescue, if my house burnt down."

"Me either," said Etheline. "I'd probably just faint and burn up right along with mine."

"It could have happened to me, if Marj and Bucky hadn't arrived when they did," Louette said slowly. She tightened her arms around Bucky.

"You two saved my life, I reckon." Marj moved protectively toward Louette and Bucky, whose eyes had drooped almost shut.

"I wouldn't be sitting here holding my wonderful grandson right now." Louette kissed the top of Bucky's head and put her arm around Marj's waist. "Poor little fellow," she said. "He's sound asleep."

Deputy Clyde bustled up, looking official. "We got a lot of cleaning up to do. We can soak the ashes good and when it all cools down, we can wet the burnt-out places on the grass and cover them with sheets of plastic. The levee sandbags helped keep most of the burnt area contained."

"I'd use tarpaulins," Oscar told him. "I sent some of the boys with Mayor Warren to get tarps from the hardware store. They're bringing chemicals to help tamp down the smell. Tell some of my guys to help you put the tarps down after the area has been sprayed. If there's not enough tarpaulins, you might use the plastic right around the edges, but it will take several days for the center of the burn to cool properly. Don't smell too good right now, but we'll air it out with big fans. Should get the worst of the odor. Enough so that folks can breathe and eat."

"People can park across the street," said Clyde. "Benjamin and I picked up the stakes and replaced the yellow tape. The grass there crinkles under your feet, like it's frozen or something. A fire sure makes a mess."

Benjamin spoke up. "I'll bring you more roses, Lou."

"That would be nice," Louette told him. She noticed the blush. "We could set them right here on the table with the paper goods. That would help the looks of that table." She felt strange, holding a normal-sounding conversation beside what had, until hours ago, been her home.

Her back yard had been seared black, almost to Shirley's yard. Blades of grass, once vibrant, alive, were now withered and shriveled. Tiny green leaves once covering the rain tree had burned off. The tree's stark limbs reached toward the sky as if in prayer. The clothesline posts had burned down to stumps.

A fireman kicked the remains and scattered the ashes with his big fire boot. Clyde called out as firemen placed tarpaulins on the sooty area where the tables would sit. "We'll have this covered by the time folks start to arrive."

Double Doc jogged up, looking as if he were out for his morning run. "What can I do?"

"You can help, Doc," Clyde called out. "We've got to get it as clean as we can for the wake."

Louette looked at the thin light toward the east. "This afternoon."

The others laughed as Double Doc jogged to the side yard and started unrolling tarpaulin, still jogging.

The sky was turning pink by the time most of the coffee, all the coconut cake, the cold drinks and firemen were gone. Townspeople who had gathered for the spectacle, stayed to drink coffee and eat cake then also wandered off, promising to come back around one o'clock.

Marj spoke up. "Stay what's left of the night with Shirley, Mom. Bucky and I will sleep at Miz Gumby's." She held Bucky in her arms.

"I want to stay with Gramma Lou," Bucky mumbled, his eyelids shut. Louette kissed his forehead.

"I'll see you later," Benjamin told her and kissed her on the lips, a warm, heartening caress that promised more to come, the thin light glistening on his bald head. Louette snuggled her head on his shoulder. It lifted her spirits.

I do love you, Benjamin, she said inside her mind. But the words wouldn't come out of her mouth. She tried to smile, a crooked twist of the lips. Her hand trembled as she squeezed his arm and pulled away.

Shirley picked up Louette's pillowcase. They walked across the yard. "Something burnt your house right to the ground; did a whopper of a job of it, too. All them firemen weren't worth a hoot."

"Oscar said the fire probably started around the stove where the turkey was baking. Something happened to the wiring," Louette mumbled, exhausted.

"What does Oscar know? Most of his training was slapping at brush fires."

"Aw, cut it out, Shirley." Louette fanned smoke from her face. "The insurance company will send the fire marshal. They'll tell us what started the fire. Railing about it won't bring back the house. It is gone from this earth, forever." Louette stared at the charred remains of what had been her home most of her life. She wound her arms across her chest. *It ain't started to hurt real bad yet, but it will.*

"Go on, Shirley. Leave the door unlocked." Louette pulled up a folding chair. "I just want to set here a spell."

Death's like a charred hole of nothing, or a burnt house. A flash of slippery gray sand, sucking down everything, the thought jarred her mind.

She shifted in the chair and whispered aloud, "I forgot to be sad about Mama and Joseph for a little while. I caused this. I was rejoicing about my wake. I was excited about being with Benjamin. Guess I must have been too happy." The sour smell of smoke not quite tamped down burned her nostrils.

Joseph would be devastated to see this. Stop it, Louette, Joseph is not just off somewhere. He's more than likely dead. But the sad thoughts kept coming. *Even if he's dead, he can't miss a sight like this, smell this awful stench. Even dead, his spirit is hurting. So's Mama's. I know mine is. You can't let it get you down. Go in and try to sleep awhile. Think of all that company. You're having a real honest-to-goodness wake, remember?* But she couldn't push away despair. It hung over her like the cloud following the little boy in an old comic strip.

Louette sat until the slowly-rising sun painted the black carcass of what had been her home, first in soft shades of pink, then with wide swipes of brilliant light. There were no cottony white clouds, no gray clouds. It would be a beautiful, clear day. What had been a house and home looked like a big fireplace without bricks. Louette shivered as she entered Shirley's back door.

Put one foot in front of the other. Time does not stop. Life goes on. Or doesn't. Nature lasts forever, not people. Nor houses. But you don't stop. You just keep going.

She made her way to Shirley's guest room and lowered her body onto the bed, still wearing her pajamas and the torn chenille bathrobe. Her sleep was jerky with nightmares— fire and quicksand, pleasure and despair. A sense of falling, then rising to meet a new day, a ripening sun.

Morning has broken, like the first morning.
Blackbird has spoken, like the first bird.

Chapter Thirteen

Louette stretched, rubbing her back as she walked to the window in Shirley's guest room. When her fingers touched the shade, it jerked and zipped to the top. She reached for a chair to stand on so she could pull the shade back down. Thinking better of it, she merely stood at the window and looked out.

She noticed the tall wooden fence Shirley's neighbors to the south had put up years before. Once painted, now it was scarred and peeling. It looked like the fence at the farm, the one Dan built across the road to the sinkhole.

A heavy sense of doom gripped her. A long time on this earth, and at the end all was gone but for the smoking ashes where her home had been, and a pervasive memory of a quicksand-sucking sinkhole. She could smell the ashes even from inside Shirley's house.

In the kitchen, beside the gurgling percolator, a note lay on the counter. "Lou, I'm gone to find us another turkey. We're fixing to have us a party, and we can't do it without your turkey dressing."

Louette showered and put on the slacks and shirt from the pillow case, leaving the new dress hanging on the closet door, the black Sunday shoes on the floor underneath.

Coffee mug in hand, Louette wandered outside and across the back yard, the grass crackling under her feet. *Just a black pile of smoking, stinking cinders.*

Her mother's room, Joseph's clothes, baby pictures of Marj, pictures of Bucky, her grandparents' pie safe, the hope chest her parents had given her when she graduated from high school—earthly reminders of her former life. All of it gone. *Utter ashes.* In that moment Louette wished she had never planned the wake.

Feeling a great sorrow, she sighed and sat down at the picnic table. She hoped the fire hadn't killed the rain tree. She loved that tree. She certainly wouldn't miss the pea vines and dried corn stalks though.

She didn't see Marj come up from the front of the yard. "Maybe it's better this way, Mama." Marj walked to where the clothesline had been.

"No," Louette responded.

"Yes. Now you can start over. Begin a new life. Living in that house with reminders of Daddy and Gramma Clara, you would have continued to grieve."

"How can you tell me about grief?" Louette hurt, like her insides were exploding.

"I know I have no right. I'm asking you to forgive me, to start over, to come home with us, to live with us." Marj reached her arms out, surrounding her mother.

A smile flickered around Louette's mouth. "You check on that offer with your husband?"

"Not yet, but he usually does what I say or what Bucky wants," Marge said, with an answering smile.

"I appreciate you asking, Marj, but I couldn't impose." Louette swiped at her cheek with the back of her hand. "No offense meant. You are my daughter, but I couldn't live with you."

"I thought you wanted to be around Bucky. If you lived with us, you could see him all the time."

Louette was silent for a moment. "What I wanted most of all was for my mother to be around Bucky while she was alive. It's no use now. It's over. She's gone."

"I told you I could not bear to see her like that. That's why I stayed away. She was suffering so."

"No. She wasn't. Not after the last bad stroke, she was just there."

"I couldn't stand it," Marj took a deep breath. "I was afraid I might do something... help her along... I couldn't have just let her lie there on the bed, helpless. She would not have wanted that. I know it."

The truth hung between them. It burned, like the fire that took Louette's house.

"Don't tell me you didn't think the same thing at one time or another." Marj grabbed her mother by the arms.

"Stop it!" Louette broke loose from Marj's grip. Fists raised, ready for mortal battle, Louette felt like she watched from the air above her.

When she came to, Marj was fanning her face with a paper plate. "What happened?" Louette's head throbbed. She felt her cheeks, flushed with anger. "You hit me!"

"I did no such thing. You swooned over in a faint." Marj sat on the dry, singed grass at the edge of one of the tarpaulins and cried, softly at first, then with gulping sobs.

Louette's anger melted. She reached for her daughter. "Shh," she soothed, folding Marj in her arms. Louette's heart ached. Marj had said the unsayable out loud.

Louette admitted for the first time to having fought the same feelings in herself. Her mother had lingered, helpless. Wouldn't it have been easier to put a pillow over her face and end her suffering? Louette couldn't set herself up for eternity in hell in order to end her mother's misery. Such a thing could have created a hole of shame in her soul. But why should her mother lie there month after month, year after year? Louette had allowed it to go on, had held back her mother by her own will, by her own need.

"You know, Mama wouldn't want us to be at each other's throats," Louette told her daughter. "We've got to stop this fighting. It's wearing us down."

"All right by me. When do we start to stop?"

"We can begin right now," Louette said, then smiled. "I couldn't go live with you though, even if I don't have a house anymore."

"Why not?"

"Mainly because I couldn't stand being around that husband of yours full-time. We mix about like oil and vinegar—him being the vinegar, of course."

"The offer is open, in case you change your mind." Louette held Marj and rocked back and forth as they stood beside the ruins. She patted Marj's back, like she had when Marj was a baby. "I loved Gramma Clara better than anybody in the world, next to you and Bucky. You know that. Don't you, Mama?" Tears rolled down Marj's face.

"I know, child. I know."

Peace settled over them, as when Louette was little and a teacher would stop fights on the playground. "Kiss and make up," the teacher would say. The kids hugged on command. First one, then the other cried. Now, as Louette and Marj comforted each other, years seemed to drop away. In this moment, grownup Marj was her child again, and Louette could offer her, as she had long ago, unconditional love and could feel it being accepted.

The funeral home crew showed up. "Where you want the rest of the tents and chairs, Lou?"

"Farther this way boys, over into Shirley's yard. Don't want people getting smut on their shoes."

Clyde and Benjamin were busily outlining what had once been Louette's house with yellow crime scene tape. Clyde had brought a roll of plastic sheeting to spread around the tarpaulins on the edge of the yard.

The roar of Shirley's automobile with greetings from a wide-awake Bucky startled Louette and Marj. "Gramma Lou! Mama!" Louette and Marj together pulled Bucky into their arms.

"I'm back with the turkey," called out Shirley. "It's cooked, straight from Oceola's kitchen, with the broth and stuff for you to make your famous dressing."

"Let me get the turkey out of the trunk for you." Benjamin pulled a grocery bag from Shirley's car.

Bucky squirmed loose. "Aunt Shirley, when does the party start?"

"Soon as the turkey and dressing's ready," said Shirley. "The fire ate the first turkey, but it can't beat us. We'll finish up with this turkey. We can't have a wake without Louette's cornbread dressing." She handed a bag to Bucky. "Here carry this."

Benjamin put the turkey on Shirley's kitchen counter and returned to help Clyde.

Marj reached out to Louette. "If you don't live with me, where will you live?"

"I don't know, Marj. Ain't thought it out yet."

Mittie's car pulled up. She rushed around to help Dan with his crutches. "Still need the crutches, Dan?" Benjamin asked, holding the car door open.

"I guess," answered Dan. "Anything gives me support, I aim to hold on to it."

Clyde held a roll of crime scene tape as he shook his head. "Flapping them things around makes you look like Ichabod Crane."

"I overheard what you said to Marj, Lou. You don't have to rebuild," Mittie told her. "You're welcome to live with us out at the farm."

"I couldn't do that."

"Oh, yes you could." Dan pointed a crutch in the direction of the farm. "We need you." He swept the crutch toward the blackened remains of Louette's home. "And it looks like you might need us."

Thankfulness welled up in Louette's heart. "My house burns down, and I get two offers of places to live within ten minutes. Can't beat that." Her chuckle came out as a gulp.

Mittie stuck her head around Dan. "You can set yourself up in your old room, if you like, or we can build onto the house to give you more space." She plunked grocery bags onto the table.

Bucky appeared at Shirley's kitchen door. "Aunt Shirley says we got to hurry if we want to get the dressing fixed." He held a stalk of celery. "This has to be cut up. And she says I'm too little to hold a knife."

"She's right," Louette said with a laugh. "Excuse me, folks, my grandson's calling."

Shirley's kitchen was smaller than hers. "Go on outside Shirley. Bucky and I will be there soon as we finish."

"You sure? I might could cut up the onions," asked Shirley.

"Stay in the kitchen and you'd learn my secret recipe. Besides, people will be coming in and those tables have to be ready."

"I can help with that." Shirley went out the door.

Bucky grinned. "You got a secret recipe, Gramma Lou?"

"No, I just want my grandson all to myself." With a stalk of celery in each hand, he rubbed his forehead against her arm. She stirred the cornbread dressing, observing Bucky. *The angle of his jaw, the way his hairline dips before his ears—exactly like my father's.*

A scene from the past sprang up: Her father yelling for them to keep away from the death trap as she and Joseph poked at the gray muck of the sinkhole. She brushed at her eyes. Past gave way to present. Bucky grabbed her around the knees. "Gramma Lou! You're crying!"

She stooped to gather her grandson into her arms. "These are tears of joy, Bucky. I'm crying from happiness." Marj, Shirley, Benjamin, and Mittie's voices floated through the window. Louette had put one p.m. on the invitations. It was almost noon, and she could see the backyard filling up with people, fast.

"You go on outside," she told Bucky. "Turkey broth and cut-up meat mixed in the dressing and zoom, it's in the oven."

In the guest room, Louette put on her new lavender dress with the white collar and her new black patent leather shoes.

At Shirley's back door, Louette paused, looking forward to greeting her family, friends, and townspeople. A crowd stood beside the charred remains of her house.

In a way, the fire, Mama dying, and Joseph leaving are the same. Tragedies I have to live through. All I have left is a pillow sack filled with pictures and a heart filled with memories. She shook her head. *Add Benjamin and his promise of love. Plus a yard full of relatives and friends.* She walked toward the tables and funeral home canopies, humming, "This world is not my home ... I'm just-a-passing through..."

Marj came up and hugged her. "Wish you wouldn't sing that song."

"What would you rather have me sing?"

"Something like 'In the Garden' or 'What a friend we have in Jesus'... "

"My garden is now ashes," Louette said. "And what kind of friend would let your house burn slam down to the ground?"

"I guess that would be a friend who wanted you to start over." Marj walked toward the tables where women placed food containers and men plunked coolers of tea and soft drinks.

Louette spotted two elderly women near where her front door had been yesterday. "How were the beds at the Osceola?" she called out, rushing to hug Aunt Rufus and Aunt Juney.

"Not as soft as mine at home, but all right." Aunt Juney placed a wet kiss on Louette's cheek. The old woman turned and pointed at the rubble, burned and blistered down to nothing. "There's something about a house," she said softly. "It has a spirit. And that one had a friendly spirit." She held Louette by the arm.

"That's the truth if I ever heard it," Louette told her.

"Wherever you go, whatever you do, you'll still have that spirit. What lived in your house lives in you."

Louette cleared her throat and turned to the wizened old woman standing beside Aunt Juney. "Hello, Aunt Rufus," she said. Her aunt wrapped frail arms about Louette's shoulders.

"You can come live with me and Juney over in Sopchoppy."

"Thank you, Aunt Rufus, but I'll be all right. I'll probably stay at the farm with Dan and Mittie while I map out a new life for myself." *What a nice thing for Aunt Rufus to say. They're kind, but old and set in their ways. They couldn't put up with me full time.*

"Now that Clara's gone, bless her soul," Aunt Rufus wiped her eyes, "maybe you can come see us more often."

"I will, Aunt Rufus. I promise." Louette and her aunts walked over to the coffee table.

"We brought chicken and dumplings," Aunt Rufus said in her soft voice. "Hope it's all right."

"Your dumplings are always the best," Louette told her.

Marj was approached by a rotund man who spoke from around an armful of doughnut boxes. "Give 'em these until the big feed, then we'll eat all them fancy desserts. Compliments of Geneva Bakery."

"None in the world better." Marj took the boxes and put them on the table. "Can't wait to put my mouth around one of those."

A neighbor, Lina Jones, who lived in the beige house next door to Benjamin, carried up a covered basket. "Where do I put these peas and beans?" she asked.

"Oh, Lordy!" Louette slapped her hand on her forehead. "I put the rest of the peas and corn in the shed freezer. We could cook them on Shirley's stove."

"Don't worry, Mama," Marj told her. "I'm sure we'll have enough. Here, take a doughnut."

"No thank you, I ate one of those things, I'd get to be as big as Shirley flopping all over the place."

Shirley walked up, her arms full. "Don't you be talking about me behind my back, Louette Kelly. Greet the visitors. Marj and I have our parts under control."

Louette approached Laverne and Jasper standing beside the ruins of the house, staring in shock over the roasted remains of the kitchen. "I knew you'd come!" She hugged them.

"What a dreadful thing to happen, Lou, and the night before your big party, too!" Jasper cocked a wary eye at the sky. "Sure hope it don't rain on your wake. There's a cloud easing up on the east looks like it might be totin' a gully-washer."

"It'd better not. That ash pile would turn into an even bigger mess."

"Lou, you've lost your house here." Laverne reached for her hand. "You could live with us. Apalachicola's not too far from Geneva."

"It's nice of you," said Louette. "But I'll figure out something. Soon's it all settles down."

Miz Gumby stood beside the tent, sipping coffee. "I could take you in, Lou. I'd be proud to have the company."

"Thank you." Louette carefully mouthed the words so Miz Gumby could read her lips. "I appreciate your concern. But I couldn't do that to you."

Bucky grabbed Louette around the legs. "But where will you live, Gramma Lou?"

Louette grinned at her grandson, so alive, so bubbly. "Actually, I thought about fixing up the old shed."

"That'd be great! Gramma Lou! I could live here with you. We could play with all the old stuff."

Marj measured coffee for another fifty cups. "Not likely, young man." At Bucky's expression, she chuckled. "But wherever Gramma Lou is, we'll visit her."

"You promise?"

"Yes."

"Lots?"

"Don't you believe me?"

"Well, I'm not always sure." Bucky hung his head.

"Bucky, we'll see your grandmother Lou as often as we can."

Bucky sighed and hugged Louette around the waist. *He's wrinkling my only Sunday dress, but I ain't complaining.*

"So how is the world's greatest grandson this morning?" It was Etheline carrying a dish covered with a white napkin.

"Bucky, give Etheline one of those hugs," Louette directed. He hid behind her.

"He may not be in the mood." Etheline smiled warmly at Bucky, who offered a tentative smile. "Ta, dah!" She held up the dish. "Clara's famous Southern spinach dash poke! By Etheline! Cooked it myself!"

"No way!" Shirley walked up. "You actually cooked poke sallet?"

"I did and put sliced boiled eggs on top."

"I thought you were joking."

"Etheline Powers does not jest, especially about something I do as seldom as prepare food to eat." Her eyes were serious. "I thought about making Marjorie Rawlings' Cross Creek okra, but decided against it, because I wasn't sure this crowd would appreciate hollandaise sauce."

Louette spoke up. "You should have fixed it; you might have been surprised."

A woman in a red, green, and yellow turban, her ample figure hemmed in by a purple dashiki, bustled across the yard carrying a huge metal pot. She put it down, a scowl on her round, dimpled face. "Best collard greens in five counties!"

Shirley plunked the pan of turkey dressing onto the table. "Why, it's Racie Mae Williams! I thought Etheline didn't never let you off from work!"

"Sometimes she do." The scowl flashed to a wide grin.

"Come here, girl, gimmie a hug!"

"Didn't know Shirley and Racie Mae were so close," said Etheline. "Did you?"

"They picked at each other something awful when they both worked at Chapman's," said Louette. "I guess they fought enough to become fast friends."

"Sure happens sometimes."

"Great to see you, Lou." The large woman turned Shirley loose and grabbed Louette.

"How you doing, Racie Mae?"

"Fine as frog hair. You look a little peaked, though. But then you got a big pile of reasons." She looked at the burnt spot. "Boy! You shoulda let folks know your house was gonna burn down—we coulda roasted a ton of fattenin' pigs and held us a great big barbecue."

"Next time I'll do that," said Louette. *Might as well laugh as cry. No way to turn back the clock.*

A crew of men led by Benjamin and Warren Roberts had put down posts and planks and covered them with stretched chicken wire to make a long table across part of Louette's backyard and on into Shirley's.

"Let's see what people brought," Louette suggested to Etheline. They strolled the long line being rapidly covered with bowls and platters.

"A hundred yards of dishes; salmonella in every bite," said Etheline.

"You don't have to eat it if you don't want to." Louette scowled.

"Oh, I fully intend to eat all of it I can. I'm going to eat 'til I pop."

"These fellowship hall tables are for desserts," Marj ordered as women brought up covered dishes.

"Bet you can't tell what's in the containers," Etheline challenged.

"What are we betting?"

"What about each guess you miss, you give Benjamin a kiss?"

Louette looked around. Where was Benjamin? She didn't like discussing what she did with Benjamin. *That's our own business*, she thought. "What about I give Bucky a kiss for the missed ones?"

"You're on." Etheline pointed. "Start with that one and go down the line."

"Chicken casserole, fried chicken, ham, ham dressing, turkey, turkey dressing, pole beans, potato salad, black-eyed peas, purple-hull peas, zipper peas, Ferris peas."

"Wait! What are Ferris peas, again?"

"They were named after one of the neighbors. You sure don't know much. Or you just missed a lot by going up the East Coast."

A tall, dark-skinned man wearing overalls put a huge pot on the table among the vegetables. "Sweet English peas and new potatoes," he said proudly.

"Well, if it's not Elijah Finney," cried Etheline.

"Best produce farmer around. Wouldn't you know he'd have sweet peas and new potatoes before anybody else," beamed Louette.

"Hi, Lou. So this is how Etheline looks growed up."

"I grew up a long time ago," Etheline told him, putting her hands on her hips. *Just like when she was a young'un*, thought Louette.

"Little Miss Rich Girl livin' on a hill. If her mama don't kiss her, nobody will," sang Elijah. The elderly friends were transported back to the playground in elementary school. Their hilarity almost drove the stench of her burned house from Louette's nose.

"Y'all want to help blow up these balloons?" Shirley, Racie Mae, and Bucky appeared with bags of balloons, tin whistles and birthday hats.

"I never heard of no balloons at a wake," Louette protested.

"I never heard of no wake for a still-living person, either," Shirley answered. "It don't hurt to have a few balloons. Makes the place look festive. Besides, it's your birthday on Monday, Lou."

"Enjoy yourself." Etheline patted her on the shoulder.

"I am. I am." *Much as I can beside my burnt-down house.*

Benjamin walked up holding something behind him, a grin as wide as the Choctawhatchee River.

Mayor Roberts looked tired and worn out. "Greetings," he called out, as he pulled Preacher Ed to the microphone. "I'm turning over these ceremonies to my friend Ed. He's by far a better politician than me."

"I doubt that, Mayor, but you did work yourself into the ground cleaning up Louette's burnt down house," a voice called out. Those gathered clapped and cheered.

Preacher Ed held up his hand. "Thank you, Mayor. Before we begin this repast, I'd like to hear a few words from Lou."

Warren shouldn't have left it up to Preacher Ed. He'll make it as much like a real wake as he can.

"You don't have to tell these folks how wonderful I am," Louette scolded him. "I ain't really dead yet." Laughter rolled around the crowd. "We are having my wake so I can see my relatives and friends while I am still alive and I can gather my roses while I may."

"To judge from all these people, you have many roses about you."

"And a few thorns," a voice called out. Laughter again.

Benjamin, in a blue polo shirt and tan cotton pants, his bald head shining, placed a bouquet of roses in Louette's arms. She glanced at the bouquet on the coffee table. *Oh, well, one can't get too many roses.*

"Mom, you're blushing," laughed Marj. She took the flowers.

"I'll get a vase." Shirley bustled away. "Don't do anything fun until I get back."

Probate Judge Simon O'Connor, sprigs of red hair sticking out over his ears, marched to the center of the gathering. He propped his left elbow on his stomach, which looked as if he had swallowed a basketball. His right hand raised a plastic tumbler. "I'd like to offer a toast," he said.

Simon was certainly taken with himself. He enjoyed the sound of his own voice but could look a person in the eye and make them believe they had his undivided attention. The crowd quieted. "I wish to propose a humble toast to our illustrious friend Louette Kelly upon the occasion of her untimely wake."

He brought his hand down and peered into his plastic cup. "What is this confounded liquid?"

"Probably a soft drink," Marj told him.

"I can't give a toast with a soft drink, and I can't use anything stronger, for obvious reasons." He nodded at Preacher Ed, handing the cup to Marj. "Sweet tea, please."

With the proper liquid in hand, the judge raised the tea high and proclaimed in his courtroom voice: "To Louette, who had the courage to do what she thought best in the face of blatant and obstinate obstructionism."

"Hear, hear," called out several voices.

"Now I know what you are, Judge" whispered Etheline teasingly. "A blatant obstructionist."

Preacher Ed touched a finger to his lips and frowned at Etheline and said, "Shhhhhh."

"Louette Kelly persevered. And that's what we need more of these days: perseverance." Judge O'Connor harrumphed loudly, as if preparing more words.

A voice called out. "Hurry up, Judge. We ain't et yet."

"Be quiet," another said.

"I'll drink tea to Louette's courage."

"Me, too," a voice added. "And to some of them other big words the judge said."

Aunt Rufus stood. "I propose a toast to Louette because she's not afraid to be old," she said, modestly ducking her head.

If she only knew. I am totin' a great big fear right now on my shoulders. Folks just can't see it.

"Hope she lives as long as you, Aunt Rufus," someone called out.

Louette remembered more lines of Robert Herrick's poem stuck in her mother's Bible: *"The same flower that smiles today, tomorrow will be dying."*

"The choir is ready to sing." Preacher Ed turned to a robed group standing in rows on a tarpaulin beside last year's garden spot. "What would you like to hear?"

"That's easy. 'In The Garden,' and 'I'll Meet You in the Morning on the Bright Riverside'," Marj called out.

"We can only sing one or the food might spoil," said Preacher Ed, a twinkle in his eye. "What about 'When the Roll is Called Up Yonder'?" He pulled out a chair and motioned for Louette to sit.

She shook her head. "I'm not ready for that roll call yet. Could we all sing with the choir?"

"You got the right idea," said Preacher Ed.

Racie Mae's voice rang out. "Let's sing something happy." She turned to the choir. "Ya'll know 'Joshua Fit the Battle'?"

"We do," roared back a collective sound. A pained look came over Preacher Ed's face.

"Whooee," answered Racie Mae in perfect pitch, then as she began to belt out the words, a symphony of voices swelled until they rose over the entire neighborhood, echoing all the way to the river junction.

"Joshua fit the battle of Jer-i-co, Jer-i-co, Jer-i-co, Joshua fit the battle of Jer-i-co..."

Bet they can hear Racie Mae's champion collard-cooking voice over five counties. Louette joined in on "til the walls came tumbulin' down, down, down."

Before Preacher Ed could stop her, Racie Mae swung into "Jeremiah was a bullfrog, was a good friend of mine... joy to the world... joy to you and me."

Even Bucky mouthed the words he didn't know as music radiated to celebrate the wake of one Louise Etta Kelly, still alive, on a fine Saturday afternoon in May. Louette sang with those around her. *Sounds of happiness,* she thought.

Preacher Ed held up his hands, then slowly brought them down. Those gathered knew what the gesture meant.

The singing stopped. The minister's hand popped up in the air again. "Time for your speech, Lou."

"Thank you." Louette's voice trembled. "A real wake couldn't have been more heart-warming. I thank all those who came, those who brought this pile of scrumptious looking food. I've got plenty of time to consider my housing problem. Tomorrow. I'll think about it tomorrow."

"Pretty good speech, Scarlett," a voice called.

"I have made one decision," Louette said. "Next year, Lord willing, if I'm still alive, my wake will be held right here on the second Saturday in May. You can be sure you are all invited."

"I'll be here!" Bucky yelled, waving a red balloon.

"Hooray! Me, too," called out Shirley.

Louette, her speech over, stood silent for a moment.

"One more thing," Mittie's voice reached out. "We can't have a wake without an Irish blessing." She pushed Dan forward.

"Gospel music and Irish prayers," muttered Etheline.

Under what was left of the blistered rain tree, a timid, red-faced Dan shuffled his feet. He held up a hand for silence. Louette took Benjamin's hand, and he took Marj's who took Bucky's. Bucky's other hand joined Dan's. All the guests responded in kind until relatives, friends and neighbors were in a big circle holding hands.

Dan's voice, thick with emotion, quoted the familiar words: "May the road rise to meet you. May the wind be always at your back. May the sun shine warm upon your face. The rains fall soft upon your fields. And, until we meet again, may God hold you in the hollow of His hand."

Shirley's highpitched voice called out: "And when the devil comes to fetch you, may you already be gone." Waves of laughter rolled across the yard.

Louette saw the preacher eyeing the uncovering of the food. "Say the blessing before this gets any more ridiculous," she whispered to him.

"We are so happy to be gathered here today," Preacher Ed called out. "If you will bow your heads... Thank you Lord, for this food, bless it and those who prepared it, those of us who are about to partake of it, and bless us to thy service. Amen."

Louette caught the eye of Aunt Rufus. "That Preacher Ed sure knows his particulars about food," the old lady observed. "The women at the long table just uncovered the last bowl."

Just like a tree that's planted by the water,
I shall not be moved.

Chapter Fourteen

Louette sat with Benjamin at her decrepit picnic table which had been dragged to Shirley's backyard. "It wouldn't have bothered me if the fire had burned up this old table," she said.

It made her happy to see friends and relatives eating, laughing and talking. The people she cared about most were right here, against the backdrop of her burned-out house.

Lively voices of children rang above the murmur of grownup conversation and the clink of spoons dipping into pans and bowls. Bucky, in the middle of it all, called out, "Mom, there are two little girls over here, and they look just alike. They cry just alike, too." The twins were howling at the tops of their lungs. *So much for them learning to be sociable.*

"I haven't seen you in a long time," she heard Jasper tell a cousin. "You still live near Bonnet Pond?"

"Yeah. Think I last saw you at a homecoming at New Zion. How long's it been?"

"Don't know; maybe thirty years? Time lopes along like a yearling. How you been?"

"Fair to middlin'," the man answered. "I'm gettin' better though."

"Bonnet Pond?" Etheline walked up with a full plate. "I always wondered why they called that place out in the middle of nowhere Bonnet Pond."

"The pond had snake bonnets around it—you know, pitcher plants. Those tall plants that close their little top hats when they catch a bug," Jasper told her. "I don't think they're there anymore, though. DDT likely got 'em."

"What a shame," said Etheline. "Did you try the tenderloin with pepper jelly?"

"Mittie brought that," Jasper bragged. "She makes the best pepper jelly of anybody."

Bucky ran by, Etheline following, then they veered toward the desserts.

The sorrow of losing her home lay heavy on Louette, but contentment and pleasure at the gathering of friends and relatives was topmost on her mind. Joy surpassed sadness.

Benjamin sat across from her, happily ladling food into his mouth. He winked at her and her heart skipped. She felt heat rise in her face. Bucky plopped down on the bench and leaned against her, meringue on his upper lip and only the Lord knew what else on his shirt. "Lemon pie is my favorite," he said. "What did you like best?"

Louette smiled. "I can't make up my mind between the red velvet cake and the coconut pineapple pie."

"I like the fudge cake too," said Benjamin.

Etheline walked up and then settled in beside them. Her plate was not so full anymore. "The butterbeans are my favorite of everything—meats, vegetables, desserts. You can't buy butterbeans like these in a store. I tried in Boston. The packages all say lima beans, but they don't taste sweet like the ones grown in gardens and frozen as soon as they're shelled and blanched."

Louette rubbed Bucky's back. "When I was little, I piled my plate with butterbeans and chocolate cake at homecomings and reunions. Didn't touch other things like potato salad or turnip greens with roots until I had eaten all the butterbeans and chocolate cake I wanted."

Etheline laughed. "One time up north when I was really homesick, I looked for black-eyed peas to cook for New Year's luck. I found a package with the words 'blackeye beans.' I stood right there in that store and cussed the whole northern United States and their disdain for peas."

"You didn't buy them? New Year's is not New Year's without black-eyed peas."

"Oh, I bought em all right. There was no such thing as hog jowl, but I put a little bit of bacon in them and they tasted almost like the ones from home. You make do when you get sent away." Etheline got a faraway look in her eyes. "Thank you, Lou, for holding your wake." She stood up.

"It was a good idea, wasn't it?" Louette looked at Bucky's face. "This boy looks like he could use a nap— maybe a bath first."

Bucky sat up straight and rubbed at his eyes. "I am not dirty." He swiped at his mouth. "And I'm not sleepy. I'm just tired from eating so much good stuff."

Gordon, ever the banker in any situation, however happy or dire, walked up. "Don't worry about rebuilding the house," he told Louette as he placed his full plate on the picnic table. "It's a good thing you borrowed money for the new roof. I checked the policy in your file and your whole house is covered. You can build a new house and we can hold the note with the same interest and payment."

"That's good to know. If I hadn't gotten the loan for the roof, I wouldn't have the money to re-build," said Louette. "I've got to roll all this around in my mind. Seeing so many of my folks and friends has taken the edge off losing my house. Maybe I ought to rethink that insurance stuff."

A smile played around Gordon's mouth. "Maybe you should," he said.

"Marj would agree to that."

"What's your favorite dish, Gordo?" Etheline asked him.

"Look at my third plateful and guess," he said, scooping a spoonful into his mouth. "Chicken pie, potato salad, peas, beans, collards, turnip greens." He peered at his plate. "I don't know what's in that casserole, but it looked good. Best party I have ever been to. Calling it a wake was a unique way of getting all these people here, Lou. Wonder if my family and friends would respond in the same way."

"Marj thought I was crazy, and look at her now," Louette pointed. Marj stood with classmates from long ago, belting out a loud laugh.

"Sometimes it works out best to be a little crazy," Etheline observed. "I never had the nerve Lou has."

Shirley sat down on the other side of Benjamin. "You look real nice in regular clothes. Maybe we could go eat at the Osceola Hotel some evening."

"I'd like that if Lou would come with us." Louette grinned, then turned her head, pretending not to hear.

The sun was far from setting when the crowd began to thin out. "We need to leave now, Lou, so we can get home before dark," Aunt Rufus said.

Aunt Juney sighed happily. "We sure put a dent in them vittles. It was a fine party, Lou. Don't think I'll need to eat for a week."

"You could stay another night at the Osceola," Marj suggested. "We'd love to visit with you some more."

"One night in somebody else's bed is enough for me," said Aunt Rufus. "Remember, you are welcome in our home any time, Marj. You too, Lou, and especially Bucky."

"We'll remember," Louette told her. "I am so glad you were able to make it."

Laverne and Jasper hugged Louette. "We'll see you next year or, better yet, come down to Apalach to see us again."

"Come with her," Jasper told Benjamin. "We'll go floundering this time."

"I'd like that." Benjamin and Louette shared a smile. "From now on, I'm sticking to this woman like glue. Long as she'll let me."

Clyde walked up. "Next year, I'm starting off with desserts," he said. "There wasn't enough room in my stomach for some of everything."

Guests carried away hampers, coolers, boxes, and bags. Soon the backyard was almost empty. "Looks like they all left at the same time," Clyde remarked, pulling full trash bags from cans in the yard. He piled them beside the street.

"I'll help you," Benjamin said, reaching out for trash bags.

Suddenly the tired Bucky became animated. "Can I pop the balloons now, Mama?"

"May I," corrected Marj.

"I didn't know you liked to pop balloons," said Bucky.

"Pop all you want," Shirley told him. "Come on, I'll help you."

With each pop, Louette thought of taps played at her father's funeral. Soldiers had stood in a row. One held a flag, one a rifle, and the other a bugle. The sound rang out over the cemetery, the woods, and fields beyond, with finality. Afterwards the soldiers gave a folded flag to her mother. Sorrow and joy struggled within Louette again.

Willie's son James sat down beside her at the picnic table. "I wish you'd come back to work at the print shop," he said. "Our bookkeeper wants to retire. We sure would appreciate the help. But I guess you'll want some time to get organized."

"It won't take me long. I'll call you one day next week. Oops, I don't have a phone, and I had just bought an answering machine."

"You can call me from Shirley's or Dan and Mittie's. Or," his eyes twinkled, "from Benjamin's."

Louette heard, but her heart didn't miss a beat. "I promise," she said.

As James walked away, Louette watched Benjamin help Clyde stack trash bags. Her fondness for Benjamin had grown by an amazing rate. She hadn't thought she could open her heart to any man but Joseph. *It's a good feeling*, she thought. Benjamin walked up. "Is this seat taken?"

"It's been waiting for you," Louette moved over slightly.

He sat beside her. "I think we've about finished the yard. That Clyde is a taskmaster."

Louette leaned against him. "I'm a little tired."

"You have a right, considering what you've been through. I'm sorry your house burned down."

"Definitely a tragedy," Louette shrugged. "But I'll survive—have to after this fine turnout for my wake."

"You know, Louette," said Benjamin, "Your homeless problem could be solved very easily."

"Easily?"

"You could marry me and live right around the corner from here."

"I'd like that," she said wonderingly. "If I only knew where Joseph is, whether he's dead or living off somewhere, if he's happy, then maybe I could turn him loose."

Benjamin's hand tightened on hers. "I take that as a promise," he said.

Clyde called out, "Could you help me again?" and Benjamin rose.

"Thank you," he said to Louette. She looked around to realize almost everyone had gone home.

Miz Gumby walked up. "The backyard looks almost lonesome now. I think I'll watch Bucky and Shirley pop balloons."

"Pop a few yourself," Louette suggested, careful to mouth the words so Miz Gumby could see them.

"I'm too old for that. I'll watch," said Miz Gumby.

"A person is never too old to pop balloons." Louette watched Benjamin and Clyde finish lining up the bulging trash bags along the street for a full block.

While Benjamin checked the edge of the yard, Clyde came over to the picnic table where Louette sat. He brushed his hands on his uniform pants and stood in front of Louette, shifting from one foot to the other.

Looks like he wants to tell me something. But what? "You found any pictures that might be Joseph?" Louette moved over as Marj plopped down beside her.

"Clyde's been checking records on unidentified people who died," Louette told Marj. "He'll show us any pictures he finds that favor Joseph."

Marj jumped up. "Clyde, what a wonderful idea."

"Nothing's showed up yet that makes me think it might be Mr. Joseph. But, I'm looking," He shifted his feet.

"Thank you, thank you, Clyde." Marj grabbed his hand, then threw her arms around him. "Why didn't we think of that all those years ago?'

"I don't know," said Clyde. He stepped backward then walked away.

"Oh, Mama," said Marj. "Wouldn't it be wonderful if Clyde figured out what happened to Dad?"

"It would. He doesn't sound too hopeful about the pictures though."

Marj turned her attention to the jars Louette had mentioned earlier. "Gramma Clara's jars are in the shed, aren't they Mama? When can we get them out?" she whispered. "I want to see how much she saved."

"I wouldn't be too impatient; you might be disappointed in the amount. I told you it's Mama's money, and it don't matter to me." She got up and walked toward the entrance to the shed.

Marj shook her head. "That's your money."

"I don't want it," retorted Louette, alarmed at her words. "Or I don't think I do. I'll tell you one thing I want right now."

"What?"

"For you to bring out that chair with the rawhide bottom. I'd like to set on it beside the shed, quiet and peaceful; my feet are throbbing from these new shoes."

"I still want to see how much money is in the fruit jars." Marj did her mother's bidding.

"Money in fruit jars?" Clyde walked up, winding a long strip of crime-scene tape into a ball.

"Now, don't you go reporting me to the Internal Revenue Service over Mama's money." Louette stood and boxed him on the shoulder.

"But, Lou, your mama's dead."

"It ain't none of your business. Mama said she saved her spare change from the grocery money. And don't you go telling anybody, or I'll sic Sheriff Messer on you."

Marj plunked the old chair behind Louette. "Sit," she ordered. "Don't fuss at Clyde, and don't go staring at that pile of burnt-up house. Smile."

"My poor old tired mouth is slam wore out from talking all day. It may not want to smile."

"Just tell me where the jars of money are," insisted Marj. "I can check it out. That money may be too moldy to use by now anyway."

"If it's real old, it might be worth more than face value." Clyde continued to roll the yellow tape. "Lou, what about inheritance tax? Shouldn't you pay an inheritance tax if Miz Clara left it to you?"

"My land, Clyde, you are like a bull dog; when you get something started you can't let it go. You come up with the most gosh-awful things. I wish Marj hadn't brought up the jars in front of you. Did anybody ever tell you you're a meddler?" Louette asked.

"All the time," Clyde answered with a chuckle. "Especially Sheriff Messer."

Benjamin walked up. "I finished checking the area, Clyde. No more trash."

"Good," Clyde told him, looking at Marj.

"Come on, Mom, quit stalling," said Marj. "We need to check out Gramma Clara's savings jars, whether you want them or not."

Judge O'Connor had zeroed in on the discussion. He rubbed the stubble on his chin. "Actually, Lou, by law, you would be responsible for an inheritance tax to the Internal Revenue Service, if the money adds up to a sizable sum."

"The infernal revenue service, if you ask me. I didn't inherit the money. Mama saved it. It ain't mine."

"Half of it might rightfully be Dan's," said Judge O'Connor. "If he wants to claim it."

Louette shook her head. "Goodness gracious, Lordy, mercy, me. Better to leave it right where it is. Mama didn't mention any jars with money in her will. I guess she forgot about them. Next thing you'll tell me I got to put Mama's will through probate again and get me a lawyer. It's common knowledge that once lawyers get their fingers into your business, they wind up with all the money. It would be better for me if she'd of buried the jars under the house like she started to."

"But, Lou, if she'd buried the money under the house it would be good and gone by now, with the fire and all," Dan told her. "I don't need the money. Mittie and I are doing fine. You need it, now you're wiped out."

"I am not 'wiped out.' See what's going on? We're arguing over money in jars. Money makes trouble." She looked thoughtful. "Most of the time it does... maybe Mama meant it for an emergency. Guess I do sort of have an emergency here." She pointed at what was left of her home.

Benjamin moved behind the rawhide chair and settled his hands on Louette's shoulders. She turned and looked up at him, acknowledging the gesture.

"Where is the money, Mama?" Marj was adamant. "Clyde is an officer of the law. Simon is a judge. Benjamin's not going to tattle it around. Tell me where it is, and we'll drag it out and count it."

"The jars are in my grandfather's World War One Army trunk in the south corner of the shed." She looked up. "Watch out for spiders."

Etheline held the door as Benjamin and Clyde moved dusty articles from Marj's path. "What if the trunk is locked? How do we open it if we find it?" Benjamin asked. Judge O'Connor followed close behind.

"I doubt it's locked. Gramma Clara never locked anything," said Marj. "But it's probably rusted shut. No telling how old the jars are."

Louette got up and eased into the shed. She realized her curiosity had gotten the better of her. She turned and walked back outside.

"Here's a footlocker," Clyde called out.

"That's Joseph's from the Korean conflict," she hollered back. "They didn't call it a war, but the boys who came home said it felt like a war to them. It's newer than the trunk, but you're getting close."

Gordon walked up to the shed. "I've been using Shirley's phone," he said. "What did I miss?"

"Marj's been having a hissy fit to get into Mama's money jars." Louette answered.

"Money jars?"

"Wait and they'll drag out the trunk and you can see for yourself." Clyde and Benjamin brought out the dried leather trunk, rusted metal bands barely holding it together, with Marj leading the way.

"Is it heavy?" Marj asked.

"Not so heavy," said Benjamin. "Just cumbersome. The handle on my end broke off."

"You were right, Lou," Judge O'Connor told her. "It wasn't locked."

When the battered trunk was placed on the grass, Benjamin leaned over and pulled the lid back. The leather had dried out long ago and was split in several places. Clara had wrapped the jars in newspaper pages. "A casual observer would think it was filled with canned vegetables or pickles," said Etheline. "How many of your mother's money-hoarding jars are there?"

As they were lined up on the grass, Marj inspected each jar. "Drag the picnic table over here," she told Benjamin. "We can count the money on that."

"Looks like too much to count," observed Gordon with a practical eye. "Why don't we take it to the bank and lock it up, then the tellers can count it when they come in to work Monday."

"I'd hoped to be back home on Monday," said Marj. "I wanted to know how much there is tonight, or at least have an educated guess."

"Count one jar, then multiply it by how many there are, then," said Gordon.

"It's too dark to count that old money. Let's do it tomorrow. I'm exhausted." Louette intervened.

"Aren't you just a little bit curious?" Etheline obviously was.

Judge O'Connor shook Gordon's hand. "Counting one jar to get an educated estimate is a good idea."

"It would be safe in the bank, Lou," said Clyde. "We could put it in a plastic bag and I could put this yellow tape all around it."

"Then we could put a note on it that says 'Property of Louise Etta Kelly,'" added Gordon. "We can place the trunk and money in the vault. It won't be tampered with and can be counted on Monday."

Clyde crammed the newspaper wrappings into a trash bag as Marj lifted the jars one by one and placed them on the picnic table.

"Wow, look at these newspaper pages, some of them are really old." Nobody paid any attention to Benjamin, except Louette.

"You're right," she said. "We ought to take these papers to the library, instead of throwing them away."

All other eyes were aimed directly at Marj. She had emptied one jar onto the picnic table. Coins bounced out. Paper money was rolled up. As she smoothed out the ones, fives, tens, fifties and a few hundreds, Gordon, the banker, whistled.

"I thought she put change in the jars, Lou," Dan said. "Where'd the bills come from?"

"I don't know, Dan. I knew she saved money in jars. I didn't ask her about it. How many times do I have to tell ya'll it's not my money?"

"How many jars?" asked Gordon.

"Twenty," Benjamin said. "Look, this one's only half full. Your mother must have gotten sick before she finished filling this one, Lou."

Louette perked up. "I could use the empty jars for canning peaches and pears."

Marj wouldn't let the others help count. Soon it was obvious she was tired. Etheline left the picnic table to stand beside Lou's chair. "I didn't want to count money, anyway," she said. "I'm worn out. Think I'll go home, Lou."

"Stay a little while longer," said Louette. "They'll all run down to the bank. Just watch."

She was right. It didn't take long for Marj to realize that counting all the money could take hours. "I suppose what you said makes sense," Marj told Gordon. "Let's go lock it in the vault."

"We are an honest bank," Gordon told her solemnly. "We pride ourselves on our trustworthiness. My conscience wouldn't let me do anything dishonest. Your money will be safe, I promise."

The squad car was full, with Clyde, Marj, Gordon, Dan and the judge. Mittie and Etheline stayed. Benjamin sat at the picnic table, cushioning his head on his arms. "You ladies had the right idea to stay. I am bushed," he said.

Let the circle be unbroken,
Bye and bye, Lord, bye and bye.
There's a better home a-waitin'
In the sky, Lord, in the sky.

Chapter Fifteen

Cleanup crews had left. The funeral home tents, church tables and chairs were gone. Louette sat in the rawhide-bottom chair, watching the sun slide down behind the trees. She watched Benjamin, asleep, with his head cushioned on his arms. She felt a rush of warmth in her veins, a promise. There was her dear, dear Benjamin, close enough to reach out and touch.

Underneath, Louette's sorrow lay dormant, muffled by her awe and delight in knowing that so many loved ones had shown up for her wake. "It was wonderful having so many come to visit," she said. *Love crept through the cracks when I least expected it.* Happiness was like a warm blanket snuggled around her.

Lights came on around the storage building and in Shirley's back yard. Behind Shirley's house, Louette could see Miz Gumby watching from the back stoop as Shirley and Bucky ran about grabbing at fireflies. "Guess they popped all the balloons. Now they're harassing the fireflies."

Louette, Etheline, and Mittie looked at Benjamin whose breath made little puffing sounds. "Looks like he's enjoying his sleep," said Etheline.

The sound of the county police car and excited voices returning to the yard woke Benjamin. He snorted. "I must have dozed," he said, and stood up.

"The jars and the money are all locked in the bank vault," Marj announced.

"Safe as safe can be," said Gordon.

"We tried to drop the judge off at home, but he wouldn't stay there," Dan said.

Marj went toward Shirley's yard where she and Bucky helped gather up the bright colored pieces of the burst balloons.

Miz Gumby sat down beside Louette. An uncommonly quiet Clyde stood before her, rolling his official police hat around and around. He cleared his throat several times. *I wish he'd spit out what he's got to say. He's held it in long enough.*

"Those things Gordo said about his conscience," Clyde announced. "I've got one of them, too, and it's been hounding me for years."

"Why would your conscience bother you, Clyde? There ain't a mean bone in your body."

"I done something really bad, Lou, a long time ago and it won't let me be."

"I knew about you and that Parkston girl," said Dan. "What y'all did on the river bank wasn't THAT bad. She'd already been with just about everybody in the county. I wouldn't worry about her none."

"You don't understand, Dan. It's worse than the Parkston girl."

"I don't know how anything could be worse than that bucktoothed girl," said Gordon. "Good thing her folks moved her off from here. She was trouble with a capital T."

"Y'all ain't listening." Clyde was clearly agitated. He waved his arms about. "I got to tell Lou something, and it's hard for it to come out."

"Okay," said Louette. "What have you done? Tell us."

"You won't be mad at me, Lou?"

"It'd be hard for me to be mad at you, Clyde. I'm so grateful you're still trying to find Joseph after all these years. What is it?"

The deputy shifted from one foot to the other and tightened his fingers around the brim of his hat. His eyes blinked in deep, tired sockets. "Lou, Mr. Joseph didn't park his truck at the depot all them years ago. I did."

Louette pushed herself up from the rawhide chair and stood stock-still in amazement, wide-eyed, sucking in his words like a drowning person struggling for air. "What?" Louette's mouth dropped. She held her breath.

"I'm sorry, Lou," said Clyde. "You said you wouldn't get mad."

"I'm not mad, Clyde. I'm shocked. Go ahead."

"I been wanting to tell you for a long time, Lou. I skipped school and walked along the dirt road out by your folks' farm. I saw Mr. Joseph's truck parked beside the barn with the keys in it. He taught me how to drive in that truck. I couldn't resist getting into it. Then I drove it some. About lunch time I parked it by the train station and walked back to school. I never told nobody. Mr. Joseph didn't take no train. He must have walked away." Clyde looked relieved to get the burden off his chest.

Louette wiped her face with both hands, shaking her head. "It's hard to believe you'd do something like that, Clyde. Why didn't you tell me? All these years I been thinking Joseph left on a train. How did he leave? You said he walked?"

"I don't know," said Clyde. "I couldn't figure it out either. Maybe he hitch-hiked or something, I don't know about that. But I do know I was the one put the truck at the train station. Can you forgive me?"

"I'm trying to understand, Clyde." Louette reached for the back of the cowhide chair, then folded over, tumbling forward in a faint. Dan's crutches clattered to the ground as he dived under her, breaking her fall.

She came to and heard Benjamin calling, "Lou! Lou! Wake up!"

Etheline rubbed her arms; Mittie fanned her. Miz Gumby had run to her house and back. She reached out a hand. "Smelling salts," she said. "Put this under her nose."

Louette looked up at a ring of concerned faces. She tried to rise, but too many arms held her. "Y'all turn me loose," she said. "I'm all right. Just surprised out of my skull. Leave me alone."

"Miz Gumby's concoction worked," said Etheline.

"Come on, Lou, stand up." Benjamin grabbed Dan's crutch and held it out to Louette, then helped her pull herself up.

"Y'all quit staring at me; I'm all right. You'd think ya'll had never seen nobody faint before." She looked around. The past pushed against her. A sense of dread swirled around her like fog. So many years. It still mattered. Or did it? How long she had hidden from life behind the memory of Joseph. Whether he had left by railway or walking wasn't the main point. He was gone. And she had used that emptiness as a shield against the pain that kept her from an appreciation of her own existence. When had joy left her, expectation, gratitude, and hope?

"Did I hear what I thought I heard?"

Clyde cleared his throat. "Mr. Joseph didn't leave his truck at the train station way back then. He couldn't have. I borrowed his truck and drove it there and left it right where it was found, at the depot." He was clearly frightened. "I didn't mean to make you faint."

"You better be telling the truth." Dan aimed his crutch at Clyde's head.

"It is the truth Mr. Dan, I swear." Clyde looked at Louette. "I tried to tell y'all before, but it just wouldn't come out, especially when the whole state put out a search for Mr. Joseph. If I'd a told the truth, my Pa, and everybody else in this county, would've killed me."

Louette stared into space. Dazed, she let the fact of what Clyde had said sink in. She held tightly to Benjamin's hand.

Her brother made menacing moves toward the deputy. "Dan, don't get so het up at Clyde," Louette told him. "He was just a teenager. He'd have no reason to lie about it now. Tell us Clyde, exactly as it happened."

"I was bored out of my skull at school, so I took off. I followed the river for awhile and then hit the paved road. When I came by Mr. Dan's farm, I saw Mr. Joseph's truck sittin' there by the barn with the keys in it. I didn't think he'd mind if I sat in it a little while." He looked wildly about as if expecting someone to clobber him.

"I didn't mean to take it. I just wanted to drive it around some. It cranked real good, like it was all tuned up and ready to go. I drove it into town before I got scared. What if my daddy found out I had taken it? He'd be mad as a wet settin' hen. And, Mr. Joseph, too. I didn't mean no harm. I just wanted to drive the truck."

Louette let out a long whoosh. "Go ahead," she told Clyde.

"I parked by the depot and walked to school. I got back before the bus loaded. Don't think anybody even suspected me." He released a deep sigh, then held out his hands, palms up. Pleading. "It was a bad thing for me to do, and I tried to put it out of my mind. But I couldn't forget it, especially when the whole county thought Mr. Joseph had run away. Maybe he did. But he didn't do it in that truck. I put his truck there, myself. I am sorry." Clyde cried like a child.

Dan's slow drawl broke in. "Our old mule, Whistler, went missing that day, too. We all thought he took off somewheres, but we never did find him. We figured he had run off. Maybe, with all the fuss over Joseph, I hadn't thought too much about the missing mule. I should've put two and two together better."

Dan pulled out his handkerchief and wiped his face. "Durndest thing. I found a button out there awhile back, when I was shoring up that fence."

Louette looked at her brother. "What kind of button?"

"Bluish white," answered Mittie. "Not off any of Dan's shirts. It's in my sewing machine drawer."

"Lord a' mighty." Louette stood up. "I worried for years about that loose button on Joseph's shirt. I meant to sew it tighter, but never got around to it. That was the shirt he had on when he disappeared." She wiped her face with her hands. "Lord a' mercy."

Marj walked up with a bag stuffed with trash and little bits of busted balloons. "What are you saying about my dad?"

For a long moment Louette looked at her daughter as if she didn't know her. This was too much information, too fast. The years rolled before her eyes, like film flickering on a screen. She cleared her throat, then looked her daughter square in the face. "That maybe Joseph didn't run away from us as we have believed all these years."

"What are you talking about? Daddy's been gone a long time. That the memory still hurts is because you have been keeping it alive, keeping it like a wall between us and between you and everybody else, including Benjamin, who loves you. For God's sake, can't you let it go? Can't you just let it be?"

"Stop!" Louette held up her hand. "I'm telling you something we have just now learned. Clyde told us he was the one drove the truck to the depot and left it there. Joseph and the mule out at the farm went missing at the same time."

A vision of the bubbling pit loomed in her imagination; a stink, like sulfur filled her nostrils. She blinked her eyes. "Maybe they somehow both died in the quicksand sinkhole."

Relief swept over her, then excitement and then a strange feeling of peace, like a healing breeze.

Marj stood, dumbfounded. "What? This can't be true." Her eyes searched Louette's face. Marj turned and Benjamin steadied her.

"Can it?" she asked. Benjamin nodded. He helped Marj to sit at the picnic table.

All was quiet, except for the pings as bugs dived onto Shirley's security lamp. Then the sound of Marj sobbing echoed over the yard.

Louette went to her and wrapped her arms around her daughter. "I'm so sorry," she said. "I wish we had known. Life might have been much easier."

Louette looked at Clyde nervously rolling his hat around in his hands. "Life is like that," she said, her voice soft. Benjamin handed a handkerchief to Marj and reached over to clasp Louette's hand.

"Can you forgive me for my bitterness toward you all those years?" Marj asked Louette. "Now that we might know what happened to Daddy, maybe we can start over."

"I'd like that," Louette said. They stood up and wrapped arms around each other with a desperation that had festered for many years. This was a revelation they had needed for a long time.

"I thought you drove him away," said Marj. "I'm so sorry." Louette held on tightly. Benjamin, Dan and Mittie wrapped their arms around the two women. Louette could feel years of hurt and anger sloughing off, like dead skin from a healed wound.

Louette pulled away and turned to Clyde. "Thank you for helping us understand what really happened. I am so relieved."

"I'm sorry I didn't tell you sooner, Lou." Clyde shuffled his feet. "I been trying. I just couldn't get it out. If there was any way I could take it all back, I would. You know that, don't you, Lou? Mr. Dan? Marj?"

"Damndest thing I ever heard," said Etheline. "Wish I had a pencil and paper." She scratched around in her purse.

"I'll call Sheriff Messer," said Clyde.

"What good would that do?" asked Louette. None of it felt real.

"Miz Gumby already called me." The sheriff walked into the yard. "She said Clyde's shocking everybody. Tell me about it."

"I tried to tell Lou before, but I just couldn't, until now." He held out his arms. "Arrest me."

"Hold on here just a minute, Clyde." Sheriff Messer stifled a laugh. "Don't go off half-cocked. Start from the beginning."

"Oh, Lord, deliver us from Clyde's re-recitation," Judge O'Connor butted in. "The mule disappeared at the same time as Joseph. Dan and the rest of us think Joseph and the mule may have gone down in the quicksand sinkhole out at the farm."

"We could find that out," said Sheriff Messer. "It might not be easy, but we could probe the sinkhole to look for Joseph and the mule."

Benjamin put protective arms around Louette and Marj. "They obviously died. Why dig them up?"

"You don't understand; it's the law," explained Sheriff Messer. "The law says a dead body has to be verified if we can find it. It don't say anything about digging around in a sinkhole. Let me be the judge on legal complications,"

Judge O'Connor broke in. "Could I interject a voice of reason?"

"Do," said Sheriff Messer. "'Bout time somebody did that."

"I can research the law, but since the Florida peninsula is a porous limestone plateau, I doubt you would find anything, even if you try digging in that sinkhole."

Louette spoke up. "It don't make sense. It's been such a long time. I believe Joseph went in there. Him and Dan's mule. We ought to let it be."

"We're agreed on that." Dan reached out a hand to Louette.

Sheriff Messer looked around the gathering. He swiped a hand across his forehead. "I know how treacherous that trembling earth can be. The statute of limitations on a coroner's inquest has long passed."

Gordon cleared his throat. "We've got another matter we need to take care of, uh, on Monday—counting some money in jars."

"Oh," Sheriff Messer laughed. "You found Clara's stash of dough. Aha! That might bring up a few problems itself."

"You knew about Gramma's hidden money?" asked Marj.

"This is a small town," said Sheriff Messer, as if that closed the subject. "Probably not more than a few thousand dollars," he added.

Marj and Gordon looked at one another with arched eyebrows. "Not if you multiply what's in one jar by twenty," said Gordon. "There's a pretty large amount."

"What do you think about all this, Lou?" Judge Simon asked gently.

"I guess I'm too tired to think."

Bucky ran from the far corner of Shirley's yard. "Gramma Lou, Mom, look at the bugs in the jar. They make lights."

"Fireflies," said Marj woodenly.

"Aunt Shirley said they're lightning bugs. Look at 'em Mom. They blink like stars." Marj and Louette gathered the little boy in their arms. He wriggled loose. "We have to get outside the big light to find them all."

Shirley walked up. "What happened? What did I miss?"

"It's too complicated," Louette gave Shirley a hug. "I'll tell you later."

"You'd better," huffed Shirley. "I'm getting in the tub. This has been a long day."

Marj raised her hand. "People, I say we adjourn. Mom and I and Bucky will go to the Osceola Hotel for the night. We can tackle this puzzle tomorrow."

Louette rose from her chair. "I second that motion," she said. "I'm numb with all this information, and exhaustion." *And perfectly willing to let Marj take charge this time.*

At the Osceola Hotel Bucky held tight to the jar with lightning bugs. "These are mine. I need them to see the way in the dark."

Wonder where he got that. There are plenty of street lights. "Let me hold them while your Mom checks us in."

"Gramma Lou, I've not never seen you and my mom hugging and crying before." A puzzled frown wrinkled Bucky's brow. "Why?"

She thought he was chasing lightning bugs. How much did he hear and see? She took Bucky's hand. "A hug usually means you care about someone. I'm hugging you now because I love you."

At the curb, she unscrewed the lid and handed him the jar. "Let's release the lightning bugs. They need to be free, outside, where they live. They'd die bottled up."

In the hotel room the rambunctious little boy became himself again. "Look! Look! I have a bed of my own!" He jumped on the sofa-turned-into-a-bed.

"Bath first," called out his mother.

"I'll get his sleepers," said Louette.

"No, no, I can do it mineself!"

"He sure reverted to role, didn't he?" Louette watched as Bucky made a mess of his suitcase until he proudly held up pajamas.

"Look," said Bucky, pulling on his nightclothes. "A button is gone."

A button. Joseph's button at the edge of the sinkhole. What did it prove? That he had been there on the day he disappeared, wearing that particular shirt. Deep in the heart of herself, Louette finally sensed it. She knew in her soul that Joseph was gone. She was free of the gnawing ache. Her thoughts turned to Benjamin. Now she understood that the yearning in her had blossomed into an overwhelming love, astonishing and real.

Bucky was asleep almost before his head hit the pillow. It was quiet in the room. Louette wondered if Marj was asleep. "Just realizing what happened to Joseph takes such a giant load off my mind," she whispered softly.

"Couldn't we just leave him there? I'd rather remember him as he was the last time I saw him," said Marj. "It wouldn't serve any purpose to dig him up, would it?"

"I don't think so. We could ask the sheriff and Simon what we can do legally. They wouldn't mislead us. I would like to hold a memorial ceremony though, if it's okay with them." Louette turned over.

"That's a good idea. We need some closure."

"You're right, Marj. We can cross that bridge tomorrow. Goodnight."

"Goodnight, Mama."

Just before sunup Louette eased out of bed, not waking Marj and Bucky. She dressed in the slacks, blouse and tennis shoes from her pillowcase. It had been many years since her last stay in the Osceola Hotel. She'd heard they had a good cook. Sure smelled like it. The kitchen was in the same place, early morning food being prepared full blast. She followed her nose.

"That famous Osceola coffee ready, Rosie?"

"Sure is, Lou. Sausage and biscuit?"

"Yes. I want it to go."

Rosie handed her a paper bag and a large coffee container. "Fix your coffee any way you want it. Where you goin', Lou?"

"Over to look at where my house used to be. Thanks Rosie."

Louette walked over familiar sidewalks through the sleeping town. She felt comforted by thoughts of her many friends. "I am blessed to live in this place," she said aloud. "Thank you, Lord."

By the time she reached the shed beside the remains of her home, the sun was just peeking over what was left of the redtip shrubs along Miz Gumby's property line. Sitting beside the shed on the rawhide-bottom chair, she watched the ruins of her house covered with tarpaulins light up with a warm sunrise glow. Louette pondered what had happened.

It's been some roller-coaster ride since you left, Mama. Marj getting out the jars was a good thing. Marj understanding that I didn't chase Joseph away is a very good thing. Now maybe we can have the relationship a mother and daughter should have. I don't feel cheated by life anymore. I was cheated by the quicksand sinkhole, that's for sure, but not by life.

"It was a fine wake, Mama," Louette said aloud. "Maybe my wake was really for Joseph. Even though he died long ago in the sinkhole, I've always felt he was here, just like with you and Daddy and all the others who loved me. Joseph must have been there in the spirit world, too. Now that I know where he is, I won't miss him like before. I can get on with my life. Benjamin has asked me to marry him, Mama. What do you think of that?"

Louette leaned the chair back against the wall of the shed. *I've got plenty of memories here.* Sunlight shimmered on the dark shadow where her house had been. *I'm sorry the house couldn't be saved. But we finally know what happened to Joseph.* She let out a sigh.

"Gramma Lou!" Bucky and Marj rushed up.

"Whoa." Louette hugged him.

"I borrowed a black dress for you," said Marj. "Come back to the hotel and get ready for church."

Louette thought it would be hard to see pity on the faces of her church friends. But most people voiced condolences, then moved aside as she and her family walked into the church. Men tipped hats and women offered hugs. Bucky mostly hid behind Marj's skirt.

"Welcome," Preacher Ed cleared his throat. "Let us say a prayer for our friend Louette Kelly who lost her home to fire. May the Lord heal her soul."

There he goes again, thought Louette, *getting his images lopsided. My house burning down didn't make me sick.*

Then she realized that what he said was really true enough. She was sick about the house. But she was also ready to take up her life and start over, with Benjamin. *We are at home in ourselves. We will get through this.*

Marj and Bucky moved over as Benjamin slipped into the pew beside Louette. He wore a blue Sunday suit, no cap, his bald head shining, right there before God and everybody. "Remember me?" he asked.

"For the rest of my life." She clasped his hand during the service.

"This is a warm, friendly church and community," he said. "I knew it before, but it took you and your wake to help me see what was right before my eyes."

After the service, Marj spoke with Preacher Ed. "I know this is quick notice, but we'd like to hold a memorial service for my dad beside the sinkhole at the farm this afternoon. Sheriff Messer and Judge O'Connor agreed that it would be acceptable and said they'd be there."

"I think that is a wonderful idea." said Preacher Ed. "Shall I bring the choir?"

"If we need a song, we can sing something simple ourselves," Louette told him.

"You always need a song," said Preacher Ed. "What about 'Farther Along'?"

"Couldn't have picked a better one, myself," Marj told him. "I called Dan and Mittie."

"I'll tell Shirley and Miz Gumby," said Louette. "What about Etheline and Gordon?"

"We'll definitely want Clyde," added Marj. "The others were all there when he cleared up the mystery about Dad's disappearance."

"I keep thinking it's a dream, that it can't be true." Louette looked Marj straight in the eyes. "But it is. True, I mean."

"I'll bring plenty of my prettiest roses for the ceremony, Lou," Benjamin promised.

"You do that." She patted his shoulder. "We'll gather in the pasture and give Joseph a fittin' farewell."

That afternoon at the edge of the pasture, a good distance from the sinkhole, a subdued group waited with Louette and Marj for the words of finality they'd long needed. Bucky ran from one to the other, excited.

Tears rolled down Mittie's face. "It'll be all right, Lou," she said.

"Dearly beloved," said Preacher Ed. "It is time now to say goodbye to husband, father, and friend, Joseph Kelly. This formal goodbye can help bring peace to Joseph's loved ones."

Louette looked around. She, Benjamin, Marj, Bucky, Dan and Mittie, Shirley, Miz Gumby, Etheline and Gordon, Deputy Clyde, Sheriff Messer and Judge O'Connor, all held hands. Bucky's eyes were wide in amazement.

In the distance she heard birds chirping and a faint cluck of hens. A calf bellowed. Dan's mule Jobe whickered. Louette thought about her life, her loss, and now of her gains from learning the truth about Joseph's disappearance. She'd have to write to Aunt Rufus and Aunt Juney, to Laverne and Jasper. They needed to know. *The truth shall set you free. It has certainly lifted a heavy burden from my heart.*

This is a fitting place for Joseph's grave. This spot we circled in curiosity, from our childhood friendship to adulthood, romping in the pasture, carefully skirting the dark waters of the sinkhole. The grass now at the edges looked frail, as if expecting to fall into the bubbling maw at any time.

Louette closed her eyes as the preacher's voice recited the final ceremony. The funeral words sounded familiar. She wasn't eager to hear them, especially concerning Joseph, but they seemed fitting.

Preacher Ed started the song and they sang, soft and low: "Cheer up my brother, live in the sunshine... we'll understand it all by and by." Subdued and pensive, they filed back to the farmhouse.

"Sipping coffee and munching on pound cake," said Marj. "That's what we do after funerals in this part of the country."

"They do the same in Boston, except they don't get Mittie's special lemon pound cake," said Etheline.

"If it's all right with you, Bucky and I will go home this evening," Marj told her mother. She stopped Bucky's protest: "School and work."

"Gordo can figure the total on the jar money. Benjamin and Etheline will help him. Be sure and save the jars for jelly-jam. Mom, you can go home with us."

"No," said Louette. "I'll stay at the Osceola for now."

"Okay, Bucky and I will come next weekend and we can take the planning from there."

"Suits me," said Louette. *Marj in charge again. Let her. Benjamin and I have some planning of our own to do.*

"One more cup and we're on the road." Marj said.

"We can use some of Mama's jar money to fix the sinkhole and put up a grave marker for Joseph," said Louette.

"And one for Whistler," added Dan, with a low chuckle. "There'll still be plenty left. You'll figure out what to do with it."

Bucky pulled on her elbow. "You think she'll really come back next weekend, Gramma Lou?"

"I'm sure of it. We have changed, for the better." This time she believed her own words.

At the Osceola, Louette woke up early. She dressed and headed for the kitchen. "I plumb forgot it's my birthday, Rosie. Could I have a coffee and sausage biscuit to go?"

"Back to your pile of ashes, Lou?"

"Lots of memories there. Got to sort 'em out."

The sun was waiting for her. Just as she rounded the corner the first rays reached tentative fingers, then flashed full-blown on the shed and yard. Men in overalls and masks worked in the ashes of her house, rolling up tarpaulins and plastic sheeting, pitching wires and frames of the refrigerator, washer and dryer into a dump truck.

Benjamin and Lige were unloading lumber. "We'll put up the swing and repair the picnic table first," said Benjamin. "Hoped we'd get more done before you showed up. This is your happy birthday."

"Load of topsoil's coming," said Lige. "They'll pile up the chimney bricks and spread the topsoil over the ashes. We want to get on the garden spot before dark; if not, first thing in the morning. Put in a few tomatoes, some onions, radishes and collards. It might be a little late for turnips."

"What about corn, snap beans and squash? The old Indian way?" Shirley rushed up.

"Those are high summer crops," Benjamin told her.

"Plant whatever you want. You know more about that than I do," Shirley said with a laugh. "I've got aprons and shoe covers. Lou and I can clean around the edges."

"Who'd a thought it? This is what a happy birthday is all about." Louette leaned the cowhide chair against the shed. "Think we could save the rain tree?"

"We can try." When Lige rubbed the black spindle, shards of bark came off.

Double Doc jogged up. "I can help when you get your rows in. I'll check back after awhile." He jogged away.

Clyde's sheriff's car drove up. "Just checking to see how the birthday's going," he said.

Willie appeared with a bright birthday banner. "The other one was ruined. This one's not as big, but it'll do in a pinch."

"Let me get some yellow tape," Clyde told him. "We can hang that between Shirley's security lamp post and the shed roof."

Miz Gumby came next, untying her apron. "Shirley and I are making you a birthday lunch, Lou."

"Well, I never," said Shirley. "It was supposed to be a surprise."

Miz Gumby didn't hear her. She waved her hand, including Benjamin, Lige and Clyde. "The rest of you are invited. Lou, don't you go off nowhere."

"I'll be right here," Louette told her. "This is turning into about the best birthday celebration I ever had." There was no other place she'd rather be. She reached out and hugged Benjamin and the two-by-four he had sawed to measure.

I've got the joy, joy, joy, joy,
down in my heart...
Down in my heart to stay.

Chapter Sixteen

A week later, early Monday morning, a subdued group gathered in the conference room at the Planter's Bank. A crew of bank employees had piled boxes and bags filled with empty Mason jars on the floor against the wall. On the conference room table was a ledger pad with lines of figures, totaling the amount from each jar.

Gordon Lassiter walked in. "You the one in charge Lou?" he asked.

"I don't know about being in charge. I thought Marj would be here for the official stuff. She said for me to tell you she'd be a little late."

Dan, Mittie, Benjamin, Clyde, Etheline, Judge O'Connor, and Sheriff Messer waited with them. Gordon looked at his watch.

A tall man with a moustache and a stern expression entered the room holding a heavy speed-graphic camera. "Who all's here?" he asked.

"Just the usual suspects," muttered Etheline. A gentle laugh eddied around the room.

"Come in Mr. Horace Greely Purefoy, esteemed journalist." Gordon reached out and shook the newspaper editor's hand.

Horace put the heavy camera on the conference table. "I'd always heard that Miz Clara had money stuffed in jars. How much did it amount to?"

"A lively sum, but not a great amount." Gordon turned the ledger bottom-up.

"Where's Shirley and Miz Gumby?" Clyde asked.

"I don't know," said Louette.

"Seems like somebody's missing. Maybe it's them. It's too quiet," Clyde grinned.

"Yeah, Shirley'd be talking a blue streak if she was here."

Sounds from the front of the bank alerted them that Marj and Bucky had arrived. "But, Mom, I want to go to the farm, not to an old bank." Bucky's voice started low and then increased in decibels as he trotted behind his mother.

"Sorry we're late." Marj motioned Bucky to sit. Louette held out her arms for him, then after a solid hug, he sat down happily beside her.

As Gordon flipped the ledger book, Judge Simon and Newsman Horace leaned over to see the figures. "You won't have to worry about inheritance taxes," Simon told Louette. "It'd have to be something like three hundred thousand to qualify for that."

"Thank Goodness," Louette whispered back.

"Would everyone please be seated?" Gordon stood at the head of the table. "This is a solemn affair. Louette, do you want the money split and checks made out to you and Dan?"

"How much is it, Gordo?" Louette asked. Getting the priorities skewed, thought Louette, then followed his eyes as he gazed toward Etheline.

"One hundred eighty-eight thousand dollars and fifty-nine cents," he answered.

"Wait!" Benjamin held up his hands. "Did you check the dates to see if any of it is old enough to be worth more than its face value?"

"Oh." Gordon's face flushed bright pink. "There may be some valuable bills. Why didn't I think of that?" Louette chuckled. *Because your eyes were on Etheline.*

"I'll check and advertise to collectors what we've got." Gordon cleared his throat. "Is it all right if we write the checks, then adjust the amount if there are collectibles in the bills?"

"Don't give me none of it," Dan told him.

"I don't want it," said Louette. "Give it to Marj."

"Make out the check to Mama," Marj told Gordon. "She can decide what to do with the money later."

"If you will sign these." Gordon held out forms. The newspaper editor grabbed his speed graphic and took a picture of Dan signing the money over to Louette.

"Where are the jars with cash in them?" Horace asked.

"We took the money out of the jars," Gordon explained. "See?" He held up a box of empty jars.

"Just a minute," Horace shifted the speed graphic. "Go stand with him Lou, maybe Marj and Dan too. I'll shoot something for the newspaper."

"What about Bucky?" Louette cringed at the idea of publicity. Her mother wouldn't have wanted a newspaper writeup about her saving money in jars.

"Ah, yes, Bucky," agreed the newspaper man. "People like to read about money and about children. Let Bucky hold a couple of the jars. There, beside that biggest box. Pile the other containers around, make it look like he's surrounded by jars filled with cash. Ah, ha!" Horace was obviously in his element. He scurried around, straightening this, turning that.

"Suits me if you'd leave me out," Louette told him, but by then he was positioning her face to catch more light.

"Here," he pulled Benjamin up beside Louette. "I'll get a picture of you together to run with your engagement announcement."

"You can take our picture, but don't be running an engagement notice until we're ready for you to."

"You got it, Lou," Horace told her. "I'm as happy for you two as if you were my brother and sister."

Benjamin looked uncomfortable. Louette tugged at his hand. "This is not our style," she said, "but we can put on a smile. Look happy."

"I can do that," he told her.

When the hubbub subsided, Louette looked around for Gordon and Etheline. In the hall outside she could hear bank employees milling around. "What's going on?" she asked. Benjamin shook his head.

"I see Aunt Shirley and Miz Gumby," called out Bucky. He ran toward the front of the bank.

The others followed to find a celebration set up. Shirley and Miz Gumby, with the help of bank employees, had filled a long table with a cake, platters of cookies, and dishes of dip, vegetables, crackers and chips. Clean fruit jars ringed the punch bowl with a "Cash Flow" sign. The cake's white frosting had JAR MONEY spelled out in red.

"This'll make a great picture," called out Horace as he posed Louette, Marj, and Bucky at the JAR MONEY cake. "Ought to sell a few newspapers."

"What on earth is going on here?" Louette caught Shirley handing a knife to Marj.

"What do you mean? I thought you liked celebrations and parties."

"I do, but not about Mama's jar money. That's a private thing."

"You know you can't keep a secret around here, especially one about Miz Clara and her jars." Shirley hugged her. "Everybody's been wondering about the jar rumor for a long time. Let them be part of the fun."

"You might be right," said Louette.

"Besides, what you gone do with all that money? What?" asked Miz Gumby. Louette reached out and hugged her. *Buzzy old woman, but I love her. She might just be a picture of me when I get to her age.*

Louette turned. It did look like the whole town was represented. *Might as well join them.* Benjamin, who was normally shy, was talking to the mayor. Clyde, who never wasted a breath without words, held fast in a discussion with Dan and Mittie. She looked for Bucky and discovered him leaned against a filing cabinet and the wall. His eyes were closed, his hands splayed against a drawer handle.

Louette poked Marj. "Look at him." They rushed over and caught him by the shoulders as he slowly slid toward the floor.

"What's wrong?" Benjamin asked.

"He's sound asleep," Marj answered.

Benjamin deposited Bucky in the front seat of Louette's car. Marj hovered.

"You two hold the fort at the party." Louette's eyes twinkled. "Bucky and I are headed for the farm. Dan and Mittie can come when they get through visiting."

"Don't you want a piece of cake?"

"Bring us some."

"We'll fill you in," Marj told her.

"What about the check?" asked Benjamin.

"Tell Gordo to do his collector search. I'll think on what to do with whatever figure comes up."

Louette hugged him. *Looks like I'm breaking out in a hugging spree. Better get out of here.*

When she cranked the car, Bucky was suddenly wide awake. "We're missing the party, Gramma Lou."

"I like parties as well as the next one, but that was too much of a to-do."

"But the jars had money, Gramma Lou. Mom said it might be a lot."

"Dan signed it over to me. It wasn't a great big amount, and it bears thinking about, and I do most of my best thinking out at the farm."

"Me too."

Louette felt better driving through town. She appreciated how delighted Gordon, Marj, and especially Horace, were about the money in the jars. But to publicize it seemed a betrayal of her mother, somehow. *Maybe Mama wouldn't really care about the celebration. Maybe I'm reading too much of Mama in it all.*

Bucky was quiet as they followed the road south. Then he seemed to spark like a firecracker again. He looked at an old falling-down building up against a hill. "What's that?"

"It used to be a tavern called The Rocks. Back when they put in juke boxes to play music, like those at the old diner where you put in quarters for a song. There was one called The Pines, on the south road to the farm. They were called juke joints. Juking was a kind of dance too."

Bucky's attention flitted to other attractions along the road. They came to a wide pasture with a trough for watering animals and a block of licking salt beside a pinoak tree. Louette gazed out at the grass sprouting green all over. *I thought this was a really big field. Maybe it shrank.*

"Look, Gramma, look! A real cow!" Louette eased the car to the pavement's edge and stopped. A cow with a glossy brown coat mottled with white stood near a rusty wire-mesh fence. Switching her tail, the cow plowed her nose into the brown grass in search of green sprouts. Off in the distance other cows and a reddish-brown bull munched in peace.

"Can I pet her, Gramma Lou?" Bucky was beside the fence before Louette could get out of the car.

"Wait, Bucky, don't rush up to her. Animals don't like that. You need to remember not to startle them."

"What do I do?"

"The way to become friends with a cow is to approach her slowly. Talk to her and see if she's friendly. You can't ever tell about an old cow. They're like cats. If they want to pay attention to you, they will. If not, just let them be." *He don't seem to have learned much of a lesson from the encounter with the mama sow. Strong willed, like his mama.* But now Louette gloried in the idea of Marj being just the way she was. *Maybe being stubborn is an asset.* Louette could feel the softening of her attitude.

Bucky's eyes widened. "How do I talk to her?" Louette laughed. Bucky leaned against the fence, reaching for the cow's nose. "Hello, cow," he said. The cow rolled liquid brown eyes, threw back her head and lowed mournfully.

A truck roared from the driveway of the farmhouse beyond the pasture. Louette and Bucky stood transfixed and watched as the truck barreled toward the road and came to a screeching halt. A man jumped out. "Git away from my animals!" he yelled.

Louette took Bucky's hand and backed up. "Who are you?" she asked.

The man had a scraggly beard and a wide swath of pale skin where his hat usually sat on his head. His overalls looked new, but he was barefoot. "I'm the owner of this here farm. This is my cow. Git on outa here."

"What's your name?" Louette was puzzled. This man was a total stranger. "I thought the Faulks lived on this place."

The man's voice rose several decibels. "I told you to git off my land."

"But this is not your land. We're standing on county right-of-way. You don't own the road, nor the right-of-way."

"Up to that there fence is my property and if you don't leave now, I'm gitten my shotgun."

Bucky held tight to the leg of Louette's slacks, his eyes wide.

The man turned purple, his eyes bugged out. He left his truck where it stood and ran back up the lane toward his house.

"We'd better go," Louette told Bucky, who remained quiet as if more amazed than afraid at the man's outburst.

"He sure is one mad man," Bucky observed.

"You can say that again," agreed Louette. They got in the car. "Most people around here are friendly."

As they drove away, Bucky turned around on the car seat. "The loud noise the cow made didn't sound like hello, or moo either," observed Bucky. "It sounded more like myrrr."

"At least that cow didn't bellow three times. There's an old saying, 'When a cow bellows three times without stopping, a storm will come a-hopping'." Bucky looked puzzled. "Guess you never heard that."

Bucky peered at the sky. "I don't see a storm. But the man bellowed four times."

"Well, the cow only bellowed twice."

"Oh. Must not count, then."

"Farmers have lots of ways of talking about the weather. 'When the dew is on the grass, the rain will come to pass.' 'When grass is dry at night, look for rain before the light.' Of course, those things might not always work, but they give farmers hope."

That was an answer. Hope. Wake up your senses. This is a magic day with Bucky. Live in the moment with your grandson.

With renewed pleasure, Louette drove. Soon the woods would be bright with yellow bells, honeysuckle, and wild azaleas, some pink and some orange. Thorny briars along fences would blossom and bear juicy round blackberries. Persimmon tree limbs and huckleberry bushes already bore tiny green buds ready to burst out and celebrate spring. The approach to the farmhouse was a long winding lane.

The "Shady Oaks" sign on the adjoining lane to her left was a sign of change to Louette. A tall wooden fence blocked some of the view. If she had driven on that left lane she and Bucky would have arrived in what felt to her like another dimension. The sprawling gated community with fancy houses had given her a startle when she saw the first one completed. Yet people who could afford big homes had as much right to be there as herself, she supposed.

She stopped at the last curve before the weather-beaten farmhouse. "See how this house is built?" she asked Bucky. He didn't answer. "That type was called a 'cracker house' because the people who lived in them were mainly workers who drove oxen to harvest pine, oak, and cypress. The driver's whip made a cracking sound to keep the oxen moving. The timber harvest began in the Midwest and moved south to the Gulf of Mexico in the 1700s and 1800s."

Bucky didn't answer. *Hush*, Louette told herself. *He can learn that stuff when he gets bigger.* She pulled the car to the front of the house and looked at him. He was sound asleep again. Beside her, curly red hair tousled, and knees pulled tight against his chest, lay her greatest delight, her six-year-old grandson. His eyes closed, his blue shirt and jeans were rumpled. His shinbones showed where the jeans had twisted above his ankles.

He looked like an angel: smooth skin, half-smile on full lips. His face reflected Louette's own expression of amazement, even in his sleep. As she wondered if she could pick him up, Bucky's eyes opened. He smiled. "We're home to the farm, Gramma Lou," he said.

"Right about that," she told him as they went into the farmhouse. Her home in Geneva had burned, but the farm was still there.

Bucky settled into bed for a nap. Louette watched him sleep. There was so much she wanted to tell him. Her history, where she came from and where she would go, was important, not only to her, but to him. He was her eternity;

what was passed from her to Marj, then to him, would be the essence of her self that would continue forever. Maybe that's what "eternal life" meant.

Soon Marj would come and take him away. But this time she felt confident that she'd see him again soon, that he would be a part of the rest of her life.

Louette sat in the cowhide chair beside the new garden when the sun rose. She watched Benjamin and Lige finish off rows for vegetables. She'd rightly enjoy putting in seedlings for peas, green beans, tomatoes, potatoes, squash, okra, onions, radishes, bell peppers, corn, cucumbers, peanuts, watermelons, and butter beans. *People speak of a new beginning, but there's actually no such thing*, thought Louette, as she sat quietly. She'd get up and help them in a few minutes, but this was a good time to think.

It had been left up to her to decide what to do with the money from her mother's jars. She didn't need another house. For the time being she would stay with Dan and Mittie at the farm and drive into town to work at the print shop. When a respectable time had passed after the memorial for Joseph, she would marry Benjamin.

When she had stopped by the print shop to tell them, Willie and his son James were delighted. "We need you to read proofs of print jobs," James told her. "You're great at arguing with suppliers about prices and amounts of paper and ink."

She'd felt a pang of missing Joseph when James handed her an estimate on a book of poetry, stapled, not perfect binding, color only on the cover. "Check this out," he'd said. "Like you used to."

Louette inspected the estimates on paper, ink—black and color—binding, and trimming. "You going to do this job free?" she called out to James.

"I hope not." James was embarrassed. "I can't believe I left out the cost for labor."

"See why we need you?" Willie patted her on the shoulder. "You got sharp eyes." Louette smiled. Remembering. *That went well.*

Louette felt lucky to have Benjamin. She had missed Joseph for so long. The pain still swept over her from time to time, but she tamped it down. *For me, heartache became a habit. But not anymore.*

As soon as the work could be completed on the lot where her house had stood, she and Benjamin would finish their wedding preparations. She'd suggested that they go over to the probate office and let Simon perform a civil service. But Marj preferred a proper ceremony.

Preacher Ed expected them to be married in the church, so she and Benjamin had told him they might consider it. It would be more to her liking to hold a wedding on the site of the old home place, with new growth signifying a fresh challenge.

Benjamin walked up with a glass of iced tea taken from the cooler beside the shed. "Thanks," she told him. "I've been thinking."

"Uh, oh," he laughed. "Be careful with that."

Louette smiled, but she was serious. "What if we donate Mama's money to the town for a public park right here, with a covered pavilion for concerts and bleachers and raised boxes for a community garden? The lot across the way belongs to the city already and it could be paved for parking, maybe some picnic tables, if there's room."

"You amaze me more and more every day," said Benjamin. "I've already ordered the materials to build you a shed for your memories over behind the caboose with the azaleas. This place will be perfect for a community park. Lets go talk to Mayor Warren."

"Now?"

"Sure. No better time." He sat his empty tea glass on the ground beside the cowhide chair. "We'll be back in awhile," he called out to Lige, who grunted an okay.

"That was fast," Louette noted as Benjamin parked at the hardware store. "Maybe I ought to talk it over with Dan and Marj first."

"Why?" Benjamin reached out and pulled her from the car, holding her close as he shut the door.

"I don't know. Old habits die hard. I'm a talker-over kind of person."

"We'll talk it over with the mayor then." Benjamin held the door of the hardware store open. "After he finishes with his customer."

I didn't realize I was getting another take-charge person, thought Louette. *He's as quick on the draw as Marj.*

"I'm astounded," Mayor Warren told Louette and Benjamin. "It sounds like Clara all right. With some of your money and some funds out of the road department's budget, we could swing it. And a community park might qualify for an improvement grant. I'll look into it."

"Gordon is looking for collectors, in case any of the money is worth more than face value," Louette told him. "The jar amount could swell. Probably not much, but some."

"We can take that into account. I'll talk to Gordon," said Mayor Warren.

"I know it'll take time and effort," Louette told him. "You know the ropes on planning and design, but we want to help."

"How long do you think it'll take to get it all together?" asked Benjamin.

Mayor Roberts put one arm around Louette's shoulders and the other around Benjamin's. "If we hit the ground running, and work like beavers, we can have this project finished and ready before summer."

"And we can hold our wedding ceremony right there?" asked Benjamin. "What do you think Lou?"

"I think that's about the grandest plan we could have. I'm all for it. Let's go right now to the Planter's Bank and get the check from Gordon, before anybody here changes their mind."

Warren motioned toward the long line at his hardware store. "You bring me some money, and I'll wait on some customers here," he said.

Louette and Benjamin walked arm-in-arm to the bank. Their miracle was happening. One step at a time.

"Joy to the world, all the boys and girls..." they sang, slightly off key.

Recipes for Throwing a Wake

In response to popular demand, Louette asked that some of her favorite recipes be included, in the event somebody else wants to hold a wake while still alive and kicking.

Of course, Shirley and Etheline insisted their recipes for poke salad and coconut cake be included. Angie's recipe for persimmon pie couldn't be left out.

A wake would be less than top notch without a bowl of Racie Mae's collard greens and Aunt Rufus and Aunt Juney's chicken and dumplings.

Louette's Turkey and Dressing

Turkey, 10 to 20 pounds
Corn meal
Celery
Salt
Onions
Eggs
Cornstarch
Sage
Worcestershire sauce

People cook turkeys for holidays and big gatherings these days but when I was growing up back during the Great Depression, folks boiled an old hen that had slowed down her laying or a rooster that tried to fight when you went into the chicken yard to gather eggs. Fryers were for frying. Frying chickens weren't fat enough for dressing or dumplings. Now you buy what is supposed to be a fryer and it's loaded with enough fat to make a washtub full of dressing or dumplings. Turkeys came from Dead River swamp when Daddy took a notion to go down and shoot one where they roosted. He knew how to call up a hen or gobbler with a short whistle he made from a reed.

Consider the number of people you're going to feed for the size of turkey. I used to get a 20-pounder, but now I buy one around 10 pounds. I also used to want a turkey hen because they were more tender, but now it's hard to tell which is which. So, just get a turkey. I use a roaster, but my roaster got roasted in the house fire. Put the turkey into a deep baking pan and make an aluminum tent over its breast so as to keep it from turning out too dry.

Some people put the dressing inside the turkey and call it stuffing, but I don't. I cut up celery and put some in the bottom and the neck cavities. It is supposed to keep the meat moist. It also flavors the drippings for the dressing or after-holiday soup.

It usually takes about 15 to 20 minutes per pound to bake a turkey at 325° F. Check it after two hours. After you cook a few, you'll figure it out. I boil the giblets (neck, liver, gizzard, and heart) and a half-dozen eggs while the turkey's baking. Put the eggs aside because you'll stir three of them into the dressing mixture at the last and use the other three for giblet gravy. When the turkey's done (If you can't tell by the wonderful smell, wiggle a leg. It almost comes off in your hand, it's done), pour the juices over the cornbread you have cooked and broken up in a large bowl while the turkey baked.

For the cornbread, I use about two cups of fine ground corn meal. Stir in a cup of milk first, then add some more if it doesn't look soupy enough, several eggs, salt and about a tablespoon of cooking oil. I used to use peanut oil or lard, but now they say canola or olive oil is better for you. Don't put baking powder into it. The cornbread might not be pretty since it won't rise much, but it'll taste better. Bake at 375° F, about 30 to 45 minutes. It doesn't have to be very brown. It doesn't matter how it looks, because you'll be mixing it up for dressing anyway.

Since Shirley hadn't baked any cornbread, I improvised by putting in dry fine-ground corn meal mixed with old loaf bread I found in Shirley's freezer. I also found a box of bought ready-made dressing mix and stirred half of that in.

Pour as much of the hot juice and drippings from where the turkey baked into the mixture as you need to make it look right soupy. Remember the corn meal (which didn't get made into cornbread) will swell up lots. The cornbread will swell up, too. After you've mashed the lumps, stir in two cups of chopped onions and two cups of chopped celery. I usually put in about three heaping tablespoons of ground sage. Go by your smell and taste.

Stir in three or four raw eggs. Cut chunks of meat, some light and some dark. (I usually cut the meat off one leg and one short thigh and about a half-cup of breast into bite-size pieces.) Stir in the meat, mix it all up, then taste some to see if it has enough salt and sage. Cut up three of the boiled eggs and stir in. Pour the mixture into a large baking pan. When I'm in a hurry, I turn the oven to 475° F for about 15 minutes, then lower it to 350° F for the rest of the baking time. Ovens are different, so go by whether your oven is higher or lower than normal. It takes about an hour. When it's done, it'll be brown on top and when you shake the pan the center should jiggle. Otherwise it's too dry. If it looks iffy, dip out a spoonful, blow on it to cool, and taste.

Young people don't often like giblet gravy. I see the gravy from jars bought in the supermarket sitting in bowls beside dressing at gatherings. In case you want giblet gravy, take the meat you cut off the neck and cut up the other giblets and about two cups of drippings. Add a cup of chopped onions and chopped celery to the mixture. Add 3 tablespoons Worcestershire sauce, and probably some salt. Taste it. Heat and turn down to simmer. Mix 2 heaping tablespoons of cornstarch with a half-cup of cold water and add slowly, stirring all the while. When thickened add the 3 cut-up boiled eggs. To serve, spoon over cooked dressing.

Aunt Rufus and Aunt Juney's
Chicken and Dumplings

Hen or fat fryer
Eggs
Dumplings
Celery
Onions
Herbs
Salt

Cut up and boil a chicken in a 5-quart pot of water until done (about 20 minutes). Put in 4 or 5 eggs and take them out after about 10 minutes. Cut meat into bite size, discarding bones, gristle and skin. Set meat aside. If you don't have outside dogs or cats to feed the scraps to, dig a hole at the edge of the garden and bury them. Or, if you live in town, put them in the garbage. Or you can buy boned chicken breasts and short thighs. Cuts down on the mess.

You can make your own dumplings if you want to, but these days they sell them already made. Get two packages. To make your own, put four cups of self-rising flour in a large bowl and hollow out a hole in the middle. Pour in a cup of warm broth and when it is cool enough dip your fingers in and work in as much flour as you need to make a stiff dough. Pour out dough and flour onto a piece of waxed paper and roll it out, adding flour as needed. Cut into strips.

Into the pot of cooked chicken broth put salt and pepper, chopped celery (about a half-cup), and onions if you want them. You can sprinkle in some dried parsley. Some people like all sorts of herbs. Go by your taste.

Get the mixture to boiling and drop in the dumplings one at a time. When you've got them all in, turn the heat to simmer and put the lid on. Stir every once in awhile to keep them from sticking together into big lumps. It usually takes about 35 to 40 minutes. When they're done, dump in the chicken meat and stir in the chopped-up boiled eggs. Let them set awhile, maybe 5 to 10 minutes, before serving.

Racie Mae's Collard Greens

Buy a big bunch of collard greens off the back of Lige's pick-up truck, if he comes around. They also usually have them in the grocery store. Collards are better in the fall after first frost. This is something lots of folks don't know. They're also good in the spring though—actually, they're good any time. Sometimes I put them in the refrigerator overnight, still all in a bunch, just to give them that frost-kissed flavor, but you don't have to do that. I bought the ones I took to the wake from the farmer's market just outside town.

I usually boil a couple of ham hocks. The taste of the collards comes through whether they have seasoning meat in them or not. I used to put in a couple of tablespoons of lard if I didn't use seasoning meat, but then doctors say lard's not good for you, so I switched to peanut oil. Now I can't hardly find peanut oil.

Clean the collards and wash 'em, wash 'em. My mama made us wash collards through five waters to be sure we got all the bugs. These days they don't usually have many bugs and they have been sprayed down with a water hose before they ever hit the store. Wash them some more anyway.

When you cut leaves from the big stem, strip off most of the center ribs. Some people throw away the big stem, but I peel it and dip pieces of the heart into ranch dressing to eat while I'm cooking.

Roll up the stripped leaves and keep adding until you have a pretty good handful. Then cut into bite-size chunks. Put about a cupful of water into the pot with the cut-up collards. Add salt. You have to watch to be sure the collards don't use up all the water. Add a little all along. Don't just leave them alone for no set time. Check 'em. After about 20 to 30 minutes on low heat, they ought to be getting close to done.

Taste. Add salt if you need to. If there's a little bitter taste, sprinkle in about a fourth teaspoon of baking soda. Stir it up good. Then after it cooks down some, add about a teaspoon of sugar. Could need more or less. Taste. Your taster can tell when they're perfect. Best collards greens in five counties!

Clara's Famous Southern Spinach
By Etheline

Pick the most tender poke leaves—those no bigger than your hand. Put on the stove in a big pot of water. Put water and several eggs in a smaller pot and boil while you clean the poke. Strip most of the rib from the middle of each leaf and throw it away. When the water's in a rolling boil, drop in the poke and stir it around. Parboil poke leaves about 15 minutes. Dip off the green scum, rinse well, then cover with water and cook again. The second cooking is to remove excessive vitamin A, which may be toxic. Pour the greens and water into a colander, then rinse really well under the faucet, stirring it around a lot. Squeeze out all the water you can.

Fry several strips of bacon in a skillet. Lift out the bacon. I put a few chopped up onions in the bacon grease, too. Then put in the rinsed and squeezed poke, stirring it around until it's done. Add the crumbledup bacon at the last minute.

After the poke sallet's in a bowl, slice the boiled eggs and decorate the top.

Chocolate Fudge Cake

Box yellow cake mix
Eggs
Oil
Sugar
Cocoa
Milk

Butter

Vanilla

Turn oven to 350° F. Put 3 ½ cups sugar into 2 or 3 quart saucepot and stir in 3 heaping tablespoons of dry cocoa. Add just enough milk to moisten, about 1/3 to 2/3 cups. Add 1 ½ sticks butter and 1 tsp. vanilla.

Put on stove with the heat turned as low as you can get it. I put out a saucer for the spoon and the butter knife I'll use to spread the hot fudge. Don't let it cook up too fast. As it cooks slowly, it gradually thickens. Stir once in awhile and if it hasn't thickened hardly at all when you start to put it on the layers don't worry, it will soak in, which makes it taste better.

Everybody has their own favorite brand of yellow cake mix. Follow mixing directions on the box, adding ¼ cup extra water. More water if you want more than six layers. (With 9-inch cake pans, allow 3/4 cup for each layer.) Spray cake pans, or swipe on oil with fingers, pour in dough. Bake 12-14 minutes.

Stir fudge mixture all along. When first three layers are done, have more layers ready to put in the oven. Put layers bottom side up on plate, to soak up the hot fudge. Dip with stirring spoon and slather the fudge over the layer, covering completely. If fudge bubbles too much, move to edge of flame or heat eye so the mixture stays hot but cooks very slowly. As you add each layer, cover it with hot fudge. Cover the sides too. If the fudge tries to escape don't let it. Use the butter knife to scotch it back up on the cake. There should be about six to eight layers. Keep back one to cool as a final cover for the top.

I usually call Shirley to hold the cake-saver so it doesn't slide around, but sometimes I manage by myself. Take the big spoon you've been stirring fudge with to poke holes in the stack and pour in hot fudge. Take the spoon and poke it down, then sort of twist it to make room to pour in fudge. I do three holes. Be careful and don't poke the hole all the way to the bottom or you'll have spurts of hot fudge shooting out. Since you won't have a little Dutch boy to put his finger in the dike, just keep spooning it back on the cake. It'll firm up. (Sometimes if it's too much trouble, I don't poke holes). After you put the saved top layer on and cover it with hot fudge, take the saucepan off the heat. Keep stirring that last bit of fudge until it thickens, then cover cake completely with the thickening fudge. If you have covered the cake and have fudge left over, drop it on waxed paper or aluminum foil for little fudge kisses. The secret of this cake is patience. Don't hurry it. It takes about two hours of your full attention to make one of these, but the taste is worth it. Have plenty of milk handy. It's too sweet to just eat a pile of. Only children and grown men can usually handle a large piece, or more than one slice. I cut the cake in a crisscross pattern for smaller pieces.

Louette's Butternut Pound Cake

One cup Crisco
6 large eggs
2 cups sugar
Two cups Swansdown Cake Flour
Three tablespoons butternut flavoring.

Into bowl, put shortening and sugar. Add eggs, mixing well. Add flour and butternut flavoring. Pour into oiled Bundt pan. Bake at 325° F. just over an hour (some ovens may vary). Let cool 10 minutes before dumping onto a cake plate. Glaze: 1 ½ cups confectioner's sugar, 1 tablespoon butternut flavor. (It may say butter and nut on the bottle.) Mix well and drizzle or slather on cake.

Prize Winning Coconut Cake

By Shirley

Box cake mix (or from scratch!)
Eggs
Oil
14 oz. bag flaked coconut
Sugar
Cream of Tartar
Vanilla

Set oven to 350° F. Separate 3 egg whites. Use the whites in the icing and the yellows in the cake mix. Use your favorite yellow cake mix and follow directions, substituting three yolks for two of the whole eggs. Divide the batter so it'll make four layers, about ¾ cup for each layer. Cook and set aside to cool while you make the frosting.

Buy a 14-ounce bag of Angel Flake coconut. I used to grind up real coconut, but they do it for you these days. Saves work. It's according to how I feel if I use all of it.

The secret of this cake is seven-minute icing. If you have a double boiler, use that. I got caught making a cake at my niece's at Mims Hill one time and I mixed up my egg whites and sugar in a small boiler and set it over a bigger one of boiling water. If you have to do that, be careful. Steam from the boiling water can do a number on your hands.

Put unbeaten egg whites, two cups sugar, 6 tablespoons of cold water, and ¼ teaspoon of cream of tartar (you can leave out the cream of tartar if you don't have any; just shake in a little salt) into the upper part of the double boiler. Mix thoroughly and place over rapidly boiling water, beating constantly. Beat with egg beater or hand electric mixer until thoroughly mixed. Cook 7 minutes or until frosting will stand in peaks. Remove from over water, add 1 teaspoon vanilla, and beat until thick enough to spread.

I mix in about half of the bag of coconut, then start layering. When I've finished stacking layers and spreading icing, I sprinkle the rest of the coconut over the cake, pressing it in. Some people mix the coconut in all at once. But I'm the one who wins the blue ribbons. So there!

Clara's Coconut Pineapple Pie
By Shirley

1 stick of margarine or butter
2 cups sugar
4 eggs
1 can flaked coconut
1 small can crushed pineapple (well drained)

Mix ingredients. Pour into 2 uncooked pie crusts. Bake at 300° F. an hour, or until brown.

Persimmon Pie
By Angie

Gather persimmons in the fall when they are ripe. Take a clean sheet out to the woods, find a loaded tree and shake it. The ripest persimmons will fall on the sheet. Be sure you don't use those yellow or just beginning to turn. They're bitter. Ripe persimmons are orange and wrinkly.

Pick the little black pips off the bolls and take out the seeds. Peelings are all right; you'd never have enough pulp if you tried to peel a ripe persimmon.

2 cups persimmon pulp
1 cup sugar
2 tablespoons cornstarch
½ cup water
2 tablespoons butter
1 teaspoon lemon juice or extract

Combine ingredients and cook, stirring constantly until thickened. Pour into baked pie shell. Cool in refrigerator until it sets, then serve topped with whipped cream. It's not hard to whip fresh cream, but it's easier to get it right from the grocery store cooler.

Author's Musical Note

Chapter headings are from gospel songs; many from church hymnals.

"Star of Hope," my Uncle E. Bert Riddles wrote and my cousin Benjamin T. (Tommy) Riddles II later adapted to his own music.

I include brief snatches of these songs to emphasize the widespread influence and enjoyment of gospel music that was a part of everyday life during the time of Louise Etta Kelly, and Louette's Wake.

A few non-gospels are mixed in for flavor.

Chapter 1:
> "The Unclouded Day." Josiah K. Alwood 1828-1909. circa 1880. In 1987 sung by Willie Nelson in a Farm Aid concert.

Chapter 2:
> "I Saw the Light." Hank Williams, 1923-1953. Williams wrote this in 1947 while returning to Montgomery from performing in Ft. Deposit, AL. His mother was driving and announced the lights of Dannelly Field Airport. It became his standard closing song for concerts and was published in 1948 by MGM Records (Wikipedia).

Chapter 3:
> "Love Divine, All Loves Excelling." Charles Wesley. *Songs of Faith*, Baptist Hymnal © 1933 Broadman Press. Nashville, TN.

Chapter 4:
> "Higher Ground." Johnson Oatman, Jr. 1856-1922. Baptist Hymnal. ©1991 by Convention Press. Nashville, TN.

Chapter 5:
> "Jesus is Tenderly Calling." Fanny J. Crosby, 1820-1915. Baptist Hymnal. ©1991 by Convention Press. Nashville, TN.

Chapter 6:

"Do Lord, Oh Do Lord, Oh Do Remember Me." Listed in *Southern Gospel Journal* online. Family Album 1968. Author Unknown. Adapted and arranged by William Farley Smith, 1986. Popular gospel song recorded over the years by many musicians.

Chapter 7:

"Revive Us Again." William P. Mackay, 1863.

Chapter 8:

"Bright Star of Hope." E. Bert Riddles. 1942. © Stamps-Baxter Music Co. Dallas, TX. Adapted 1986 by Benjamin T. (Tommy) Riddles II.

Chapter 9:

"O Happy Day." Philip Dodderidge, 1692-1751. Published posthumously in 1755. Refrain from *Wesleyan Sacred Harp*, 1854.

Chapter 10:

"Precious Memories." J. B. F. Wright. *Favorite Songs and Hymns.* ©1938 Stamps-Baxter Music and Printing Co. Dallas, TX.

Chapter 11:

"All Creatures of our God and King." Frances of Assisi, ca 1182-1226. Translated by William H. Draper. ©1926, renewed J. Curwen & Sons, Ltd. International copyright secured. Reprinted in Baptist Hymnal, 1991, by Convention Press, Nashville, TN.

Chapter 12:

"I'll Meet You in the Morning." Albert E. Brumley. © 1936 by Hartford Music Co. in "Lights of Life." Stamps-Baxter Music and Printing Co. *Favorite Songs and Hymns.* Dallas, TX. Sung in early 1960s by crossover pop musician Skeeter Davis (Mary Frances Penick) (1931-2004).

Chapter 13:
   "Morning Has Broken." Eleanor Farjeon 1881-1965. © Eleanor Farjeon in *The Children's Bells*. Oxford University Press. Reprinted by permission of Harold Ober Assoc. Inc., N. Y. in the Baptist Hymnal. ©1991. Convention Press. Nashville, TN. One of Cat Stevens' most popular songs in the 1970s.

Chapter 14:
   "I Shall Not be Moved." H.F.M. ©1939 StampsBaxter Music and Printing Co. *Favorite Songs and Hymns*. Dallas, TX.

Chapter 15:
   "Let the Circle be Unbroken." Ada R. Habershon. Music by Charles H. Gabriel. Recorded in 1907.

Chapter 16:
   "I've Got the Joy, Joy, Joy, Joy, Down in my Heart." George Willis Cooke 1848-1923. Played in American Television series *Wilfred*. Sung by Granny (actress Irene Ryan) in episode of 1960s TV sitcom, *The Beverly Hillbillies*. (Wikipedia).

Other songs in the book:

   "When the Roll is Called up Yonder." James M. Black. 1893. This song was sung in the Academy award winning movie *Sergeant York*, 1941.

   "I'll Fly Away." Albert E. Brumley. Brumley recorded the song in 1931. He worked for 34 years as a staff writer for the Hartford and Stamps-Baxter publishing companies, then founded the Albert E. Brumley and Sons Music Company and Country Gentlemen Music, and bought the Hartford Music Co. He wrote over 800 gospel and other songs during his life; the Country Song Writers Hall of Fame inducted him in 1970.

"This World is Not My Home." Albert E. Brumley. © Alfred E. Brumley. 1939. Stamps-Baxter Music and Printing Co. *Favorite Songs and Hymns.* Dallas, TX.

"Corrina, Corrina," (Where You Been So Long?), A country blues song, first recorded by Bo Chatmon and the Mississippi Sheiks (Brunswick, December 1928). It was copyrighted in 1932 by Chatmon and his publishers, Mitchell Parish and J. Mayo Williams.

"Joyful, Joyful, We Adore Thee." Henry van Dyke. 1907. Music "Ode to Joy," from the 9th Symphony of Ludwig van Beethoven. *The Baptist Hymnal.* Convention Press, Nashville, TN.

"Farther Along." Rev. W. A. Fletcher. 1911. Stamps-Baxter Music Co. Dallas, TX. Also W. B. Steven. *Favorite Songs and Hymns.* © 1937 Stamps-Baxter Music Co. Dallas, TX., in Starlit Crown.

"Rest For the Weary." Samuel Y. Harmer. 1939. © Stamps-Baxter Music and Printing Co. *Favorite Songs and Hymns.* Dallas, TX.

"Joshua Fought the Battle of Jericho." 1870. Bantam Books. © 1948 by Sylvia and John Kolb.

"Jeremiah Was a Bullfrog." Written by Hoyt Axton, released in album *Joy to the World* in 1971. *On Three Dog Night 4th Studio Album,* 1970; heard in *The Big Chill* movie, 1971.

"Shall We Gather at the River?" Robert Lowry, 1864. First published in Happy Voices, 1865. Part of this song was sung in the Academy Award winning movie, *Trip to Bountiful,* 1985.

"In the Garden." C. Austin Miles. March 1912. This hymn was sung in the movie *Places in the Heart*, which won two Academy Awards in 1984.

"What a Friend We Have in Jesus." Joseph M. Scriven, 1819-1886. Scriven wrote this hymn in 1855 to comfort his mother, who was across the sea from him in Ireland. It was originally published anonymously, and Scriven did not receive full credit for almost 30 years.

"Bringing in the Sheaves." Knowles Shaw. 1874. © 1933. The Broadman Press. Nashville, TN.

ACKNOWLEGEMENTS

This is a work of fiction, rooted in real place and time. The routes through the Wiregrass, the Constitution Oak at the junction of the Choctawhatchee and Pea rivers, the buildings—including the old library in Apalachicola and the Osceola Hotel in Geneva, even the juke joints on the line separating Alabama and Florida— were there during the time of Louette and her supporting actors in this dramatization of Wiregrass life.

I am basically a story-teller. Say a word and I can tell you a tale of something that happened to me, or to someone I knew, or didn't know but heard about. Shaping the stories into a novel has been a years-long work in progress. I could not have put this together without the encouragement of my family and friends.

Brenda Ameter, my teacher and friend at Troy University, Dothan campus, prodded me into entering the first draft in a USA TODAY newspaper competition for top 100 university scholars, where it stuck. Dawn Radford fell in love with Louette as she and Adrian Fogelin helped me settle on such things as plot and point of view. My daughter, Alda Thomas, read and re-read, edited and advised. My granddaughter, Merri Rose Fink (credited with "Cover and design") rounded out the finished product with her various talents.

Persis Granger and the Fiction Among Friends writer's retreats have been a carnival of cheerleaders. Our gathering of writing sisters on St. George Island, Florida each year are always a hoot-and-a-holler. I cherish the friendships of these fantastically gifted women, including Gina Edwards, Mary Lois Sanders, Peggy Kassees, Rhett DeVane, Pat Griffith O'Connell, Susan Womble, Debbie Cooper, Evelyna Rogers, Linda Terburg, Roberta Burton, Amy Kirk, and Liz Jameson. Talented writers all, they gave me courage to continue. So did Rosemary Daniell and her Zona Rosa group. Howard Denson III, Sharman Ramsey and the *Nuts to Us!* crowd, Jerry Hurley, Ron Harris, Ralph Grimaldi of Writers of the Forgotten Coast, and friends Nancy Campbell, Emmy and Bill Butterworth, Ed Breslin, and many more. Thanks to you all!

AUTHOR with laptop, leaning against a giant pecan tree in the back yard at Mims Hill.

Photo by Debra Brackin

Sue Riddle Cronkite, born 100 yards inside the Geneva County Alabama line, grew up in Holmes County Florida.

Her first newspaper job was for the *Geneva County Reaper*, working with the late Karol Latimer Fleming and Joel P. Smith, where she became editor, then publisher.

Sue's journey as a servant of the people of the South included time as owner of the *Graceville* (FL) *News* and *Hartford* (AL) *News Herald* during an era where women were mostly at home. She served as interim editor of the *Southern Star* in Ozark, AL, during the Cuban Crisis.

While living in South Alabama in the early 1960s, Sue spent time as a correspondent for the *Birmingham News*. She then moved to Starke, FL, where she covered area news for the *Bradford Telegraph*, and worked for University of Florida Press.

Sue also worked with the Geneva Chamber of Commerce, *Seafarer Magazine* and Florida *Times-Union* in Jacksonville, during her early Florida years.

A return to Alabama settled her into a decade long run at the *Birmingham News* as copy editor, assistant state editor, assistant editorial page editor, and writer for the Metro desk. Sue Cronkite was one of a handful of women, in the 1970s, who were the first to serve on editorial boards of major, big city newspapers in the United States.

In her later years, Sue has served as managing editor at the Talladega (AL) *Daily Home*, and news editor at the *Clearwater* (FL) *Sun*. She worked as managing editor at the *Rome* (GA) *News-Tribune*, and *Decatur* (AL) *Daily*. She was executive editor of the Dothan (AL) *Wiregrass TODAY*, reporter for the *Apalachicola* (FL) *Times*, and the late Tom Hoffer's *Franklin* (FL) *Chronicle*.

Sue has also served as correspondent and fact-checker for *Life Magazine* and taught journalism at Jefferson State College.

Sue Riddle Cronkite has been winner of many short-story contests, including the F. Scott and Zelda Fitzgerald Museum (Montgomery, AL) fiction award for "Tobacco Velvet."

Louette's Wake is her first published novel.

Made in the USA
Columbia, SC
01 September 2019